The Journalist

JOHN REID YOUNG

First published in 2021 by Reidten Publishing.

For farmer Bob and other lifeguards

CONTENTS

This story is fictional. Characters and names are either the product of the author's imagination or are used fictitiously. Any resemblance to actual persons, living or dead, is entirely coincidental.

Chapter 1 – Resentment

What was about to happen stung him to the core. It breached his normally impenetrable nerve. It tore into his sometimes arrogant self-confidence, brutally shattering the illusions he'd so naively crafted in his mind over the past few months.

The evening had begun well enough, though, with hope and expectations sparkling at Rosie's Cantina. The wild west, batwing doors opened and closed like waves on the shore and the music swung almost to the same rhythm as the eager, Friday-night revellers flowing in and out of the popular Mexican restaurant.

Rosie's was on the slopes of a volcanic cone, just above Los Cristianos, and added even more glitter to the newest American-style timeshare complex in the bustling holiday resort on the Canary Island of Tenerife. It was the kind of place that had begun to attract the new, beautiful and affluent people, both holiday-makers and locals with high expectations for a great night out and, perhaps, for love.

It was early July, 1988, and the man with the blue cotton shirt and cream chinos was one of them. He had arrived at just before eight and sat on one of the bar stools, looking towards the doors every time they swung open. He was becoming restless. The date had been for eight o'clock and it was now a quarter to nine. He could not remember her ever being on time but his military discipline, inherited from his father and enhanced by a spell in the Army, could never deal with punctuality issues. Nevertheless, he knew he would melt the moment he saw her, and indeed he did.

"Your table is ready, Sir," invited the head waiter, ushering Jamie and Olivia away from the excitement around the bar and up the staircase to the airy, terraced restaurant area overlooking the pool.

Olivia was at her most attractive. She wore a light-blue backless dress, simply adorned with a pearl necklace. Her mane of chestnut hair was parted sideways into a high bun with loose strands hung down to partly cover her left cheek. Her earrings, glittering against her brownish skin, were tiny silver dolphins. They had been a gift from Jamie when they parted company at the end of his last visit to the island.

She was the daughter of a successful Spanish lawyer in the capital, Santa Cruz, and the only heiress to a considerable fortune on her mother's side, with properties in the Canary Islands and Madrid. Jamie Ryder was a descendant of a long-established British family on the Spanish island whose business interests, which included farming, fruit exports and the import of fine English china and furniture, had faded considerably since his father, Will, died when Jamie was still in his early teens. Jamie planned to revive some sort of business, although he had not discussed the matter with his mother yet and would need her approval. He expected fierce opposition from his sister and brother-in-law, Manolo, whose personal ambitions included making quick money from the ravenous new construction boom. It was no secret that he could not wait to get his hands on the old family estates and buildings. Property development was all the rage, legal or not, and that included persuading certain politicians to reclassify farmland to enable the building of lucrative housing estates and holiday apartments.

Maria, Jamie's mother, still owned a small farm in the lush, northern hills of the island, planted with vines, apples, and plums. Jamie had loved the freedom of the farm since he was a child. He knew every tree, every goat track, and every smell in the unspoilt and remote nature of the pine and chestnut forests above the orchards. Whilst there was evidence of renewed interest throughout the islands in producing fine wines, Jamie had always thought Las Rosas, their *finca* above the town of Tacoronte, would make a unique riding club.

Jamie and Olivia had been childhood sweethearts, and this was their first evening together for nine months. Jamie was twenty-seven and had recently completed a five-year commission in the British Army. He had thought long and hard about continuing with his career in the Army and had been highly considered within the Regiment. In fact, his commanding officer had tried his utmost to persuade the young Lieutenant not to resign.

It had been a tough decision because he loved his life in the

Regiment. Right now, however, Jamie felt like the happiest man in the world. He was, after all, in the company of his gorgeous Spanish lass to whom his heart had belonged for so long. Dreams of this moment had kept him alive on those bitter, freezing winter exercises in Norway, and alert in the heat of jungle training with the BFB in Brunei. She was all he wanted, and it was going to be a special night.

The cooling air of the terrace, the rosé wine which Olivia chose, and the laid-back effect of the balmy island night had come together to create the perfect blend for what Jaime had in mind. A romantic dinner for two, a drive in his mother's old MG and a stroll onto the small beach at Los Gigantes. That is where he and Olivia had first become lovers and where he intended to put one knee on the sand before enjoying a night of passion on Sundowner. Sundowner was his father's ageing Fairey Swordsman motorboat, which Maria still kept moored at the marina under the stunning Los Gigantes cliffs.

However, that is not what happened. In fact, Jamie's romantic ambitions were all but lost before the waiter could even take their order. He noticed two men taking their seats against the balustrades at the far corner of the terrace. One of them was the last person he wanted to see.

"Olivia, don't look now but your father has just sat down at a table over there."

She didn't need to look over her shoulder. She already knew her father would be at Rosie's Cantina. Her *papa* had decided to invite colleagues, and a new client, to dine at Rosie's after he found out his daughter was meeting Jamie there.

"Oh, didn't I tell you? *Papá* has a group of friends for an after-business dinner tonight. But, don't worry, he's only my chauffeur tonight. He's not going to meddle!"

"Um. No, of course. Forget it. But I was counting on it being just us, all night, and with no one in sight except tourists."

"Oh, dear Jamie. You are such a sweetie and so sensitive. This is so romantic, my love. Don't let the sight of my old man spoil things. Come on, let's celebrate with some more of this lovely wine!"

"Well, yes. This is quite nice wine, but it should have been chilled for longer."

"Really? You know me, I wouldn't have a clue. To me it's just wine."

"But you'll come with me to Los Gigantes afterwards, won't you? I was hoping we could celebrate on the boat, like in the old days."

"That sounds nice, Jamie", she said, putting the wine glass to her lips.

"Good. In that case there won't be any need for your father to be your chauffeur tonight, will there?"

"I suppose not, but I can't promise anything. I'll have to ask him before we go."

Olivia was not being entirely open, and Jamie sensed it. It began to dawn on him that his sweetheart, on their first night together after so many months, might not be thinking of a night of passion and love. His hopes suddenly began to crumble, and there was nothing he could do to stop disillusion and surprise showing in his eyes. Jamie's instinct, one that appeared out of nowhere and without warning, like an enemy sniper, suddenly told him that something in Olivia had changed.

There were two important reasons. One was that her father, Alonso, had never approved of her daughter's relationship with an Englishman. Jamie had always been aware of that, of course.

The other reason, vital and more destructive, was that during the past nine months Olivia had been dating, and apparently falling in love with another man. Jamie never had a clue. He was not prepared. Nobody had warned him. Telephone calls and the occasional letter from Olivia had never hinted that anything was brewing on the island. Jamie's time and self-interest had been absorbed entirely by his duties in the Army. He never saw it coming. Perhaps he had been naïve in his self-esteem. Perhaps it was because he had never had time to fall in love with another woman.

Olivia's other man was older than Jamie and didn't have her English lover's dashing good looks, but that no longer seemed to matter. He was permanently on the island, whilst Jamie was always thousands of miles away, playing games with guns. Besides, her new boyfriend not only oozed charm and spoiled her without mercy with promises and endless gifts. He was also an amazing lover, toying with her in ways her Englishman would never have contemplated.

There was something else too, something that still mattered in certain families. As far as Olivia's father was concerned, her new man would also inherit a considerable family fortune from property development in the booming island tourist industry. So he entirely approved of the relationship. In fact, it was he who had introduced the man to Olivia. Alonso was always quite open about it and had told his daughter to make sure she did not disappoint him. This was a threat, of course, but she did not see it that way. The new boyfriend, already influential in political circles, especially within the new Canary Island Nationalist Party, which was pulling all the strings since the end of the Franco dictatorship, had a future. Olivia, it appeared, could not resist that, almost as much as Alonso and his partners.

"I think I would rather you went and asked your father now, Olivia. I just want to relax, you know. I won't, knowing that he is over there, waiting to pull you away from me. He has already glanced this way a couple of times. If he does so again, I'm going to get the waiter to find us another table."

Jamie's tone was different. Olivia knew he meant every word. Jamie had suddenly lost the more reserved, English charm that had always amused her mother. What Olivia could never have imagined were the feelings that had begun to churn in his stomach and that his smile, charming as it might appear, was now quite false and icy cold.

Olivia looked surprised at first but then sighed, smiled nervously, and blew a loose strand of hair off her cheek. She carefully and deliberately put down her napkin, just as the waiter returned with some *nachos* and *guacamole* to open their appetites, stood up and walked towards her father's table. It was laid for six, and Alonso was sitting at one end. Some of what Olivia had told Jamie was true. He *was* expecting others.

Jamie watched her bend down and whisper into Alonso's

ear. He poured himself some more wine and looked down at the table, so he didn't see Alonso peer around his daughter at him. It didn't really matter. Olivia returned and was sitting opposite Jamie within a couple of minutes. She gave a slight shrug of her shoulders, sipped at her glass of wine, and dipped a nacho in the sauce. There was quite a long silence before Jamie spoke.

"Well?"

"I'm sorry, Jamie," she said, without looking at her Englishman. "My father is insisting. He says we have been invited by a very important man to a party on a yacht in Santa Cruz after dinner. He needs me to accompany him."

"I see. Just you. Not us? Very well," said Jamie, rather stiffly.

"What about your mother? Why doesn't he take her instead?" continued Jamie. "Is that very important man more important than me?"

Jamie flinched, cursing himself. He wished he hadn't said that. Very feeble of him. Olivia did not bother to reply, not immediately anyway, and this time it was she who went on the offensive.

"My mother is in Madrid. Jamie. I am truly sorry. Actually, there's another reason why I can't come with you tonight. I should have told you long ago, in my letters or when you called me. But then, that wasn't very often, was it?"

Jamie attempted another of his stiff-upper-lip smiles. He thought he knew what was coming, a more direct hit. He was absolutely right.

"Come on, Jamie. It had to happen. It was alright for you, with your British Army friends and having fun all over the world. I was here all alone. He was here. You never were. You know you were always more in love with your stupid army than with me, anyway!"

Olivia realised immediately she was so wrong to have said that to her childhood sweetheart and she buried her face in her hands.

"I'm so sorry," she whispered, searching into his eyes, begging with her own for him to accept her apology and, at the same time, for sympathy.

But her remark had cut too deep into Jamie's natural defences. For a moment Jamie gazed away to his left, over the balustrade and up to the darkening sky. *How dare she?*

"My darling, I left *her* for you." The whispered words wrenched at his heart.

"What do you mean?" asked Olivia, suddenly feeling almost relieved. *She really hadn't understood, had she?*

"Surely you know perfectly well what I mean. You've just said it yourself. I left my *other* love for you. I've resigned from the Army. I am no longer going to be a Captain in the Regiment next year. For you, I no longer serve in Her Majesty's armed forces. You were going to be my queen, Olivia. Forever."

The reserved manner remained intact, but Jamie had stiffened like a dog that had met an enemy. All his public-school charm vanished into another swallow of wine and a glaring glance over Olivia's shoulder at that other table. He wanted eye contact with Alonso, but this time he didn't get it. Instead, he decided to put a swift end to the misery.

"Look, I think it would be more suitable if you got up and left, rather than I. Don't you think so? A man can't leave a lady stranded, if you know what I mean."

"Please, Jamie. Don't. Not like this. Let's just enjoy this evening, for old time's sake. I feel so sad, myself. *Por favor, amorcito.* I beg you."

"Olivia, don't you see it. You have crushed my heart." Jamie's last whispered words came from the back of his throat, and his eyes looked as if they should be emptying with tears.

"My love, I'm so sorry."

It was then that Jamie lost his gentlemanly courage entirely.

"I've been a bloody fool, Olivia. I've given up a bloody wonderful career for you. I've no words to describe what I feel except, well, I don't know. But all those sweet letters you wrote. Everything you said on the phone, all our whispered conversations on those dark nights, tempting me to imagine your nakedness. Ah, yes, I expect you were probably in bed with whoever this wretched guy is, acting like a cheap whore!"

Jamie's words were now coming out in a spitting tirade. It was so unlike him and, once again, he regretted every word. However, it was too late, the damage was done. As the waiter brought their main course of beef and chilli tacos and offered to top up their wine glasses, Olivia burst into tears, grabbed her small, cream and blue handbag, stood up and left. She never said another word. She didn't even stop as she brushed past her father. Nevertheless, Jamie saw Alonso gulp some wine before he stood up to follow her.

Jamie looked up at the waiter and half smiled in apology. The waiter shrugged and waited for him to react, fully expecting the young English client to rush down the steps after his girl. However, he did quite the opposite. Whether Jamie was hoping Olivia would return or not, he began to sample what was on his plate. The waiter, with an impassive look on his face, shrugged again and went to attend to another table.

He no longer had an appetite, of course. When Jamie caught the waiter's eye again, he called him over.

"You can take these away, thank you. Just bring me the bill. Oh, and a whisky."

"*Si, señor!* A whisky." The impassive look changed to one of delight. This was becoming interesting.

"What brand would you prefer?"

"Any old whisky. Just bring it, please. Thank you. With two lumps of ice. And *la cuenta*. Don't forget the bill, please."

The waiter disappeared, but returned, almost immediately this time, as if eager not to miss the next episode of this affair. He was carrying a tray with a glass, half-filled with ice and a bottle of Glenfiddich.

Jamie nodded. As the waiter poured the whisky, he noticed Alonso had returned to the table in the corner and was looking straight at him. When the Spaniard was certain Jamie had caught his eye, Alonso gave him a sideways nod, offered a chuckling smirk, and began to talk to the other members of his party. They had obviously not missed the fun and Jamie imagined, rightly, that he had become the source of their amusement.

Olivia did not return, of course. It was the end of a teenage love affair and perhaps of a friendship that had lasted for so many years. Jamie felt everything falling down around him. Where there had once been such longing and expectation for a future with the girl he adored, there was now total emptiness. That was, until he looked across at Alonso's table once more. If that man, the one who had given him that greasy smirk a few minutes ago, had ever become his father-in-law, perhaps life with Olivia would not have been so idyllic. Jamie straightened himself, took one last swallow of the whisky and stood up to go, attempting to regain some of his self-control and dignity. First, however, he would pay his compliments to Alonso and he strode over to the table for six. He would act as he had in the jungle when dealing with the senior member of a tribe.

"Good evening, *don* Alonso. I hope you are well," he said, bowing slightly, but keeping both hands behind his back. He did not feel like shaking hands.

Alonso did not say a word, but there was that sideways nod again, this time without the smirk.

"Please give my best regards to your charming wife when she returns. I gather she is in Madrid again. Enjoy the evening, gentlemen," he said, offering a smile and a prolonged look into the eyes of each of Alonso's five friends. Satisfied that they had captured some kind of message, Jamie turned and walked towards the staircase.

***

When Jamie slid into the MG it was as he left it, topless. The twin carbs hummed in unison as he revved the engine and sped the car down the street and then left towards the first of the new roundabouts. They were certainly getting on with the new roads to cater for the ever growing tourism industry. With the hood down, the sudden cool air blowing through his blond hair produced a welcome sense of relief.

However, the wine and whisky didn't give him a moment to settle on any particular thought once he was on the open road from Los Cristianos to Los Gigantes. On the contrary, what had just happened at Rosie's Cantina flashed by repeatedly, like the lights of oncoming traffic, on occasions dazzling him in and out of a blend of sad, positive, and what-the-heck moods. Visions of Olivia hung listless at the back of his mind and every corner on the road brought back a fond memory, only to find it crushed once again by the knowledge that she had gone forever.

Those faces around Alonso's table also played tricks with his mind, coaxing his anger. Whatever message he had intended to send them with his parting smile, he didn't really know. Alonso's sniggering face, and the other men apparently enjoying the Spaniard's game, bugged him. The five men with Alonso were just there for a night out, perhaps, but Jamie was determined that they were all now the enemy. The one who had been with Alonso from when he arrived, also a Spaniard but older, with cheeks and neck stuffed with years of oily food, looked as if he had sat behind an office desk forever. A dark, smooth-looking man dressed in white and boasting large gold cufflinks, had also caught Jamie's eye although, as Jamie bid them a good evening, he did not seem to acknowledge Jamie's presence at all. Perhaps it was deliberate. He didn't look Spanish. In fact, his appearance was more north-African, possibly Moroccan. Next to him, there was another Latin gentleman. His face flashed in and out of Jamie's thoughts because it was so ugly. It had the scars of a youth tortured by diabolical acne, and the poor man also possessed an unfortunate brown, hairy birthmark just above his right eyebrow. However, it wasn't so much the man's ugliness that played a role in Jamie's thoughts. It was the man's ruthless stare, never for an instant losing eye contact as Jamie, albeit sarcastically, wished them a pleasant evening. The other two members of Alonso's party looked British. One of them certainly was. He was the only one with a pint of beer in front of him. The one next to the North African, of slighter build, also caught Jamie's attention, not because he also didn't take his eyes off Jamie but because, for some reason, his face reminded Jamie of Pablo Falco, a Canary Islander who had tried his hand at being a racing driver in Formula 3.

It was still quite early by Spanish standards when he drove down the hill on the one-way system through the small resort of Los Gigantes and towards the marina; but Paddy's Bar, on his left as he drove past, was bubbling, as it always did, with loud voices and music. Jamie drove the MG to the right, along the quay, and found a space near the pizzeria at the end of the line of cafes, shops, and bars. He then walked back to where Sundowner was moored, showing signs of having been all but abandoned for too long. Jamie had spent the day cleaning her up for the occasion, but she still looked in need of some love, probably even more so than himself. He stepped down into the galley.

Two champagne saucers on the saloon table brought the evening's events back immediately and he felt his guts begin to churn again. He had placed them there earlier, before going out to meet Olivia. They would not be needed. He sat down and stared emptily at the fine crystal. Then suddenly, he stood up, opened the fridge, and reached for the bottle of Moët. He would drown his sorrows.

Jamie searched in the pocket of the blazer which he had chucked earlier that evening onto the berth in the twin aft cabin and took out the little box, tightening his grip around it and almost crushing the fragile container. He opened it and pulled out the ring, which he placed gently beside the bottle and crystal saucers. It was a simple, delicate, brown rose cut diamond, but it had cost him a fortune. Then, choking back a flood of tears, he cried out loud.

"Olivia. Why? Please, oh God, why?"

A loud round of applause and laughter coming from one of the quayside bars brought him back from the brink and he stood up. He never opened the Moët & Chandon. In fact, he replaced it on the shelf in the fridge. He left the damaged little jewel container on the table, but he put the ring back into the same blazer pocket. He was damned if he was going to sulk in the boat all night. A blend of wine and whisky still stirred false courage, and unclear thoughts whirled through his head, prompting him to drink more, but not alone.

He stepped up into the narrow entrance at Paddy's and sat down on the nearest vacant stool at the bar. They were the same two barmen, the moustached owner, and his younger assistant from the next village. Jamie remembered them from his previous visit, three years ago, but hoped they would not recognise him. The last time he drank at Paddy's was when an army chum came to stay. His friend's behaviour had got them both literally thrown out of the bar.

Two *Arehucas* rum and cokes later, he decided to move on. All the girls were either the wrong shape or attached to sunburnt Brits. He wasn't going to make the same mistake as his friend by chatting up someone else's woman.

Walking down a side street behind a pub called the Green Corner, he noticed a board signalling to a disco down a narrow staircase.

Why not? he thought to himself.

The music was different, loud but different. A touch less *here we go, here we go* and more cosmopolitan. However, the place, small as it was, was relatively empty apart from two couples smooching on the dance floor, a Spaniard propping up one end of the bar and Paul Newman's double at the other end. In between, a couple of German girls were entertaining the barman.

Jamie joined in the conversation. These German ladies were the right shape. More drinks, flashing disco lights and smoke of all densities and aromas led to a dance or two and then to one of the Germans following Jamie back up the steps and down the road to the marina.

The sound of a seagull and shouts from the quay awakened Jamie at around nine. The sunlight danced with dust particles inside the blue curtains covering the twin portholes and it was becoming hot. Jamie's head thumped to the rhythm of booze and disco music. He tried to remember as he let his eyes become accustomed to the light. It was only when he turned on his side, and found himself staring at a half-empty bottle of Moët, that he began to recollect. He stood up and clumsily put on the pair of boxer shorts and the blue shirt he had worn before stripping naked. It reeked, a mix of cigarette smoke, sweat and alcohol. Jamie stepped into the saloon.

The German girl had gone. Jamie suddenly realised he didn't even know her name. Whoever she was, she had been considerate. Except for the bottle with the remains of the champagne, she had cleaned up all evidence of their drunken night of sex. Jamie sat down at the galley table and put his face in his hands. A feeling of guilt, the same he had felt after one particular night out with the lads in the Norwegian city of Bergen, at the end of a cold weather survival exercise, made his guts churn.

It passed though. It always did. After devouring a sandwich and swallowing two cups of coffee at the café on the corner, Jamie felt better. His head ached almost as much as his heart, but he was going to take Sundowner for a spin under the cliffs before heading home to Puerto de la Cruz.

Sundowner was built at Hamble Point in 1972. Jamie's father, Will, had intended to keep her at Lymington, where they had a small cottage for whenever they needed a break from Tenerife. However, when he was diagnosed with the cancer that eventually got the better of him, Will decided to have the boat shipped out to the island where he could enjoy it regularly for as long as his health permitted.

As soon as Jamie passed the end of the harbour wall, he pushed the throttles forward making the twin Perkins Saber turbo diesel engines launch the old boat over the still water in Los Gigantes Bay. He took her as close to the cliff as he knew he could, under the shadows, and then turned towards the Teno lighthouse, pushing the throttles right forwards. Sundowner was reaching her limit of 26 knots when Jamie spotted the dolphins and reduced speed to a gentle 17 knots, sharing the natural freedom of the ocean with them for a few minutes. One or two fishermen were out, but not as far as Teno point where the trade winds and meeting currents creased the surface of the sea with warning streaks of white. It was time for a quick dip before heading back to the marina, and Jamie made for the little cove under the great Masca *barranco*, the most spectacular of all the ravines that have cut great gashes through the island over millions of years.

The water in the bay was crystal clear and Jamie could easily make out the sandy bottom, broken here and there by occasional clusters of black volcanic rocks, the favourite hunting grounds for so many marauding fish. He eased the throttles and let the bow move ahead slowly towards the shore, to the right of the rocky promontory used by the boats that ferry hikers from Masca back to the marina at certain times of the day. When he was in about two fathoms of water, he chucked the anchor over the side and sneaked backwards under minimum power, letting the line pay out until he was certain it had held. There were no other boats in sight, except one further out to sea, so Jamie took off his shorts and shirt, and dived in naked.

He swam to the shore and back and pushed himself up onto the bathing platform. Jamie sat there for a while with his legs dangling in the water. He gazed back towards the mouth of the Masca ravine. Long ago, when they were in their mid-teens, he and Olivia had camped for a night there with a group of friends, just above the pebbles, after an afternoon hike down from Masca village.

Jamie looked down into the water as the memories gushed back once more. That was the night he and Olivia had begun to fall in love, the first time they had kissed, skinny-dipping under the stars.

Jamie put on his shorts and stepped down into the aft cabin. He took the engagement ring out of his blazer pocket and went back up to the deck. He stood behind the wheel, started the engines, and let them idle. Jamie placed the brown rose cut diamond ring beside the navigation compass above the main dashboard and went to haul in the anchor.

By the time Jamie returned to the wheel and began to push the throttles forward, a couple of speed boats were coming to join him in the small bay. It was time to go. It was also time to say goodbye to the past. He picked up the ring, pressed it hard against his lips and threw it over his shoulder. Just like the future he had planned with his childhood sweetheart, it would quickly disappear, buried into the sand by the constantly changing currents in Masca Bay.

Chapter 2 – Revenge

Later that same afternoon, 1,700 miles north of the Canary Islands, another boat was cutting a smooth course around the western corner of Bere Island, in Ireland's Bantry Bay. It was the Sallygirl, a cheerful-looking Fisher 30. She was fluttering, not with sails filled with sea breeze, but with clothes of all shapes and colours hung along the guard rails, from bow to stern, to capture the last of the evening sun. Sally, after whom the boat was named, was now hurrying to gather in her washing. The forecast had been correct. There was what looked like another summer downpour not far ahead, just past the ruins of Dunboy Castle; the landmark, in a state of ruin since it was burnt down by the IRA in 1920, was fast disappearing into the veil of dark cloud just above what was left of the castle.

At the helm was Sally's husband, Pete Rennie. He was using the motor to gently chug the Sallygirl towards their anchorage at Lawrence Cove, along the north coast of Bere Island. The couple were towards the end of their first Atlantic cruise. They had enjoyed stunningly good and safe sailing for most of their round trip to Madeira and the Azores but were absolutely exhausted after having been pursued by one squall after another over the past few days. They were looking forward to a much-needed stopover.

Peter, always meticulous in preparations, had plotted a course for Lawrence Cove, a safe haven for yachts and once a small British Army outpost. The plan was to spend a day or two catching up on sleep and perhaps to explore the island on foot. They would then catch the ferry over to Castletownbere on the Beara peninsula to order supplies as well as some new lines, a backstay adjuster, and one or two other bits and pieces for the Fisher before setting off on the last stage of their adventure. It was going to take them up the west coast of Ireland and then east across to Crinan, on the Sound of Jura in Scotland. That was where they kept a permanent mooring for their usual summer sailing. There was a small post office store in Rerrin village, just above the cove, but it would not have all the supplies they required and certainly not the spares for the boat.

Further up the lane, along from the store, Fergal Breslin, a man with a slightly rounded waist and legs that never moved very fast, put down the binoculars on the window ledge. The shower had passed, and the early evening was beginning to clear. He had been watching Pete and Sally busily washing down and tidying up on deck for quite a while. In fact, he had been making mental notes of every movement on the Fisher ever since Pete turned her bow into the light breeze and anchored. Now, with the sun beginning to play at making rainbows over the mainland, there was little more to spy for. Fergal knew he had seen enough to make the call. He locked the door to his room, went downstairs, and cheerfully informed the landlady that he was nipping out for a beer. He did go up the same lane to the pub but, before entering, he went to the telephone booth on the corner next to the store.

"Fergal here. I think we've got one," he told the man who answered the call in Castletownbere.

"You sure?" It was Patrick Collins, the commander of the local Active Service Unit, a six-man cell chosen to carry out the operation for the IRA.

"Yes. A good little boat with a high-up wheelhouse. Plenty of room below, I reckon."

"How many?"

"As far as I can see, it's just a man and a woman. Late fifties, maybe a little older," replied Fergal.

"Can you see any tender?"

"Yes. Looks like a fibreglass dinghy in front of the wheelhouse."

"Fine. Call me at 11.15 tomorrow. By then you should get an idea if they are staying or not. I'll tell the others to prepare themselves, just in case. No drinking tonight. I'll need you to be alert in the morning. They'll probably come ashore at some point."

***

16

Patrick Collins was what British intelligence referred to as a *volunteer* activist, which means that he had almost certainly never been identified by British or Irish security forces. He lived and worked in the fishing industry at Castletownbere, where he owned his own wholesale fishmonger's shop on Dinish Island, just across the bridge from the mainland. That is why he had been chosen for this particular operation.

Collins had been a valuable asset for several years, using his highly successful business, Cork Whitefish, as a cover for smuggling small arms and other forms of contraband into Ireland. When he was finally arrested in 1990 it was because he was suspected of having received a small shipment of weapons destined for the dwindling hardcore of the Irish Republican Army from a visiting Russian ship. Ships from the Soviet Union and former USSR states often came to Berehaven Harbour to buy and process fish. MI6 had established, with the help of an informant, a connection between IRA diehards and the Russian arms mafia. Investigations had also previously connected Collins to an arms deal with the separatists in the Basque region of Spain.

Indeed, this new mission in 1988, which had been planned for more than a year, consisted of hijacking an innocent yacht to transport an important consignment of weapons from northern Spain to Ireland. The vessel didn't have to be very large. It just needed to be a sturdy, seagoing boat with ample room below decks. Essentially the boat also needed to have an inoffensive appearance. That is why they had gone for a private pleasure craft.

Patrick Collins was also required to persuade a Spanish-speaking sailor to help take the yacht to and from a port in Spain's Asturias region. Apart from having a good knowledge of the sea, the Spaniard would be required to interpret, if necessary, in the Spanish port. One would expect that task to have been the most difficult, but it hadn't been. Collins was well connected with a good many Spanish trawlermen, often purchasing excess stock from them as they did their business in Castletownbere, where they took on gallons of fuel for the next trawl. A good load of money under the table goes a long way when necessary. In the middle of May, the right Spaniard happened to cross his path.

Spain has one of the biggest fishing fleets in the world. It has immense fishing grounds of its own, benefiting from a narrow, continental shelf which is extremely rich in a variety of fish resources and runs along the entire periphery of Spain's coast, from the Mediterranean to the Bay of Biscay. Their trawlers, however, especially those with bases in Galician ports like Vigo, also reach far into the north and south Atlantic, and even as far as Tasmania and pacific waters, often fishing under foreign flags to get around restrictions to quotas. Several trawlers use Castletownbere, a hive of fishing activity, as a convenient trading post and refuelling station. This brings opportunities for local businesses, so they are very welcome. The only sector which isn't too keen on having foreign trawlers in their backyard is Ireland's own trawling community.

In that respect, as the Spanish trawler fleets grew, particularly in the latter half of the 20th century, so did their ambition and domineering attitude towards smaller fishing nations. As a result, there have been numerous incidents involving Spanish trawlers, accused of bullying smaller, Irish craft, overfishing and using illegal methods in British and Irish waters. That is the reason the Irish Navy has been so particularly vigilant since the 1970s. On occasions though, according to Irish fishermen, the Irish authorities have been tougher on their own people than on the foreigners.

***

In May 1988, in the beautiful and historic city of Santiago de Compostela, the Tuesday parliamentary session in Spain's autonomous region of Galicia appeared to be moving along placidly as usual. There was no reason why it shouldn't. The Popular Alliance conservative party governed with a huge majority. That was until it was the turn of Xose Manuel Beiras, leader of BNG, the left-wing Galician independence party, to ask his question.

Little of what he said, if anything, was expected to rattle the system. However, the two questions he made to the President of the Junta during his one, brief intervention that morning were not on the agenda and woke all their honourable deputies up. In fact the questions touched a very Galician nerve. They went straight to the heart of the region's pride and joy, to its principal industry, the beloved fishing fleet.

"What does his *señoría* propose to do about yet another illegal capture of one of our trawlers in international waters by Ireland, and the arrest of five crew members, and does he agree with my article in today's *La Voz*?" It only took him two minutes, from the moment he walked down the aisle over the red carpet towards the lectern, to when he returned to his seat on the third row, but it grabbed everybody's attention, not least the President of the Junta.

"I thank *señor* Beiras for bringing the subject up and I assure him that I am indeed aware of the reference his *señoría* makes to the totally unjust arrest of one of our boats. I have already contacted the Irish authorities and have requested its immediate release," replied Fernando González Laxe, President of the *Junta*.

He was not telling the truth, of course. However, as he answered more questions regarding domestic policies from other deputies, he knew his staff would be reading Beiras' article and trying to find out what the hell was going on in Ireland.

An hour later he was put through to the Ministry of Foreign Affairs in Madrid. The Minister, Francisco Fernández Ordoñez, of the ruling Socialist Party, was not available. He was currently in Brussels, coincidentally negotiating fishing rights.

By the time Fernández Ordoñez returned his call in the early evening, González Laxe had already had three conversations with Brian Patrick Lenihan, Ireland's Foreign Minister. Although reports suggest the Irishman had always remained calm, the first exchange had been heated, judging by the words spat out by the Spaniard, with adrenaline running high and with mounting pressure at home making his Latin temperament bite. The second was more diplomatic, as more information filtered through as to the reasons for the arrests and regarding the evidence provided by the Irish fishing authorities. The Spaniard had no alternative but to lower his tone. The third was like a chat between old friends, as quick solutions were promised, and assurances of fair play and continued cooperation were accepted.

According to snippets of information, this new incident in May 1988 had very nearly turned into something like the one in October 1984. On that occasion, Irish fishery patrol boats had fired on and sunk a Spanish trawler after it was found to be fishing illegally in Irish waters. The Irish Defence Ministry reported they had been left with no option after the Sonia, the Spanish trawler, had apparently attempted to ram one of the Irish patrol boats in heavy seas.

An unfounded rumour, within British intelligence circles, was that the Sonia may have been transporting weapons or drugs destined for clients in Ireland. Why else would she have used such dangerous tactics to avoid capture when, in the past, trawler skippers and therefore the companies that owned them had simply been punished with, and accepted, a large fine?

This new case was just one of many in recent months. It involved a boat called the Lolariz, from Riveira in Galicia, and was owned by the powerful Sedalto group. Its skipper had been warned two years earlier, when the boat received a visit from Irish fishery inspectors whilst it tried to sell boxes of undersized hake at Castletownbere. On this occasion, the Lolariz was intercepted by two Irish Navy Service patrol boats and was caught red-handed using an illegal 3mm mesh net in a foggy sea 90 miles southwest of Ireland and within what is known as the *Irish Box*, which is thought to be an important spawning area for many stocks. It meant the boat was again catching under-sized and baby hake, considered a delicacy in the best restaurants in certain regions of Spain.

The Lolariz was escorted into Castletownbere harbour and detained. The Captain and crew were also placed under house arrest aboard their vessel, pending trial. They were under surveillance at all times but were permitted freedom of movement within the town. They were also expected to be on call any morning to be driven to the Galway District Court for the hearing.

This would not take long, for the Irish had got the procedure down to a tee. A representative from the Spanish Consulate in Dublin would be on hand, probably with an agreement, signed by the trawler's owners, Sedalto, for the payment of a massive fee. This would effectively release the crew but not the trawler. The vessel would be permitted to sail once the money was in the bank, usually within a week or two.

***

In May 1988, for some inexplicable reason, the representative from the Consulate, Manuel Contreras, told Judge Mary O'Neale that there would be a slight delay because Sedalto were going to appeal against the charges on the grounds that, by the month of May, the hake would normally be mature enough to be within the size limits. In other words, whilst they were not denying the use of 3mm mesh nets, they said there was no proof that they had in fact caught under-sized hake. However, the Consulate would take care of paying the bail for the captain and crew of the Lolariz. Mary O'Neale had no option. The vessel was to be held at Castletownbere until after the appeal, in three or four weeks. The skipper and crew were free to return to Spain if they wished.

Patrick Collins, the volunteer activist, silently acting for what remained of the Irish Republican Army, already knew this was going to be the outcome. He had been informed by someone who had a contact at the Consulate's International Trade desk. He also knew Alvaro Cousillas, the skipper of the Lolariz, because he had bought fish off him on a couple of occasions. So Collins, who was waiting for Cousillas close to where the trawler was tied up, went up to the blue minibus when it arrived to drop off the Spanish crew in the harbour.

"Alvaro!" Collins greeted the trawler captain and offered him a hand to shake. "How are you doing, hey? Life treating you well?" he asked, ignoring the fact that the Spaniard had been to court after allegedly being caught in the act.

Cousillas nodded and shrugged.

"Can we talk a minute?"

21

Alvaro Cousillas nodded again and followed Collins along the pier to MacCarthy's bar.

"Cracking! Pint, mate?"

Alvaro, as an experienced trawler skipper fishing in foreign waters, was required to know a certain amount of English. In fact he spoke it remarkably well for a foreigner. Consequently he was already familiar with what he would find in a traditional Irish pub. In fact, he and the crew knew the bars in the port area well enough, after years of fishing these waters.

"Bulmers, thank you". He asked for a cider. He always did prefer cider, although swore there was none like the famous Asturian equivalent.

Alvaro was in his mid-fifties. He had made a good bit of money and owned a nice little plot of land back home. It had a stone cottage and the two fields around it were protected by woodland and a small stream flowing along the edge of the wood. His wife worked at a supermarket, nearby at A Pobra Do Caramiñal, and she made the most of Sundays when their sons would bring the grandchildren for the day. Alvaro, more often than not during the fishing seasons, missed out on that family life. He was also very tired. A trawlerman's life is one of the toughest in the world and, however lucrative the job might be, he was beginning to feel older than he was. In fact, he had been toying with the idea of taking some sort of early retirement, doing something with his fields and taking his other passion more seriously, which was reading history and writing. Collins' offer presented him a potential passport to freedom, not enough to retire on completely, but a little bit to put away. It was a huge risk to take, but the money was too tempting.

Collins and his controller had it all worked out. Alvaro was to go home to Galicia with the rest of the crew, supposedly to enjoy a well-earned holiday until the Lolariz was released and could begin to *faenar* again in Irish waters. That might not be at least until the end of July. However, Alvaro Cousillas would not take his usual trawler-skipper's break in August and September before returning for the winter fishing season. His family should remain totally ignorant. As far as they were concerned, Alvaro would be back on the Lolariz to carry out another stint of trawling for other seasonal fish, to compensate for lost time earlier in the summer.

On his return to the Lolariz Alvaro would receive a million pesetas in used bank notes before departing from Ireland on the next trawl. That was the equivalent of just over 6,000€ today. It was a pretty sum in those days. There would be another half a million pesetas waiting for him in Dingle prior to sailing a boat to Spain. On completion of the job, having returned to Ireland with the goods, he would receive the remaining one and a half million. The deal was simple.

Sensing that Alvaro was not totally convinced, Patrick Collins hinted he was likely to get a bonus when the job had been completed and a smaller amount, as a sign of good faith, if he agreed to transport the merchandise. The IRA man had no intention of keeping his part of the deal, once the job was done, but Alvaro was not to know that.

"Maybe I do it, Patrick. But, with one condition. No drugs. If drugs, I don't do. You understand?" It was a good sum of money he was being offered. Alvaro had to suspect the merchandise was drugs.

"No, mate. No drugs. I despise people who deal in drugs. You don't need to know what is in the boxes, but here," he said, leaning across the wooden table outside MacCarthy's. "I suppose there is no harm in telling you. But you tell nobody, yes?"

"Yes. I swear it on my mother."

"Very expensive stuff fallen off the back of a lorry. You understand? High technology components for modern aircraft design, and other small parts made in Germany. Very good quality material which cost a fortune. Are you OK with that, mate?"

"I think. Yes, let me think. I tell you tomorrow". It still didn't add up, but the Irishman had been so persuasive.

"Alright Alvaro, but I must know tomorrow morning, or I'll have to ask someone else, OK? Oh, and there will also be a few cartons of cigarettes. Usual stuff, you know. Anyway, you know where you can find me. The back entrance."

"OK. *Está bien.* But, you wait. Please, not tomorrow. The day after. OK? I must think."

Patrick was not going to make a fuss, not when he nearly had the man in his pocket. They agreed on a time. Thursday morning at 11.00. Collins told Alvaro where to find him again, but no more.

One day after the court case, Cousillas told his crew to begin packing their bags. They would be leaving mid-morning that Friday for Cork Airport to catch an evening flight to Vigo. The same blue minibus that had taken them to the court and back would be there early on Friday for the drive across to Cork. He told them they would go out on Thursday evening for a pub meal and a drink or two to celebrate, but they were to spend the time they had washing down the decks and the holds and making the boat ready for the next trawl. He wanted his Lolariz to look like a pretty Spanish woman. That the boat's hull looked like that of a common, foreign whore didn't matter in the least. They were a happy lot. So was Alvaro. He didn't mind smuggling cigarettes, and the high technology stuff, stolen or not, would not be a problem. If he were caught, he might be locked up for a while, but he would have the money.

On the Thursday morning Alvaro told his men he was off to negotiate with a wholesaler for future business. He did go to see a wholesaler. It was Patrick Collins, and he was waiting for Alvaro in his office at the Cork Whitefish warehouse on Dinish Island. As instructed, the Spaniard did not use the main entrance, next to the open and rusty, roller shutter doors. Instead, he walked, hands in pockets, to the rear of the building, past the empty dog kennel and between racks of cable reels. At the end of the racks, slightly to the right, there was a green door. It was the back entrance to Patrick Collins' tiny office, and it was open. The fact that Cousillas had turned up meant that he had accepted to do the job.

"Here you are mate," said Collins, swivelling his chair around and reaching inside an old, open safe. "Here's a little something to keep the wife happy."

Patrick handed the Spaniard a folded, black plastic bag which Alvaro immediately unravelled to peep inside. It contained a used airmail envelope which he also opened. He calculated there must have been a wad of at least one hundred of the green 1,000 peseta notes.

Alvaro looked up and offered the Irishman a toothy grin. In reply, Patrick Collins held out his hand to shake the Spaniard's. This step of the operation had begun successfully.

"You smoke, yes?" Collins knew perfectly well that the skipper of the Lolariz smoked like a chimney and handed him a packet of American cigarettes. He then opened a drawer on the desk and took out a box of matches. He shook it and threw it over to the Spaniard.

"There is a telephone number on the inside, under the matches," Collins said. Call that number as soon as you know the date you are to return for your trawler. It will not be me who answers. Just say *this is Lola*, and then the date you come back. OK? You got it?"

"Yes, I understand. This is Lola."

"You like it? *Lola*?" said Collins, chuckling at the sheer cleverness of the name, the first four letters of the name of the Spaniard's trawler.

"When you arrive back in Castletownbere, call the same number again. This time say *Lola is home*. Alright, mate. *Hasta mañana*."

Alvaro half smiled this time, to accompany another nod, at the Irishman's attempt to utter a couple of words in Spanish. Patrick Collins stood up. The deal was done. The meeting was over. Alvaro left the way he had come.

***

Fergal Breslin had been using the binoculars again since the crack of dawn, keeping watch across the water in Lawrence Cove at the Sallygirl the morning after Pete Rennie had thrown the anchor over the side. After a dark and still night it had turned into a beautifully clear day and Fergal had also enjoyed watching gulls and divers as the sun began to warm the early, mid-summer morning. Nothing much else happened except for the yacht moving position with the flow of the tide.

It was the woman who appeared on deck first, at just after 09.30. She had a steaming mug of tea or coffee in her hand.

Fergal observed as she looked around taking in the scenery. Then she disappeared again. Half an hour later both she and the man were on deck lowering the tender. A few minutes later the man was rowing them to the shore. That was when Fergal hurried down the lane to Murphy's shop, where he pretended to look at the notices on the windows. Maureen, the owner, opened every day of the week, even on Sundays until midday or thereabouts, depending on the weather. Patrick Collins had guessed right. The first thing the Rennies did was visit Maureen's store to purchase one or two essentials. Fergal followed them in. The newcomers exchanged pleasantries with Maureen, who was busy behind the counter, preparing a list of some kind. While Sally went about her business picking up milk, a carton of eggs and other short-term stocks from the shelves, Pete Rennie asked the lady if she had any maps showing paths on Bere Island.

"Just the one, sir. You'll find it in the corner, over there by the window. There's a good bird book too. Do you like birdwatching, Sir? Lots of birds here, you know."

"Ah, thank you. I've heard there are one or two old gun emplacements. Are they easy to find?" That did not seem to interest Maureen at all, and she returned to her list. But she did ask the question Fergal was about to ask in casual conversation as he bought himself a packet of fags.

"Staying for long, sir? You'll find the remains of the British gun batteries up this way," she added, signalling behind her with a finger over her shoulder.

"Um, no. Thank you. Probably off again on Tuesday morning. But we're taking the ferry over to the mainland tomorrow morning."

It was all Fergal needed to know. He slipped out of the shop and made his way to the telephone box, lighting up a cigarette on the way. He closed the door behind him and waited inside, filling the booth with smoke. At exactly 11.15, as instructed by Collins, he dialled the number.

Patrick Collins was sitting in his favourite armchair, strategically positioned for watching sports on the television and for a wide view over the bay from Coffey's Height. He

26

reached for the telephone on the table in front of him.

"Fergal?"

"Looks like they are here until Tuesday morning. I think they are doing a bit of hiking today and tomorrow they'll be taking the ferry. Want to grab the boat tomorrow? They won't be here then."

"No. We'll do it tonight. They might change their minds and sail earlier. No, the sooner the better, mate. I'll get the boys. Are you sure they'll be out hiking?"

"That's what they told Maureen. They'll be out for a bit, I reckon. The man asked for a map and about where the gun emplacements used to be."

"Interesting. Right, you just let me know if there are any changes. If they don't go for a hike, give me a bell. If I don't hear from you, we'll go over and check the boat out this afternoon while they are out for their walk. We'll be there at three fifteen."

Just as in any operation, it was essential to check the target out before they took any chances. On this occasion it would entail inspecting the sailing boat's instruments, sails, motor, and navigational aids. Fergal didn't have that kind of precise ability to think and to plan. He didn't understand why, if the Rennie's were going to be ashore for a long walk, leaving the boat sitting placidly in the water, Collins couldn't just jump aboard and sail it away into the horizon. As far as he was concerned, it was as easy as stealing a car, which he was an expert at. This wasn't like borrowing a car, however. The moment Pete and Sally discovered their boat missing, they would immediately raise the alarm. Searching for a stolen yacht in Irish waters was not as difficult as it might seem. The authorities would be onto them in no time with a patrol boat and perhaps even a search and rescue helicopter. No, it had to be done at night, with their owners aboard the vessel.

As for the innocent English couple, if they didn't make trouble, Collins had in mind to leave them as close to the shore as possible, in a remote cove just east of Garranes, on the peninsula which was beyond the cliffs from Dunboy Castle. The Rennies would be allowed to use their tender to row to the cove's small beach. There were the remains of an old jetty on the east side of the inlet. Above it, stood an abandoned fisherman's hut. It was on a flat bit of grassland, alongside two upside down rowing boats. Patrick would tell them to shelter there for the night. The couple would be given water and biscuits to keep them going for a while. There was a track leading up the cliff, but it was too dangerous to climb at night without a torch. It would take them most of the next day to walk from the cove, through the craggy hills above the cliffs and as far as the Ring of Beara road. As for the Sallygirl, they would sail her as fast as they could during what was left of the night and into the next day as far as Dingle. Collins liked to have every detail carefully worked out. His only fault was that he never found it easy to change an idea once his mind was set.

"Right you are, Pat. I'll keep an eye out for you."

"No, you bloody well won't, Fergal. Keep your eyes on them, mate. Don't lose bloody sight of them. Go for a hike yourself, if necessary. I want no surprises, Fergal. Alright, mate? Oh, by the way, how did they come ashore?" asked Collins.

"They rowed."

"Yes, mate, of course they bloody rowed. I didn't think they would swim it. But, did they beach it or tie up on the pontoon?"

"It's on the shore. Why?"

"Nothing. Just in case something screws up and we need you to put the dinghy out of action."

"Easily done. Anything else?"

"No. Up to us now, Fergal. Just stick close. You've got the radio. Shout if anything's up."

No sooner had he hung up the phone, Fergal noticed the English couple return to the tender and row back out to the Sallygirl. He went back to his perch at the window of his rented room. He made himself a mug of coffee and waited. An hour later, Pete and Sally Rennie were in the tender again, rowing back to the shore. When Fergal walked down the lane and looked towards the water, at the bottom of the grass bank where they had pulled up the dinghy earlier, he couldn't see them.

"Bloody hell! Where the shite are they?" he swore under his breath.

He was about to run back to use the walkie talkie, out of range from the store and possible listeners, when he spotted them walking round the back of the old pontoon shed. This time they had pulled up along the west side of the ferry mole, using the ramp which was out of sight of Rerrin Village. He chuckled to himself with relief. Fergal knew what Collins would say and do if he got things wrong. On the surface, Patrick Collins was an amiable, sometimes smooth-talking Irishman. If he felt threatened or if he lost his temper, however, he could be the nastiest piece of work in town.

Both Pete and Sally wore small backpacks. Fergal assumed they contained the usual windcheaters and possibly a nice, picnic lunch. He put the binoculars to his eyes and pretended to look out over the water. When they were at a safe distance, striding up the hill towards the east of the island, he began to follow.

***

Three hours later the sound of a high-speed craft cutting through the water could be heard rounding the western tip of the cove. A colony of seagulls, which had been taking it easy outside the rocky outcrop that split the cove in two, took to the sky in an irritated state of alarm. Collins had arrived in the rib with two of his team. Like him, they had worked as *volunteers* in this unit for several years. They looked and acted like normal guys out for a Sunday spin. However, they were equally ruthless and obsessed in their hatred for the British and the Protestants in Northern Ireland.

The gulls began to settle again on the same patch of water as Ciaran, who was driving the rib, throttled back, and let the boat creep gracefully towards the Sallygirl. He pulled her up with a gentle kiss against the yacht's port side, out of sight of Rerrin village.

They acted swiftly. While Ciaran waited in the rib, prepared for a quick withdrawal, Brendan Daly, who was to skipper the yacht out of the cove and would also be the one to accompany Alvaro Cousillas to Spain, went straight to the wheelhouse. Collins stepped below to inspect the forward cabin, the saloon, and the galley before lifting off the engine hatch below the wheelhouse. The Yanmar motor looked well used but in good condition. There was half a tank of fuel, about 12 gallons. The freshwater tank was also about half full. It all looked well maintained. Everything was neatly in its place. In fact, everything in the boat looked as if it had a place. It was tidier than any boat or home he had ever seen. Even the auxiliary Suzuki outboard motor looked as if it were polished daily. The boat might not look so homely in a few days, however. The forward berth would be dismantled to accommodate wooden crates. The galley and saloon would be transformed to make room for other boxes and space could be used on deck if necessary. Brendan and Alvaro could take turns to sleep in the saloon, where the single berth, on the starboard side, was hidden under a large chart table.

"Looking good, Bren?"

"Yep. Ready to start her up any time."

The helm and instruments on the console looked as if they had been polished for an inspection, even the chart plotter, the radar, and the autopilot, which was on the ledge above. To the left, a new-looking radio and depth sounder completed the instruments. Brendan Daly liked what he saw. The only other essential item was an old compass which was enclosed in worn, polished brass. It had been beautifully inscribed with the words *Sallygirl - te digna sequere*. The compass looked as if it had been screwed in as an extra fixture and almost took pride of place. The Latin inscription was of no interest to the Irishman.

Collins peeped inside the head, which was on the port side forward of the saloon. The sparkling cleanliness made no impression on him. He just made sure there were only two toothbrushes. He turned his attention to the saloon again, looked around the shelves, opened a locker and had a good old sniff around, trying to get even more of a feel about the couple he was going to wake up in the middle of the night. He didn't want any surprises.

Apart from carefully opening a locker or two, Patrick Collins tried not to move anything out of place. The last thing he wanted was for the Rennies to suspect their boat had received a visit when they were ashore. That was before a framed photograph caught his eye. It was next to the family one of Pete Rennie with his pretty wife and what must have been their son and grandchildren. It was a photograph of three smiling British Army officers standing in front of a Ferret armoured vehicle. For the two on each side of the senior officer, it had evidently been an immensely proud moment.

Patrick Collins did what he had set out never to do in any circumstance, which was to touch or move any visible object. This photograph made him instinctively change the rules. The game had changed because the image meant that he was possibly on a boat that belonged to a retired British Army officer. He picked up the framed photograph and turned it over to see if there was any reference on the back. There was. A typed label simply read: *N. Ireland, December 1971. A happy day for the Coldstream Guards in between the horrors. With General Robert Ford and Captain Anthony Pollen.* Underneath, near the bottom part of the frame, there was a scribbled note which had probably been added later. It lamented: *Poor Tony, a great friend and bravest soldier was brutally murdered by the IRA.*

Patrick could feel his normally calm mind begin to entangle itself in a maze of thoughts. The horrors Pete Rennie had referred to on the back of the photograph were not only the war against terrorism itself in Ireland, which people still call *the troubles*, but most likely referred to two particular incidents which shattered the original trust which both Protestants and Catholics, who were sick to death of the violence radical groups in Northern Ireland, displayed towards the British troops when they first arrived to bolster the Royal Ulster Constabulary. Peter Rennie, then a Lt. Colonel, was alluding to Operation Demetrius and to the infamous Bloody Sunday Bogside massacre in which British paratroopers shot dead twenty-six unarmed civilians during a protest against detention without trial.

Pete Rennie, then thirty-eight years old, was on leave in England when the massacre occurred in January 1972. However, he had been in Ireland, and played a limited role in Demetrius, a British Army operation in August 1971, which most servicemen wish had never been conceived. Liaising with the RUC, the Army launched a series of dawn raids on Irish homes. As a result, 342 people suspected of having links to the Irish Republican Army were arrested and interned without trial. Worse still, twenty innocent civilians died. The operation was a disaster from start to finish. Not only had the operation been prepared on faulty intelligence, but it also boosted the IRA's popularity at a time when divisions were beginning to appear in its hierarchical structure.

What Patrick Collins didn't know was that Peter Rennie's friend in the photograph, Captain Anthony Pollen, an old-Etonian and member of a very Catholic family, was captured by the IRA whilst he watched a parade and took photographs dressed in plain clothes. His body was discovered with a bullet in the head. The IRA claimed they had executed a member of the SAS.

The only thing Collins remembered, and what was making him seethe with anger and hatred, was that his sister was one of those civilians arrested and allegedly tortured during Operation Demetrius. He assumed, rightly or wrongly, that the men in the photograph must all have been a part of Demetrius and had therefore been involved in his sister's interrogation, using what the European Court of Human Rights, seven years later, referred to as inhuman and degrading questioning techniques.

His thoughts flashed back and forth to when, because of his sister's treatment by the British, and poisoned with hatred, he joined the ranks of the IRA at the age of 22. Suddenly, however, those thoughts were interrupted by the radio crackling to life on his belt. It was Fergal.

"Patrick! Why the hell didn't you answer. I've been trying to bloody contact you for about half an hour. They're back early. They're in the tender and rowing out to the boat now!" The panic and alarm in Fergal's voice was patent. He knew Patrick would blame him, whatever happened.

"What? Shit, mate. I told you to keep me posted all the time. Stay with it, man! I'll speak to you later."

Collins put the photograph back on the shelf as carefully as he could and shouted at Daly to get back in the rib fast. Ciaran heard the shouted order and was ready when they jumped in.

As he did, Collins gave the yacht a shove to move the rib away and Ciaran pushed the throttle down a touch, letting the rib move gently away from Sallygirl, using her as cover to hide their presence from anyone on the village side of the bay. When they were about sixty yards away, Collins saw the blond head of a woman appear. It was Sally climbing back on board. She was followed by her husband who began to tie the tender to the stern. They had not noticed the rib and its occupants, but it had been too close. As soon as the craft rounded the reef Ciaran pushed the throttle down and the rib skid away, sending the gulls into a frenzy again.

"Change of plans, boys. Ciaran, straight to Dinish," shouted Patrick as the rib skimmed round towards the west. "Need to get something. Drop me at the ramp, Ciaran and fill the tank. I'll see you both tonight at MacCarthy's. We'll head back to the cove at 23.15."

Brendan and Ciaran nodded their understanding and looked at each other. It wasn't the first time their commander had changed a plan at the last minute.

By the time Collins stepped onto the ramp a couple of hundred yards away from the Cork Whitefish warehouse, it was 17.30. Being a Sunday afternoon there was nobody about and he walked straight across open ground before disappearing between the racks of cable reels. Inside the office he picked up the telephone and made a call. Yes, he told the person at the other end of the line, he was one hundred percent certain the photograph on the yacht belonged to a member of the British armed forces from the time when sister Mary was done.

He put down the telephone and grabbed the sailing jacket which hung behind the door. He would need that at night even though the daytime air was warm and sticky. He then opened the grey, steel cabinet in the corner. On the left side, under a stack of files, there was a cardboard box marked *Fishing stuff*. He took it out, placed it on the desk and unfolded the flaps. He took out the old woollen jumper to reveal two Beretta 92 pistols sitting neatly on top of several boxes of cartridges. Collins released the magazines on both guns. One was full. He introduced it back into the pistol and put that gun into his jacket pocket. The other was empty and he carefully inserted ten 9x19mm Parabellum cartridges. He put the second Beretta into a small backpack, together with the old jumper. He picked up the telephone again.

"Patrick here, Martin. We're going fishing tonight. You alright with that?"

"Sure. Where?" Martin was the oldest member of Collins' sleeping unit and knew exactly what Patrick implied when he said they were going fishing.

"I'll fill you in at MacCarthy's. At 20.45 before the lads join us." That picture on the boat had made Collins modify his plans. Better be safe with one extra hand. The last call was to his wife.

"Something's come up, love. I'll be home on Wednesday at the earliest." There was no need for any other explanation. She was used to it.

"Tell Abby and Ray, will you love? Make sure they're in the shop early on to open up. Ciaran will be there at six to take a delivery." Ciaran was not only a member of Patrick's unit. He was also employed by Cork Whitefish and Collins would release him tonight once the Sallygirl was secure and under way.

It was now 18.30. Patrick had time for a kip before going to meet the lads at MacCarthy's at nine. He stretched out on the office floor and rested his head on the backpack. It was a hard floor, despite the dirty, old carpet, but he had slept there before when on IRA duty. This time, though, those images of Ballymurphy, of his sister Mary, and of the framed photograph on the Sallygirl, would not let him close his eyes.

***

Two and a half hours later Patrick Collins had briefed

Martin on his part in the mission before Brendan and Ciaran joined them at MacCarthy's, and they were all enjoying a pint and a bite to eat. A little further south, on Bere Island, Peter and Sally Rennie were playing an after-dinner game of draughts aboard their yacht in the peaceful waters of Lawrence Cove. It was so nice to be able to relax and do absolutely nothing after the last few days of rough sailing in the Atlantic. They had been for a lovely walk and had seen plenty of birds, as the lady in the shop told them they might, but Pete had been extremely disappointed by the ruined state of the old gun emplacements.

"Fancy a tipple, darling love?"

"Hmmm. Oh, yes. That would be lovely, darling!" It usually meant Pete would expect some fun and games under the duvet, but Sally didn't mind.

"If there's any of that Blandy's Madeira left, that would be wonderful."

"You sure, Sally?" enquired Pete, peering at his little wife from over the rim of his glasses. "You always say it makes you fall asleep."

"Just a tiny one, darling mine. Promise I won't go to sleep. We can have it up on deck. It's such a clear sky. Whose turn is it?" she added, looking down at the draughts again.

"Yours, my love. That's why you always lose. You don't concentrate. Have you been moving things about on the shelves since I got the pictures out?" Pete asked as he went over to open what he called his little drinks cabinet at the bottom of the locker. Whenever they were in port or at anchor in calm waters, he liked to fill the shelves with his favourite framed photographs.

"Oh, dear. I've not dusted for a while. Sorry, darling!"

"No. It's not just dust. It's more like dusty salt. Did you move the pictures around?"

"No, darling. Why should I? Listen, are we going to finish this game or are you fetching me a drink?"

"Don't worry, she'll be given a good spring clean back at Crinan. We'll finish the game tomorrow. Come on then, let's go and look at the stars," he said, handing Sally a sherry glass with the superb Madeira they picked up half-way through their cruise in the Atlantic. He poured himself a Scotch and followed her out into the night.

There was no moon, and the stars were trying hard to light up a very dark night. If it hadn't been for the dusty salt on the shelf, this was going to be a cosy, romantic evening. That photograph had been moved, however, and if it wasn't Sally, then who had moved it? Pete Rennie could clearly tell that someone had come aboard while they took their walk. The perfect angle at which he always insisted on placing the pictures, like a march-past on the parade ground, had been disturbed. It was obvious because one of the frames was now placed slightly out of line. It was at a different angle. Anyone not so meticulous and tiresomely attentive to detail would not have noticed the minute divergence in the pattern of things on the shelf.

Was he just imagining things or had there been an intruder? Pete Rennie tried to make himself believe the picture might have been disturbed by the movement of the boat when the ferry last ploughed into the bay. It must have produced quite a wake. He decided not to worry his wife. However, before settling down to gaze at the stars, Pete excused himself to go to the head. Hung behind the head door there was a small, amateur watercolour of a coat of arms. On the top there was some sort of animal carrying an arrow in its mouth. In the middle of the coat of arms, in between triumphant laurel leaves, two hands each held a horseshoe. Underneath was the same moto as on the Sallygirl's old brass compass, *Te Digna Sequere*. Pete turned the picture around and scribbled a message on the back. It simply said, *If you have read this, SOS. Please call Anthony Rennie Tel: 0189620186.*

What he sipped with Sally under the stars didn't taste like his favourite whisky and Pete had lost all of his romantic charm long before they both finally went to bed. His unusual lack of interest and the sip of Madeira soon sent Sally into a profound sleep before he finally began to snore.

At just after one in the morning Fergal only just distinguished the black shape entering the cove and followed it round the rocks to where it virtually came to a halt. He also thought he noticed there were four and not three heads keeping low under the stars. He put the binoculars down for a second, as if he needed to think about the fourth man, and then searched for the shape again. What he saw confirmed his first impression. There were four men and two of them were now using paddles to ease the rib towards the yacht. As the rib moved out of sight, touching the Sallygirl's blue hull as gently as a playful fish, he would not have seen Pat Collins hand the second Beretta to the fourth man, to Martin. Fergal quickly scanned the shore and the sea. Just like every other night since he had taken up his post on Bere Island, Lawrence Cove, and the village of Rerrin were dead calm.

Collins went first. He was followed by Brendan and finally, Martin. They crouched in the wheelhouse, listening for any sign of life. Once more, Ciaran remained at the ready on the rib. The doors into the wheelhouse and at the top of the ladder leading below were wide open to let the air in. That was one less source of noise. It also let them listen out for any movement. There was none. All they heard was the uneven rhythm of heavy snoring. It came through the partition to the forward cabin, which was slightly ajar. Brendan Daly crouched at the top of the steps whilst Martin followed Patrick down into the galley. Both held their pistols pointing towards where the snoring came from. As they made their way through the saloon, they also heard the fainter, purring sound of a woman's snores. It gave Martin reason to grin, despite the tense moment of the operation.

The two men were well drilled. They didn't make a sound. Pete and Sally never stood a chance. They were in deep sleep right to the very last, when the two Irishmen stormed in, turning their happy life of retirement into a sudden, horrendous nightmare. There was no time to react, not even for an ex-soldier like Peter Rennie. They were lunged at with astonishing violence. Gloved hands, stinking of the fish market, were shoved hard into their faces, twisting their noses, and squeezing their lips so hard that, in Pete's case, his lips were pierced by his front teeth. He would have fought back, but Martin had the muzzle of his Beretta up against his forehead, and both he and Collins were growling at them not to move or say a word.

"Not a sound or your wife gets it!" shouted Collins, signalling for Brendan to come forward.

In a matter of seconds, both Pete and his wife had been shoved, face down on the deck and were dragged into the galley and saloon area. Cushions were grabbed and placed over their heads, to smother Sally's cries and any sound her husband might be stupid enough to make. Pete felt a knee come down hard on his neck. His smothered plea about being unable to breath was pointless. His arms were then twisted round his back and he screamed in pain. Collins put his own knee hard down on Sally's middle back while Brendan helped Martin use a fishing wire to tie Pete's hands behind his back. He used another piece of wire to tie Pete's legs together just above the ankles. With her husband immobilised, it was then Sally's turn, and she too screamed with pain.

"Bastards! What do you want?" shouted Pete Rennie, the moment he felt he could move his head sideways.

"Shut your bloody mouth you bloody English swine!" The immediate reply came from Collins, just as Martin forced a piece of rag deep into Pete's bleeding mouth and used tape to strap it in. The treatment received by Sally was no less rough and violent and the two were left there, lying helplessly on the wooden deck, Pete with half a head in the forward cabin and his legs protruding into the galley, and Sally with her head unceremoniously shoved between her husband's thighs.

Moments later, Collins gave the orders. Brendan went to the wheelhouse, turned the key, and pressed the button on the console to start the boat up while Martin hurried along the deck to the bow. He hauled in the anchor as Brendan took her forwards slowly. Presently, from his perch at the window, Fergal watched the Sallygirl round the rocks and head out of the cove. Ciaran, in the rib, followed them out.

Dark as the night was, Fergal also made out how the rib then sped out in the direction of the mainland while the yacht turned westward. Fergal's job on this particular mission was done. It had taken almost three weeks of tedious watching for the right boat to appear, and he could now leave this wretched place. In the morning he would catch one of the ferries and return to his normal routine as an unemployed member of society. He would report to Patrick in a few days for his bonus.

Two hours later, well past the remains of Dunboy Castle and heading south into open sea from Disert, Brendan turned the Sallygirl into the tide to point her into a westerly direction, hugging the coastline. Collins and Martin had already begun to clear the shelves and lockers, chucking overboard everything they would not need, including the framed photographs, books, clothes, shoes, and toothbrushes. Anything that might give a hint that the Sallygirl once belonged to Pete and Sally Rennie was disposed of.

"Nearly there, Patrick," called Brendan from the wheel.

"Right. Martin, get the dinghy down in the water. Brendan, slow her down to a minimum. We'll release the cargo, open up the mainsail and catch this nice breeze."

Collins then went and stood over his two innocent victims.

"Right, my lovelies. It's time to say goodbye. You don't know how lucky you are. I'm in a good mood. You won't be tortured like my sister was in 1971. Now, don't try anything stupid, Colonel. We're going to untie your legs and you're going to come up on deck with us. We're going to put you in your little dinghy."

Pete Rennie knew from the very moment Patrick snidely called him Colonel that they were in the hands of Irish Republicans. He was aching all over but tried desperately to think of some way he could fight back. There was none.

At least, he thought, they were not dead, and they would have the tender. No point in putting up a struggle. These guys were capable of anything. He told himself to keep calm and to save their lives. Martin stepped down into the galley after having put the tender in the water. He lifted Sally and sat her on the saloon bench. She began sobbing in terror again when Collins took the strapping off her mouth. He then helped Patrick undo the wire around Pete's legs and they shoved him next to his wife, but they left his mouth strapped with the dirty cloth stuffed inside as if to prevent him saying anything. Rennie just groaned unintelligible words.

Martin took Pete first. He stood him against the safety rail on the deck, facing astern towards Bere Island. Pete Rennie was able to see their tender skimming the surface of the water like a playful dolphin behind them at the end of a line. He glanced left where he could make out the cliffs and the blacker contours of what looked like a rocky inlet. It offered hope. They could row that if the Sallygirl could be taken a little closer, out of the currents. When Sally was shoved to his side against the stern guard rail Pete looked into her eyes. He tried to reassure her with a slight nod towards the cliffs.

There was even more hope for them when Brendan turned the Sallygirl towards the shore, as planned, to dump the English couple as far into the inlet, east of Garranes, as he dared. They were going to be alright. Nevertheless, not even Brendan Daly suspected what was about to happen. In fact, he was never aware of what did actually happen until daylight when, in between watches and enjoying a mug of coffee on the stern deck, he noticed the empty tender still riding the wake behind them.

"Well, Colonel Rennie, this is it", said Collins, who now stood beside him. "But before you go, I'll let you into a secret, *old boy*. You're not my target. You're the icing on the cake. Just tough luck, mate."

The pitch of Patrick Collins's voice got higher and higher as he began to spit out the words, a blend of sarcasm and hatred.

"You should never have come this way, especially having been with your lot in Northern Ireland. Remember Demetrius? You were there, Mr Rennie, together with your friend Mr Pollen. Yes, Sir. Photographs can be so very treacherous, can't they? My sister Mary was one of the many of us you tortured. Seventeen years ago, my dear Colonel. You must remember. This, by the way, is for my sister."

Collins put the Beretta to the back of Sally's head and pulled the trigger. Before Pete Rennie had time to register, he too was dead, with two more bullets. One pierced into his temple and went through his right eye, as he turned to see his wife crumble to the deck. The other made a hole in his skull just above the ear.

Pete and Sally Rennie were never seen again. No bodies fitting their description ever washed up on the shores. Eventually the family could only accept the inevitable logic proposed by Her Majesty's Coastguard repeatedly. This assumed that the Sallygirl must have hit bad weather in the Atlantic and tragically disappeared into the profound depths of the ocean. Perhaps the yacht had suffered catastrophic damage in a collision with a foreign ship in the dark of a night. The Irish Coastguard were of the same opinion, and no yacht named Sallygirl had been registered at any Irish marina. There was no evidence that she had visited any port in Ireland. It was believed Mr Peter Rennie had simply never sailed her into Irish waters.

They were wrong, of course. Unknown to anyone, except Patrick Collins, the other four men in this operation and a sixth, unnamed contact, the same Fisher 30 was quietly lifted out of the water and taken behind the Dingle Sailing Club sheds towards the middle of July. The boat also had a new name. Painted in white on a prettily carved and rounded wooden board which had been screwed onto the port side, at the stern, was the name *Hannah* and underneath, in smaller letters, *R.Y.C. Southampton*. That carved board gave the Hannah a nice touch. It was also intended to hide a neat rectangular cavity which had been cut into the hull to coincide with the port locker, under the deck seating. On the inside, any trace of there ever having been a locker had been concealed and painted over. It was just another precaution. Into that cavity, and behind the wooden board, Collins introduced a sports bag packed with English £50 notes for delivery in Spain. The bag had been protected from any water seeping in by placing it inside two bin bags.

As far as the men put to work on the vessel were concerned, the Hannah had recently been purchased and the owner wanted her given a radically new external appearance. And so it was. Her original blue hull was sanded down and painted a bright, canary yellow and her fading woodwork was given a beautiful new coat of varnish.

A week later, the Hannah was back in the water, ready for her next voyage. This would take her two-man crew, Brendan Daly and Alvaro Cousillas, down the south west coast of Ireland and then on a south easterly course. They would sail across the Celtic Sea before heading south, past the Brest peninsula and then in an arc around the Bay of Biscay. They would then hug the north coast of Spain, as far as the coastal town of Luarca. Until then, a berth had been reserved for her at Dingle marina. Nobody was to know. Nobody really cared. She was just another boat, although her sparkling new colours, especially the canary yellow hull, did attract curious looks. Had anyone stepped aboard and below decks, however, they would have found one or two items missing. The galley table was no longer there, and neither was half of the seating. There was also a gaping space where the port bunk in the bow cabin should have been. It had been adapted for storage.

Chapter 3 - The Spanish Connection

The weather in the Canary Islands was typical for the time of year. The heat in the early part of July had been intense, but the cool north easterly breeze and a sea of cloud covering the northern valleys were providing welcome respite. Maria was sipping a mid-morning cup of coffee on the veranda. She had just returned from a walk with the dogs along the top of the cliffs and was enjoying the view across the Orotava Valley towards Mount Teide. The great volcano's peak was peeping through from above the cloud. During the day, the donkey's belly, as the Canary Islanders love to call that dense cloud which keeps the northern valleys cooler, would melt away and then return moodily like indecisive waves until after dark. Then the heavens would open, after a glorious sunset over the sea, revealing a dazzling spectacle of stars.

Maria heard the MG pull into the drive and then the wheels crunching on the pebbles as Jamie parked outside the front door. She was delighted to have her son home, but she had been devastated when he announced he had resigned from the Army. Like any mother, she was very worried and at the same time tremendously sorry for her son. Jamie had since admitted that leaving the Army had been a dreadful mistake.

When reality sank in, after a few days and nights crawling the bars and clubs in Puerto de la Cruz, Jamie also began to feel let down. He discovered, when booze loosened the tongue of one of his oldest friends, that he was probably the only one not to know that his beloved Olivia had been dating another man. Jamie decided not to dig deeper. If he had, he might have damaged even more of the friendships he had treasured since he was a child. When he stopped licking his wounds and feeling sorry for himself, life became infinitely better.

Maria didn't feel sorry in the least that he and Olivia had put an end to their relationship. Secretly, she had always hoped he would meet a nice, English girl. However, seeing how utterly depressed Jamie had become, and hearing him come home in the early hours night after night, sometimes worse for wear, was draining her.

"Good morning, Jamie," she said as he stepped out of the study onto the veranda. He kissed his mother on the cheek and poured himself a coffee.

"I didn't hear you come in last night. Does that mean you've been out all night again?" she enquired, with no attempt to disguise her disapproval.

"Morning Mummy! Actually, no, I didn't go out last night. Nothing much going on a Sunday, anyway. I thought I'd have an early night. Here, I've brought you yesterday's Telegraph and the *Diario de Avisos*." He put the papers down on one of the old rattan armchairs and strode over to the edge of the garden.

"Thank you, darling. I'll look at those when I've finished pruning the roses," she added, following him onto the lawn and under the avocado tree. The English papers always arrived a day or two late and Maria found the editorials in the *Diario* quite good.

"I got up early and went down to the travel agent. Mummy, I've decided to go back to England."

"Oh?"

"Yes. I'm sorry, but I'm going to have to put the *finca* project on hold for now."

"Yes, of course. What are you going to do? Is there a chance of the Army having you back? Well, I'm quite pleased about the *finca*. That can be something for the future, though. I mean, you are going to have to battle that one out with your sister, you know, and I'm feeling too old to have to deal with family squabbles, especially when it will have to involve Manolo." Manolo, Jamie's brother-in-law, tended to grab anything he could and would undoubtedly ensure his wife entered into a lengthy court battle to claim anything going.

"Oh, poor mummy. You're not old at all. But, please don't worry about Fiona. When the time comes, I'll make her an offer not even Manolo can refuse."

"Good. That's taken a weight off my shoulders. And the Army?"

"No, Mummy. That's finished. Once you're out, you're out. I'll find something else. That's what I was going to tell you. I was on the phone to Scott Cousins last night. He suggested there might be a job for me in his father's marine insurance business. Scott thinks I've a fair chance, especially as I speak French and Spanish. I'm flying back on Saturday and am meeting him in London on Monday, before going down to Lymington. You don't mind me using the cottage again until I sort things out, do you? Actually, most of my stuff is there anyway."

"Of course not Jamie. The cottage is there for us all to use, and I am so glad you have been able to keep it full of life these last few years," said Maria before falling silent for a moment. She had not been back to Lymington since Will was diagnosed with cancer.

"That's good of Scott. He always was one of your best friends at school. I remember his mother very well. She was such a hoot. She gave me a bowl of strawberries and cream when I came to watch you play cricket. We got quite tipsy on champagne."

"I was thirteen, Mummy. How can you possibly remember that?"

"Actually, it was her husband's beautiful, white Rolls I remember most. A cricket ball left a dent on the bonnet. Gosh, it was funny. By the way, darling, I've written to Uncle Henry. I hope you don't mind. He's very well connected, you know. If nothing comes of your meeting with the Cousins, he might be able to help you. Why don't you talk to him?"

Their mother and son conversation drifted from Jamie's future to the weather, and then to how Jamie thought the MG's twin carburettors needed tuning up. He plucked a couple of decent sized avocados off the tree while Maria walked slowly back to the veranda. When Jamie joined his mother again, she had picked up the *Diario de Avisos*.

"This sort of thing makes me so angry! Oh, dear, oh, dear! It'll be the topic of conversation at my ladies meeting on Wednesday. How terribly embarrassing!"

Maria was the only foreign member of a group of

distinguished *señoras* who met for a *merienda* every Wednesday afternoon. It was the front-page article in the local paper which her Spanish friends were undoubtedly going to relish bringing up in the conversation. Their meetings, over cups of coffee, tea, and cakes, usually concentrated on fund-raising for the Red Cross, organising their husbands' political careers or exchanging rumours about what so and so was doing, with whom, and with what intention.

The normally serious and objective daily newspaper had, as its central headline stretching across the whole page, a title that could well have come from one of the British tabloids, which Maria detested, but often glanced at furtively when she went to the English library in Puerto de la Cruz.

Either there was little news to talk about or this, according to the paper's editor, would be the story of the year. The headline, *LA MAFIA INGLESA EN TENERIFE,* and the extensive article, which continued into the central pages, was not so much news, but official confirmation of what had become public knowledge in certain circles. A big chunk of the new English time-share business in the south of Tenerife was being run by a man suspected of involvement in criminal activity in the UK, specifically in the 1983 Brink's-Mat robbery at Heathrow Airport.

There was nothing that embarrassed Maria more than the constant trickle of news coming from tourist resorts like Las Americas, on the south of the island, about the behaviour of lager louts from the British Isles. Worst of all is that it always seemed to be the British and never any other nationality causing the problems. Their street fights and drunk and disorderly behaviour seemed to be routine in pub and night-club districts like the infamous *Las Verónicas*. However, this story went much deeper. It talked of serious, organised crime, and not just about the thuggish ways of certain elements of British tourists on the island.

"What's embarrassing, Mummy?"

"We are, Jamie," she said, sitting down on one of the armchairs.

"We British. The entire world used to look up to us. Just

46

look at this headline. It tells everyone that we have a British mafia on the island. I thought there was only one mafia, the Italian!" said Maria indignantly.

"If you're going into the kitchen, will you ask Carmen to bring me some fresh papaya juice. I'm just going to sit and read for a while. But look at his face," she continued. "The man appears so innocent, doesn't he? I wonder if this is just one big tale thought up by his Spanish competitors for the new time-sharing apartments, or whatever they call them. On the other hand, don't you remember Paco? He was such a sweet looking man, and so very charming, and yet he turned out to be the biggest crook in town!" she added, referring to quite a good family friend who had been tempted into politics.

Jamie wanted to get on and change for a game of tennis at the British Club, but he put his hands on his mother's shoulders and peered down at the open newspaper, at the picture of the man she said looked as if he wouldn't hurt a fly.

"Bloody hell!"

"Jamie. Please! You know I don't like that kind of language."

"No. Sorry, Mummy. It's that face. I know the guy."

"What do you mean, know him? How?"

"No, of course I don't know him, but I saw him at the restaurant the other night when I was with Olivia."

"That's a relief. Even gangsters go to restaurants, darling. I remember, when your father and I were in Lausanne, on our tour of Switzerland and Italy…"

"It's not a relief at all, Mummy," interrupted Jamie. "That man was sitting at Alonso's table in Rosie's Cantina. In fact he and Olivia's father seemed to be very chummy indeed."

"Are you sure, darling? I mean, it *was* quite a difficult evening for you."

"Oh, yes. Absolutely positive. I had a good look at all their faces. He looks a bit like Pablo Falco, don't you think? One or two of the others looked like really nasty pieces of work."

"Who?

"Never mind, Mummy. A racing driver. What do they say his name is?"

"John Palmer. It says the *Guardia Civil* are cooperating with Scotland Yard. They are investigating him and his associates. Oh, dear, oh dear, oh dear, I really am going to be in for some questioning on Wednesday."

"Mummy, you're going to love your tea party on Wednesday. You know you are. What's more, you'll have a snippet of information up your sleeve to fend off their sniping," said Jamie, teasing her.

"What information? What on earth are you talking about? Now, please go and tell Carmen to bring me that juice. Oh, and be a love and get my hat. I think I left it next to the typewriter."

Jamie duly obeyed his dear mother and went to speak to their faithful old maid. But he was very interested in what Olivia's father could possibly be involved in. Should he call her to warn her to be careful? For a moment he thought there was still a chance to make amends. But the sudden feeling of elation was only momentary.

"Carmen says she will make you a jug of juice and bring it out in a minute. Maybe I'll snatch a glass too before I go. The weather is very sticky," he said, peeping out onto the veranda. "Anyway, I'm off to the club but I'll see you for lunch, Mummy," said Jamie, hoping that was it.

"I'll have to get Mingo to water the garden again. Now, tell me Jamie, what will I have up my sleeve on Wednesday?"

Maria sometimes gave the impression she had her head in the clouds, and she did most of the time, but she was astute and determined. Jamie could not help smiling and walked over to her. He bent over, kissed her cheek, and whispered his top-secret information.

"I would love to be a fly on the wall at your tea party. When you feel they have had their fair share at the new British scandal, shut the dear ladies up, especially that conniving little friend of yours, Lucía de los Campos, with astonishing information that will have them gossiping for months. Inform them that you have an inside source who saw the same Mr Palmer, or whatever the English gangster's name is, conspiring over dinner the other night with Olivia's dad,

Alonso. Tell them your informant suggested they were going to an all-night rave-up on someone's yacht in Santa Cruz. That will keep them happy."

"Oh, yes! I certainly shall!" she said, turning round to look at Jamie over her glasses with a mischievous sparkle in her eyes. "Whose yacht?"

"No idea. But Olivia was going to be there too, probably with her new man." On that note, Jamie left his mother to think over her strategy.

Maria did indeed enjoy the Wednesday tea party and revelled with her insider information. She also found out that Alonso's wife had decided not to return from Madrid, self-exiling in her large apartment across the way from the Sorolla art museum. A highly intelligent and refined lady, Tenerife had sometimes been a little too *insular* for her and she often took herself, Olivia, and her other two children to visit her family on the mainland. On this occasion she had travelled alone, with the excuse of going to see Olivia's younger brother who was studying at university in Madrid. Close friends informed acquaintances, and acquaintances reported to other eager ears that she would not be returning to the island because of Alonso's continued womanising.

Lucía de los Campos, who had the longest and most viperous tongue, told her friends that Alonso had also begun to enjoy long nights playing poker on a yacht with foreign friends, including a Lebanese gentleman, and that he was often flown to and from the harbour in a helicopter belonging to one of his new friends.

In the following weeks more information about this Mr Palmer and his dodgy business dealings filled pages in the local Spanish press, as well as in a growing number of international publications, including the English Island Gazette. Then, quite suddenly, those particular news items disappeared when Spanish politics took centre stage again. There were one or two rumours floating about that the local English publications had been warned to shut up.

***

By that time, Jamie Ryder had left the island. He telephoned his mother regularly until the middle of August. He told Maria he was in a place called St. Mary's, on the Scilly Isles, and that she was not to worry if she didn't hear from him for a couple of weeks. He needed time to think things over. Jamie sounded increasingly happy, but Maria did worry, of course. What on earth was he up to? Jamie was quite well-off for a young man of his age. His father had left him shares and a good bit of money in the bank, but this going off on an apparent *sabbatical* to think things over was just not on.

The only comfort, something that brought back the occasional twinkle to Maria's eye, was that their old friend Henry Clark had replied to her letter, showing an interest in Jamie. He had also begun to make it a routine to telephone her every Friday evening.

Henry Clark, Uncle Henry as they fondly referred to him, was Jamie's godfather. He and Will Ryder had shared rooms at Cambridge in the late 1930s. Whilst Henry always had his head buried deep in Shakespeare and Byron, Will had been a hard-playing sportsman, occasional student of geography, and indomitable party man. Their differences blended into a remarkable friendship and understanding which was cruelly cut short in the war. They both volunteered for service, of course, immediately war broke out. However, whilst Will soon found himself on a troopship bound for Aden in North West Africa, a childhood leg injury left Henry to his studies and to civilian wartime duties. These included an interesting assignment with the RAF Intelligence Branch at Medmenham, in Buckinghamshire.

Will and Henry met again at a college reunion not long after the war ended. Their friendship grew even stronger although Will eventually returned to work in the family business in the Canary Islands, and Henry began to travel, quite often for prolonged periods. However, when he wasn't travelling or writing, he became a frequent winter guest at the Ryder house in Tenerife. During those visits, he not only enjoyed the cheerful company of his old college mate. He also became his wife Maria's closest ally, or perhaps it was the other way round. Henry had always been a lone character and never appeared to show any interest in the opposite sex, but after Will eventually succumbed to the illness, his fondness for Maria blossomed into something more than just friendship. She became his discrete confidant, and he confided in her a great deal more than she already suspected, both professional aspects of his life, which would make one or two British institutions shudder if they were ever disclosed, and those of a personal nature. In turn, while finding great pleasure in his gentlemanly ways and wicked sense of humour, Maria sought his advice, comfort, and support.

***

The Saturday morning flight which had taken Jamie back to England landed at Gatwick Airport bang on time and Jamie was off the train to Victoria by mid-afternoon. He hopped into a London cab and asked the driver to take him to Durrants, in George Street. Durrants Hotel had been the Ryder's base whenever they went to London. As a boy, Will would take Jamie boating and to London Zoo at nearby Regent's Park and he would end up with the sorest of feet when Maria insisted he accompany her for a bit of culture at the Wallace Collection, almost on the hotel's doorstep.

Durrants was a charming sort of place. It always seemed capable of maintaining a very old-fashioned Englishness about it. Jamie found that nothing much had changed when he took his room key from the young receptionist and walked along the corridor to the left, past the small dining room, and to the lift close to the bar. Jamie wondered if the barman would be the same Italian who never seemed to age. He might pop in for a beer sometime before taking a train to Lymington on Tuesday morning.

In fact, Jamie went to the Durrants bar that very evening. After telephoning his mother he walked around the block into Blandford Street to see if Le Lutèce, his favourite restaurant in the world, was still there. It was, and what was intended to be just a brief visit for a glass of wine and some garlic beans, turned into a slightly longer evening, with a bottle of claret shared with André, the chef, and his latest assistant and girlfriend. Consequently, when Jamie left the tiny restaurant at just before eleven, he was feeling pleasantly merry. That feeling led him to the foolish conclusion that he should have a nightcap at the Durrants bar.

As usual, it was not busy. There was just a couple, sitting in the corner and almost devouring each other. The barman, the same ageless Italian waiter with the same, black, rectangular-framed glasses, was trying to make the clock move faster by getting a whisky glass to shine more than the hotel's collection of silver.

"Mr Ryder, it is a pleasure to see you again." The last time Jamie was in the bar must have been three years ago, but the Italian seemed to have an innate ability to memorise faces. The fact that the previous time Jamie had drunk there was with a couple of fellow lieutenants might also have had something to do with his remembering Jamie's name.

"It's good to be back."

"What will you have, Sir?"

"Well, it's been a long day. Just a malt whisky, please. A small one, though".

"Right you are, Sir."

When he placed the whisky and a small, silver bowl of peanuts on the bar in front of Jamie he astounded the young client by showing off his mental capacity to even greater heights.

"And, how is the Army treating you, Sir?"

Not only did the question take Jamie by surprise. It also knocked a little bit of that merriness out of his mood. He knew he would regret having resigned from the regiment for the rest of his life.

"That's an awfully good whisky. What is it?" asked Jamie, thinking of how he should reply about the Army. There was a surprising fruitiness to the malt. It was mellow, quite sweet and warmed the soul.

"Glentauchers, Sir. A very fine one. You won't find it in too many places, but if I might say so, it may be one of the best," the barman said, showing Jamie the bottle.

"Yes. Really excellent. I'm afraid the Army and I parted company a couple of months ago. I did my five years. It was time to move on," Jamie lied.

"Yes, indeed. There comes a time for new adventures. I was in the Italian Army many years ago and, before becoming a piece of furniture at the hotel, I also spent time in the Carabiniere."

"Really?"

"Ah, but that was a long time ago. Believe me, Mr Ryder, it is much easier being a piece of antique furniture."

"Yes," chuckled Jamie. But I'm sure you must have had a fascinating career. When did you come to London? I remember my father saying you were one of the only things that never changed at Durrants, apart from the wafer-thin toast at breakfast!"

"Being a barman can have its interesting moments," he said, winking as he handed over a bottle of champagne and a couple of flutes to the giggling couple. They had obviously decided it was time to take things further with a passionate night between sheets.

"That young lady," he whispered, "is a regular client, and she also has quite a few regular customers who buy her drinks from me."

"Oh, my goodness!" said Jamie, understanding the kind of regular client the lady must have been.

The Durrants bar closed at mid-night for guests, and that is when Jamie also went to his room, alone. But, before he did, the conversation between the Italian barman and the ex-soldier drifted casually from Italy and the Canary Islands to the ups and downs of life in London. Then, quite unexpectedly as far as Jamie was concerned, it jumped to being an officer in another army.

"Would you be interested in working in Oman, Mr Ryder?"

"What? Um, no. Why?" During his time in the Army Jamie had heard that one or two soldiers went on to make some quick cash as training officers in Middle East countries and suspected what the Italian was referring to. However, that an Italian barman in London should ask him such a question caught him off guard.

"You would receive a salary you could never dream of, and

you would not be the only one. Several of you British soldiers still help the Sultan of Oman. Another whisky, Sir?"

"Um. Yes, please. Why not? By the way, I'm curious," said Jamie, trying to fathom out a connection. "Yours is an odd question for an employee at the hotel to ask. I mean, you've told me you also have a military background, but this is different."

"Actually, Mr Ryder, the hotel does not employ me. The bar is mine," he said, placing another tumbler of whisky in front of the young client. "Although it is an integral part of the Durrants building, I have a lease on the premises."

"I see," said Jamie, trying to read into the Italian's eye. He didn't see at all. He was astonished. If the man behind the bar didn't work for the Durrants, who did he work for? There was no way he could be making a decent living from this tiny bar, especially when it was nearly always empty. Could the bar simply be a cover for other forms of business?

"Will you be staying for long, Mr Ryder?"

With the knowledge that Mr Ryder would be staying only until Tuesday morning and with a look in Jamie's eye suggesting that he was open to all offers, the Italian provided more information. Basically, he knew a man who knew a man.

By the time Jamie and the Italian parted company it had become evident to the guest that this quiet Italian who ran a bar in one of London's oldest, family-run hotels, had several occupations. One of them was as a recruiter of ex-military personnel for one or two foreign countries and organisations. On this occasion, the foreign country was the Sultanate of Oman, a close ally of the United Kingdom for many years, whose military forces were led by British servicemen and whose government was still closely administered by British subjects.

***

On the next Monday morning, Jamie Ryder took a cab to the address in Philpot Lane, close to Lloyd's in Lime Street. He pressed the button for number three. The inscription on the brass plaque read *Bennett and Cousins – Marine Underwriters.* At 11.00 his old chum, Scott Cousins, introduced him to his father and they began what turned out to be a brief interview. Jamie was on the street again by 12.15. It seemed to him that perhaps Scott had been rather too hasty suggesting there might be a job for him the moment he knocked at the door. Jamie felt despondent, of course, but realised he had gone to the interview totally unprepared. He had no idea the marine insurance business was so extraordinarily complex and as tricky as Mr Cousins explained. It had been more of a lecture on the ins and outs of underwriting that he received, rather than a friendly, old-boys-network interview and an open door.

Scott's father did leave a door semi-ajar but not immediately. There would be an opening, but not until January or February, and that would be conditional on Jamie obtaining a certificate in marine insurance, or at least on him having begun the required course provided by Lloyd's. The man was kind and understanding, but he was not going to be lumbered with someone who just needed a job, Army officer or not.

They shook hands on a go-away-and-think-about-it basis and Scott promised to look him up soon. Actually, he mentioned the old boys' summer cocktail party on Friday, 22nd July. Wasn't he going? Why didn't Jamie telephone Mr Mark Robertson? Scott was sure their old headmaster would be delighted to add him on to the list of old boys attending, even at this late stage. Yes, it was earlier than usual this year, but how lucky that Jamie just happened to be in London.

On the train down to Brockenhurst, before hopping onto the Lymington carriage, Jamie began toying with the idea of contacting his old Platoon Commander at Sandhurst, Captain Alan Smith. He was now Lieutenant Colonel, of course, but he and Jamie had kept up a sporadic correspondence since he passed out of Sandhurst. He doubted it very much, but there might be a way back into the forces. There had to be a way.

Jamie now had two half-open options with which to tidy up the mess he had got himself into by leaving the Army. One sounded exciting enough, and he knew he could do it. It would be a different sort of assignment to what he could only assume was mercenary-type soldiering in the Arabian heat. The other, which he also knew he could get to grips with and would certainly provide a magnificent income and security in the long run, just didn't have that edge. In other words, action. Actually, it would, especially if he was assigned Latin American clients, but he wasn't to know that.

All that kept flashing through Jamie's mind was himself, walking down the streets of London, dressed in a pinstripe suit and with an umbrella swinging beside him. It simply wasn't him. Not yet anyway. There was a third way, of course, and that was to pick up the pieces left behind on the island of Tenerife. Scott's father was absolutely right. Jamie needed to go away and think. So soon after the bust-up with his childhood sweetheart, he was in no emotional state to make clear decisions about an immediate future.

The cottage in Lymington was just as he had left it. It hadn't been long since he closed the front door to return to Tenerife and Olivia. The slight aroma of lavender in the air also meant that Joan, the cleaning lady, had been warned of his coming by Maria. She had stocked the fridge for him with fresh milk, cheeses, ham, eggs, bacon, and other goodies. There was also a note for him under the vase on the dining room table with freshly picked wildflowers. *Welcome home, Jamie*, it said. It also told him that Joan would be in on Wednesday morning, if he needed any washing done. Joan had a habit of spoiling him whenever he spent time in Lymington. It *was* almost good to be home.

During the following days, Jamie took long walks in the New Forest, got to know almost every boat in Lymington marina, and had a solitary round of golf at the nearby Walhampton golf course. He also became restless.

Colonel Smith returned his calls just as he had given up hope. But hope was not something his old Platoon Commander offered, at least not in finding him a way back into the Army. The alternative, he said, and which indeed sparked a hint of enthusiasm in Jamie, was to join the Territorial Army. Smith was willing to help him there.

"Better get a proper job first, though. The TA likes people with a steady track record," he said.

"My advice, Jamie, is to steer clear of Italian barmen," Smith said, laughing loudly down the phone. "There are proper channels, you know!"

"Oh? Do you mean there is still an official British military presence in Oman?"

"Indeed. But my advice is to be careful there. It might sound cushy and like a bloody good income, but it won't last long, if you ask me. There's too much politics."

"So?"

"If I were you, if it isn't official, I wouldn't touch it with a bargepole."

"My trouble, Colonel, is that I don't really know what I want to do at the moment, but I need to find something to do pretty quickly. It wouldn't do me any harm, would it?"

"Listen, son. Look around for something else. These people are always preying on us. They know we get bored in civvy street. Having said that, I would go back like a shot. The best posting we ever had."

"Again? You mean to say you've been there?"

"Yes, Jamie. Loved my time there. But we were there to do a job."

"Of course, Sir."

"Yes, I was there in 1976. Bloody marvellous place. Wonderful people. We did a fine job too, and still do. I can't believe some character is recruiting ex-Army guys. You sure it was Oman and not the UAE? No, Jamie, stay out of it. Enjoy civvy life. Go for that pinstripe job."

"Definitely Oman. I thought it was a bit odd too. Thanks for your advice, Colonel".

The conversation ended there. Jamie agreed to call the Colonel to tell him what he was going to do, especially if he wanted his nudge when it came to applying to the Territorials.

When he put the telephone down, Jamie stepped out onto the tiny, upstairs conservatory which overlooked Bridge Road, and spent what was left of the morning gazing at the trees and fields on the other side of the water being swept yet again by a wet gale. He did love England, even when the weather was so terrible. He made up his mind. He would enrol for the marine certificate course Mr Cousins had suggested and take it from there.

After half a pint and some scampi and chips at the Ship Inn on the quay, Jamie enquired. The next available place for the course was in January. His next call was to Scott Cousins and the reply was a more positive one.

"Good man. Keep in touch and call us when you start the course."

If the course was not until January, Jamie had nearly half a year to kill. He should have hopped on the first plane home to Tenerife and returned to London after Christmas. But thoughts of Olivia lingered, and he simply couldn't face bumping into her, casually or not. He would have to one day, but not yet.

Jamie decided to do exactly what Cousins had told him to do, which was to go away and think, but not in Lymington. Instead he decided he would make use of the English summer, if it ever arrived, to explore the parts of Devon and Cornwall he didn't know. The weather had been appalling since the day he arrived in England, but Jamie decided he would grab his backpack, get on a train and head west. First, however, he might as well see if he could join Scott at the old boys' cocktail party. He had not attended one for five years, always with the excuse of being on standby, or somewhere remote on a military exercise. It might be fun and, who knows, it was always an opportunity, not only to meet an old chum or two, but also to make interesting contacts for the future. He telephoned the school office. Of course he could join them. They would be delighted to see him again.

***

Jamie was greeted by his old headmaster and his wife at the Oxford and Cambridge Club in Pall Mall and was swept away by a wave of handshakes and a few familiar faces at the old boys' cocktail party.

It was fun and yet, the more hands Jamie shook, and the more he was asked what he was doing with his life, the more out of it he felt. He politely kept up with the small talk but, at the back of his mind, like a continuous drip of frustration, he felt a sense of embarrassment, like being out first ball in a game of cricket after playing a stupid shot. It was as if the Army had been his safety net. It was no longer there, the confidence. Whilst the sound of laughter and excitement around him ebbed and flowed to a crescendo and the champagne and Pimm's took effect, so did the thoughts that dominated his mind. Although he tried hard to listen to all the ambition and positive talk around him, in his head there was another feeling, one that he had already begun to sense days before returning to England. One can only describe it as one of blame. Stupidly, he felt that, by voluntarily leaving the Service, he had let the side down and was therefore no longer one of the team, no longer doing his duty.

That was until Ruth Eaton came into his life. Jamie had begun to apologise to his old headmistress for having to leave the party so early when she grabbed his arm.

"Nonsense!" she said. "You're not going anywhere Ryder. I'm not letting you go without meeting someone. Come with me, Jamie. Does your mother still live in the Canary Islands?"

"Um, yes. Tenerife," he replied as she dragged him through to the adjacent room.

"I think Ruth was on one of the other islands. Is there one called Las Palmas? Anyway, she speaks Spanish, too. Now, I saw her a minute ago with Charlie Sampson. Ah, there she is, by the window," said Mrs Robertson, leading Jamie in that direction.

There had been a lot of people mingling in and out of the rooms occupied by the party and Jamie had not noticed her before. Now he did. She stood, sideways to the window, looking out onto the street below. It had begun to pour with rain again in London, but enough of a light produced a delicate transparency through a short, navy blue, strapless, cocktail dress. Jamie couldn't help noticing an enticing figure and a thick wave of blond hair which just touched her bare, slightly tanned shoulders. She looked deep in thought and, perhaps like him, not wallowing in the fun.

"Interrupting your thoughts again, Ruth?" asked Mrs Robertson. "If you are not careful, my dear, I shall make you *drink* that champagne. This is the Jamie from Tenerife I was telling you about."

A smile lit up Ruth's face, and Jamie held out his hand. The delicate, prolonged touch of her hand in his, and a penetrating, highly intelligent look in her eyes sent what felt like a gently breaking wave through his body. It was as if a draught of air had brushed his skin. It was her voice, though, and her quiet manner, which struck him most. While all around them there was loud laughter and a confusion of voices competing to be heard, hers had an almost childish ring to it. Jamie was struck suddenly by an instant desire to embrace a woman he had never even set eyes upon before. With Olivia it had been the natural course the teenage friendship had taken. This wasn't simply a physical attraction. It went far beyond that, and it was the unexpectedness of it all that made his words slow to come out, with a rather old-fashioned form of greeting.

"How do you do?"

"Hello. Um, well, I was just thinking I might get a little wet, actually," was her curious, almost teasing reply.

"Well, I'll leave you to it, then," said Mrs Robertson, returning to the mélange of bodies and din. She had done her bit.

"You mean the rain? I think you'll be alright if you stay a bit longer. It's only one of the showers Michael Fish mentioned in the forecast last night," offered Jamie.

"Yes, what a summer! It just hasn't stopped. I'll have to wait until it passes."

"You were going?"

"Yes, I was. By the way, I'm Ruth".

"Jamie Ryder. Mrs Robertson mentioned something about Las Palmas."

"Wow! Did you see that?" A flash of lightning lit up the darkening sky through the window. It took Jamie to Ruth's side, almost close enough to touch her.

"Oh, yes. Las Palmas. I spent a year working at the British School in Gran Canaria. Mrs Robertson told me you were from Tenerife."

"Well, yes, but not exactly."

"Well, yes, or not exactly?" pressed Ruth with an enigmatic

smile.

"From Tenerife, in that the family home has been there since the middle of the 19th century. But British, so not exactly from Tenerife. Bit of a mix, perhaps, but sometimes we think we are more British than the British."

"Oh, I can understand that absolutely," said Ruth with emphasis on the absolutely. "Yes, quite a lot of the English I met in Las Palmas were very superior."

"Yes, the Las Palmas people always think they are better than us in Tenerife. The rivalry between the two islands, especially in political circles, is as intense as it is between the Scots and the English."

"Oh, so you people in Tenerife know that you are very much inferior!" That enigmatic smile again. For someone so petite and quietly spoken, this Ruth showed amazing strike capacity, thought the ex-soldier.

"They certainly brainwashed you on that other island, didn't they? They are just upset that Tenerife was chosen to be home to the regional island Parliament in 1982, after Franco's dictatorship. No, we, in Tenerife, are a cut above," he retaliated, hoping to establish a point.

"Really? Actually, I was referring to the haughtiness of the British I met in Las Palmas. They appeared to think they were superior to almost everybody except the Germans."

"Oh, look, it's stopped raining!" said Jamie, pointing through the window and changing the subject. Tactically, his military training had no answer to the line of conversation, and he disliked politics intensely.

"Clever move, Mr Ryder! You are right. It is time to go."

It was all clever talk, and perhaps absurd. It was governed by that nervous touch which sometimes appears when two young strangers meet for the first time and chemistry reacts immediately to uncontrolled impulses, on occasions spoiling what might be a perfect combination.

"Not at all, Miss Eaton, but don't go just because it's stopped raining. Not just yet anyway. Please. By the way, would you mind terribly if we began again? Did you enjoy Las Palmas?"

"Yes, let's begin again," she said, offering her hand for him to shake once more.

"I am delighted to meet you, Miss Eaton!"

"I'm pleased to have met you too, Jamie, really. I'm sorry if I sounded odd, but I've been a bit down in the dumps lately. In fact, I wasn't going to come at all tonight, but my mother more or less forced me into it. I'm glad I did now," she said, lightly touching his sleeve.

"Las Palmas?"

"Oh, Grand Canary was fun. I went there after graduating in modern languages. The idea was to get some experience before going on to South America and an English teaching job in Peru."

"Peru? Gosh, that's brave."

"Not really. In the end I never went to Peru. I realised, in Las Palmas, that I loved being with the really young ones. I'm not sure I'd have the patience to teach older kids."

"What, babies?"

"No, not quite. The school didn't have a kindergarten, but in my spare time I earned a little extra au pairing for a wealthy Spanish family."

"Even braver than going to Peru!"

They both laughed and then fell silent, although they could almost have been speaking to each other with a lasting look into each other's eyes. All around them the din became louder and yet they had time for silent reflection. Mrs Robertson glanced over at the couple standing at the window and smiled. Was that really Ruth laughing out loud?

"I would have stayed in the Canaries, but my father died suddenly, and I came home to give my sister a hand keeping an eye on my mother." Ruth said, her voice returning to that childlike softness and gazing out of the window again.

"Oh, I am sorry."

"Don't worry. It's been a year now. A heart attack, lucky Daddy. But it was a shock for Mummy. She took a while getting back to her old self. Well, she'll never be her old self, of course. It was as if she had lost much more than the man in her life. But she's OK now. I hear you were in the Army,

Jamie." Ruth clearly wanted to move away from anything that might trigger her emotions.

"Yes, indeed. For a while. But I resigned from my regiment earlier this year."

"I bet that was braver than teaching in Peru or changing nappies!" said Ruth, with that lovely smile returning. In fact, both she and Jamie smiled with their eyes, eyes that, so soon after being introduced, already appeared to converse without a word being spoken.

"Brave of me being in the Army? Not at all. Like you and your babies, there is nothing brave about doing what you love most."

"Brave for leaving the Regiment, I meant. Why did you leave the Army if you loved it? I don't understand." One day, Jamie was going to have to know how to reply to that question, but not yet.

"Can I answer that another day? But, yes, the Army was all I ever wanted."

There was another moment of silence as both Ruth and Jamie looked out of the window, a lull that was interrupted by yet another tray of canapés. They both declined another glass of champagne. In fact, Ruth had hardly touched the bubbly in her flute and Jamie realised the lady he had been chatting to so easily was about to leave. He had to make the move.

"Listen, I'm living down on the south coast, at Lymington, but I'd love to meet you again. I'm at a loose end at the moment, although I did have plans to go down to explore Cornwall in a day or two. I can pop up to London and take you to my favourite French restaurant. Better still, will you dine with me tonight?"

"Oh, Jamie, I'd love to, really, but I've got to go and pack my bags. My mother and I are leaving tomorrow morning. Maybe another time."

The look in Jamie's eyes, the sudden empty feeling, the disappointment was plain for Ruth to see and she put a hand up to straighten his tie, playfully, as if to console him. She too, was sorry to have to leave him.

"Look, if you see me out, I'll tell you about my secret

hideaway," she said, putting her glass down and offering her arm to Jamie. Ruth looked into Jamie's face and there was almost a giggle when she noticed it light up with pleasure.

"Secret hideaway? I am most intrigued, Miss Eaton," said Jamie as they walked together down the stairs and through the entrance hall to the front door.

"My mother and I are going to the Isles of Scilly. She has a cottage there."

"Scilly? That's one heck of a long way away for a secret hideaway!"

"Yes, I suppose it is! But it is also where I work. I flit between the little primary schools on the islands, getting infants started. I took a teaching post there. When Mummy comes back to London at the end of August I'll just stay on."

"Oh, I am sorry. I was hoping you might let me take you out one day. May I write to you?" asked Jamie, rather forlornly again, as they stepped out onto the street.

"I've got a far better idea. Didn't you say you were going to explore Cornwall?"

"I did."

"Explore a little further! Come and see me on the isles! You have to take the ferry from Penzance," said Ruth waving down a cab.

"I shall, but…"

"I live on St Mary's," interrupted Ruth. "The cottage is in Trench Lane. The last house on the left. Having been in the Army you should find the name easy to remember. It's just round from the airport, if you would rather fly!" she added, as Jamie opened the cab door for her. Then, unexpectedly, Ruth turned round and before Jamie could utter another word, pressed herself against the man she hardly knew and kissed him on the cheek, temptingly close to touching his lips with hers.

As Ruth's taxi drove away, it began to pour with rain again, but Jamie stood, frozen to the pavement. What had just happened? He brushed his cheek with his fingers, as if to be certain of what he had felt. An hour ago he was about to excuse himself for not staying for longer at the old boys' summer cocktail bash. Now he felt as if his school reunion had been a pivotal event in his life.

Jamie was soaking wet when he returned to the party. He was not going to stay, but he did want to show his gratitude for having been permitted to invite himself at the last minute. He especially felt an urge to thank his old headmistress. What for, he wasn't sure. Nothing had happened, and yet it had, and she knew it. She always had a knack for reading the minds and hearts of her boys and girls, and she always knew where a gentle push or a little guidance was required.

"My goodness, Ryder, you look like a water rat. You had better get out of those clothes at once," scolded the old headmistress. Then, as Jamie Ryder turned to go, she added, "I do hope you and Ruth meet again one day. She really is the best, you know. One of our first girls when we became co-ed. Such a shame about her mother's depression after her father died. Keep in touch. Oh, and now that you are back in England, come and see us more often. You were always one of us."

"Thank you. I shall. Goodbye."

***

The day after meeting Ruth, Jamie began to plot his Cornwall trip but, instead of a grand tour, he decided to cut it short, following the coast from St. Ives to Sennen Cove, just round from Land's End, and thence to Mousehole. There were two reasons to visit Mousehole. One was because his father had often joked at the fact that it was one of the delightful Cornish fishing ports he dragged his mother to on their honeymoon. The other was that it was close to Penzance, from where Jamie fully intended to take the ferry to St. Mary's Harbour on the Isles of Scilly. He could not get Ruth out of his mind and he was going to accept her parting challenge to seek out her hideaway.

Jamie bought a one-way coach ride to St. Ives for 5th August. He took the precaution of booking a B&B in St. Ives for the first night of his travels and left the rest to chance, but he made a rough calculation and reckoned on being at Penzance a week later. He thought he would treat himself and booked his last night before going to the Scilly Isles at the Lobster Pot Hotel in Mousehole. When he told his mother, in Tenerife, she was quite emotional.

Jamie spent an hour at the Lymington Library, just a few streets away from the cottage, where he found more information about the Isles of Scilly. The booklet included references to accommodation on three of the islands. They all sounded like perfect *hideaways*. There was one that especially caught his eye. It was a B&B situated at Porthloo, a mile north of Hugh Town, the main town on St. Mary's, and it was called Annette's Cottage. Jamie had a favourite aunt called Annette. It was described as a 1920s granite house with wonderful sea views towards the colourful St. Mary's harbour.

A couple of evenings later, after yet another soggy walk up and down the pontoons in the marina, Jamie picked up the telephone and dialled the number for Annette's Cottage.

"Hello," the lady replied.

"Oh, yes. Good evening. Annette's Cottage?"

"It is love. How can I help you, dear?"

"Well, I was hoping you might have a room available for the middle of August."

"Just a minute, love. Now, let me see. Yes, there's a couple leaving on Saturday, 13th. Would the 15th be alright for you, dear?" Jamie couldn't help smiling at the alternate usage of the words love and dear. So typically country-English and inviting.

"Yes, that would be perfect, thank you, but I don't need a double room. A single would be fine." There was a slight pause.

"On your own, sir. I see. Most people who come here are couples. How long do you intend to stay?" The voice seemed different now, almost suspicious, as if it was very odd that a single man should want to reserve a room. The love and the dear had suddenly disappeared.

"To be honest, I'm not sure how long I shall be staying for. At least a week, maybe longer. If it helps, I can pay you for two weeks and then play it by ear." There was another pause. The lady obviously needed to think this one out.

"That won't be necessary, sir. But I'll book you in provisionally for two weeks from 15th August. I'm afraid I will have to charge you for a double room, though."

"No, no. That's fine. I quite understand."

"You see, it's the season and it all goes quiet in a couple of months. We've got to make the most of visitors, you understand. We close for the winter at the end of October. Sorry about that, sir."

"Yes, of course. Well, I look forward to seeing you in August, then." Jamie was expecting that to be it, a room booked, and arrangements satisfactorily agreed with the lady at Annette's Cottage. But it wasn't.

The fact that a gentleman had wished to book a single room at her B&B had aroused her curiosity. It just wasn't what she had been accustomed to. She didn't have single rooms. Men, on their own, just didn't stay at Annette's Cottage. The kind of people who stayed at her cottage and for whom she provided breakfasts and an evening meal, if requested, were generally couples and, mostly, middle aged and older. Very occasionally, but increasingly in recent years, there would be middle-aged men arriving with men, but she did her best to turn a blind eye to that kind of thing. However, a gentleman visiting the island on his own? That was most odd.

"If I could just take down your details, sir."

"Oh, yes. Sorry. Of course."

"Name and address, sir?" Jamie provided the family's Lymington address. There was no need to go into Canary Island details.

"Age, sir? I'm sorry. We have to know that."

"Twenty-seven."

"Yes, I thought you had a young voice. Most visitors tend to be much older, you know", she added, allowing Jamie to note, once again, a tiny hint of suspicion in her voice.

"Telephone number, sir?"

There was a longer pause after Jamie had provided his number in Lymington and, for an instant, he thought the line had gone dead.

"Your profession, sir?" The lady at Annette's Cottage had

clearly been thinking about whether she should ask him or not.

"Um, journalist. I'm a journalist," he fibbed.

"Oh. Well, then! A journalist!" Jamie almost thought he heard the lady sigh with relief. The pitch in her voice was certainly a touch higher.

"Yes. I'm going to write an article about life on the islands," he fibbed again.

"Right then, love. It will be a pleasure to have your company at Annette's Cottage. I shall look forward to meeting you, dear. Thanks very much, love. By the way, I'm Mrs Martin. You can call me Cath."

Jamie put the telephone down. A *journalist*? He had no idea why he had told the lady he was a journalist. He had lied, of course, but what on earth had made him come up with that one? A journalist? Why hadn't he just been honest and told Mrs Martin, who was a perfect stranger after all, that he was between jobs and hoping to fall in love with an island infant school teacher?

Then it dawned on him. He really was screwed up. Making the biggest mistake in his life, leaving the Army, and then the heartbreak of being dumped by Olivia. All those things had so tangled him up inside that he felt ashamed of what he was. It was the same feeling he had at the Oxford and Cambridge Club before being introduced to Ruth. This was just absurd. Inexplicably, he felt the need to have a valid excuse to be anywhere and to do anything, and that included giving misleading information to a dear lady who owned a B&B on the remote Isles of Scilly. Why should she care?

She did care, of course. She cared a great deal. Having a single man renting a room during the summer season was most unusual. If he were a writer, that might just be acceptable. But a journalist! That was like winning the Grand National, especially if he was going to publish an article about how wonderful the Isles of Scilly were.

Jamie almost picked up the receiver to dial the number for Annette's Cottage again, to apologise and to open up to Mrs Martin. However, he began to chuckle to himself instead, remembering the sequence of his conversation with the landlady. The moment she discovered that he might be a journalist and ceased to be a suspect, single man, the loves, and dears had returned to her country chatter. Jamie suddenly couldn't wait to meet Mrs Martin and felt good. He took himself down to the pub for a pint and something to eat.

***

That night, just before last orders, a telephone rang somewhere in Ireland.

"Hello?"

There was total silence. Alvaro was not expecting a woman's voice to reply.

"Hello. Who is that?" it prompted.

"Oh. Sorry. Sorry! This is Lola," said Alvaro Cousillas, anxious now and giving the reply he had been instructed to use by Patrick Collins. He was calling from the telephone booth in A Pobra Do Caramiñal, just along the street from the supermarket where his wife worked. She was on duty restocking the shelves, and he was there to take her home.

Then he completed the message.

"August five, OK?" he said.

"Ok. Right you are. 5th August," the woman's voice said before Alvaro heard the receiver being put down.

It was the second time Alvaro had used the telephone number to provide information about his imminent arrival. The first was in June, when he returned to Castletownbere to take the Lolariz on the last trawl before returning to Galicia. It was also in June when he paid one last visit to the Cork Whitefish office to collect a brown overnight bag containing a million pesetas. On this occasion, Alvaro was returning to Ireland on his own, not to join his crew for a trawl, but to sail a nice little yacht for a good bit of pocket money.

***

Jamie Ryder's bus journey to St. Ives was a total blur. It was the weather. The 5th of August was as bleak and wet as almost every other day since the middle of July 1988, a year that produced one of the worst English summers in memory. Jamie had even considered delaying his backpacking adventure because of the continuing rain, but the forecast was for an area of high pressure to move into the United Kingdom from the south west, bringing warmer temperatures and sunny spells. So he took the chance, not so much to enjoy touring the unique Cornish coast, with its pretty villages and old fishing harbours, but because he needed to discover if that girl on her island hideaway really was who he imagined her to be.

When he managed to hitchhike his first lift, on 7th August, on his route westwards towards Sennen Cove and Land's End, the country was full of summer smells, birdsong and busy insects flitting about in the sunlight. Jamie also began to make annotations about whatever caught his imagination, like the quaint names of inns and cottages, and he drew the odd sketch of coastal landscapes and landmarks. Having told the landlady at Annette's Cottage that he was a journalist he might as well get into practice before beginning his new career in journalism on the Isles of Scilly.

***

The weather was similar in the west of Ireland when Alvaro, the Spanish trawler skipper, looked out of the hotel window and across towards the trawlers parked on the other side of the water in Berehaven Harbour. The room had been booked for him by Patrick Collins and he had followed instructions exactly. He used the room telephone to make the call and was put through by the sweet girl behind the reception desk at the Beara Coast Hotel.

"Hello?"

"Lola is home," he informed the same woman who had replied on the previous occasion.

"Right you are."

That was it. There was no need for any other information or chatter. There was nothing more to do except wait. He was tempted to take a walk down to the pier to talk with one or two of the Spanish trawlermen, but he could not risk being recognised. Nor could he chance going to MacCarthy's or one of the pubs he and his mates used to frequent in between trawls. No, he needed to remain anonymous. He could venture only as far as the hotel bar and restaurant in the evening. He would have an early night to be ready and alert in the morning.

As ordered, the Spaniard was ready and waiting at 09.45 on the hotel doorstep when the pale green Ford Escort pulled up outside. The driver, a big, strong-looking man in his forties, got out of the car and helped Alvaro shove his case and holdall into the boot. It was not until a good ten minutes later, heading north on the R571 after leaving Castletownbere behind, that the Irishman introduced himself.

"Brendan Daly," he said, offering Alvaro a hand to shake. "You can call me Bren."

"Alvaro. Nice to meet you Mr Brendely."

"Just Bren, mate. Brendan."

"Bren. OK. We go to boat now?"

"Yes, mate. The little lady is at Dingle. A bit of a drive, I'm sorry to say. About two and a half hours, mate. We will stop to pick up a beer and a sambo for lunch on the way."

"Is OK. No problem. Good breakfast in hotel. Sambo? What is that?"

"Sandwich, mate. Butty."

"Ah, sandwich. Yes. I understand. Bacon butty!"

"That's it. *Si señor*."

After another twenty minutes the Irishman, who was to sail the Fisher with Alvaro to Spain and back, thought he had better break the ice again.

"The boat is very good, mate. We sail on Wednesday."

"You, Brendely, are coming in boat too?" asked Alvaro. Collins never told him who would be crewing the Hannah with him.

"Yes, mate. We're going to be pals for over a thousand miles. I hope you like Irish stew!" joked Brendan, thinking he would go crazy if the man next to him was going to be as talkative as this. Alvaro could be quite jovial, however, if the right subject was touched.

"Oh, yes, but when you taste my *fabada*, you will wish I was your mother," responded the Spaniard.

"Fa what?"

"Fabada. The best bean stew in the world. My wife is from Asturias. She makes a good fabada."

"But we'll be farting like the English. The boat will be

stinking like shit! Funny you mention Asturias. That's where we're heading. A port in Asturias. I can't remember the name. It's on the charts. That will be where we pick up the stuff and where you'll do the talking."

"*Perfecto.* In that case, *Mister* Brendely, you will also sample the best cider in the world. Compared to what we Spanish have in Asturias, your Bulmers is like the sweet juice of an English apple. You like the English, *no*?" Alvaro Cousillas joked, trying to impress the Irishman with his own humour.

It was not a good idea. Alvaro had just stepped into a minefield. It was like trying to get a Basque to utter the words *Viva España* whilst playing a game of *pelota*, the traditional Basque game played in a vast court with three walls. A look of utter distaste appeared on Brendan's face.

"There are no sweet apples in England, Alvaro. Better remember that, hey *amigo*. The English are a heap of rotten apples, sour to the core, all shiny on the outside but full of worms on the inside." Brendan's words came spitting out of his mouth, like lice-infested fruit, almost threateningly, as if the Spaniard were to be reprimanded and blamed for something.

Alvaro was stunned by the reaction. After all, he had only been joking. He had only been trying to make friendly conversation. He remained expressionless and stared at the road ahead. He wasn't too sure if the man next to him was aware of the impression he was making. He didn't want the big Irishman to know either. Alvaro wasn't too sure how to take the lesson, if it had been intended as a lesson. He was no easy man to deal with himself, and hoped it was not a warning of what the company of the red-faced man might be like over the next days at sea.

Alvaro had heard of the eternal rivalry between the English, the Irish, the Scots and the Welsh in football and rugby and in pub banter. However, this outburst exhibited deep hatred.

Alvaro was a fisherman, but he had always had a passion for history and was an avid reader in those moments of solitude aboard the Lolariz, reinforcing a solid Spanish education, which included general knowledge and lengthy lessons in philosophy. He also knew about the IRA and was aware of the divisions in Ireland. Nevertheless, he didn't understand the profound sentiment of hatred. His first impression was that Daly's were the words of a person with a tendency for instability. Unless he was mistaken, the man's temper was very fickle. He would have to bite his tongue on occasions and just get on with finishing the job he was being paid for so handsomely.

The silence, the lack of conversation after Brendan's last comments, was almost soothing until another line of thought began to toy with Alvaro's imagination, as he enjoyed the sheer beauty and virginity of the Irish countryside. Patrick Collins had told him he was being paid to sail to Spain and to interpret, if it became necessary, on a job to pick up pieces which had fallen off the back of a lorry, contraband industrial parts. *But what if there was something else?*

The money persuaded Alvaro to move those thoughts to the back of his mind. Perhaps it was just Brendan, the man he was to try to be friendly with. Maybe he was betraying the mind of someone brainwashed by political, cultural, or religious radicalism, as so many of his own countrymen had been over the years. He would just have to tread carefully.

"All being well, we should be back in Ireland in a couple of weeks," said Brendan Daly, suddenly interrupting Alvaro's thoughts. His tone was pleasanter, calmer again. "I'm sorry to say we won't have much time for your Spanish cider, mate. We'll be there for a day, maybe two at the most, before getting straight back. Get the job done and no messing about."

But there was a more serious note to his tone, as if he realised that his outburst had been uncalled for. In fact, Brendan had remembered Collins' last command, as they drank at MacCarthy's the night before. "Bren", he had said, "No drinking. Self-control at all times, no matter what. Remember, the Spaniard is not one of us".

The silence between the two men returned as Daly sped the Ford Escort through the pretty Irish countryside and hugged the coast in Kenmare Bay. It also gave Alvaro time to turn things over and over in his mind about whom he might be dealing with. He kept those thoughts to himself. He wanted the money. He just needed to keep calm, no matter what this Brendan bloke said or did to distract him.

By the time the two men arrived in Dingle, it was mid-afternoon. They had taken longer than Daly had anticipated, stopping more than once, first in Killarney for a pint and a sandwich, which turned out to be a pie and chips, and a second time for Brendan to empty his bladder behind a stone wall. In Dingle, Brendan first drove into the Texaco petrol station to fill up and then along The Tracks and into Strand Street, just past a fish and chips shop on the corner. He turned around near the fields at the end of the street and came back to park on an earth patch, facing the water.

"Right mate. Here we are. Let's grab your stuff and I'll show you to your new home."

Five minutes later, Alvaro Cousillas and Brendan Daly were on the Hannah, not so long ago the Sallygirl, a happy, gentle English couple's retirement toy. The Irishman pointed to the forward cabin.

"Put your stuff in there. This bunk's mine, under the charts," said Brendan, putting one of his bags on the berth which was on the starboard side between the galley stove and the saloon ladder. He had left another holdall in the wheelhouse. Alvaro noticed everything was incredibly clean and tidy, except for cardboard boxes with food supplies for the voyage. He also realised there was no galley table and that half the seating had been removed.

"On the return trip we will take it in turn to sleep in here. Your cabin will have the crates."

"OK. No problem," said Alvaro but, as he shoved his case through the partition into his sleeping quarters, he stopped and turned to Brendan.

"You have something for me, Brendely?"

"Oh, yeah! Sorry. Brendan, mate. The name's Brendan! Bren for short. There, in the laundry bag. It is hanging up behind the jacks door, mate."

"Jacks? What is jacks?"

"The toilet, mate. The fecking head. On your left. It is behind the door."

Alvaro nodded and, after chucking his holdall on the starboard berth, the other having been removed to make room for merchandise, he opened the head door and closed it behind him again. As he did so, he wondered if Brendan Daly had deliberately forgotten about the money or whether such an important item had slipped his mind.

Alvaro found a white cloth bag, the laundry bag as Brendan had called it, hanging on a hook on the door. Inside, at the very bottom of the bag, he discovered a brown paper bag. In it was his cash. There was a neat bundle of five hundred green, one thousand peseta notes. The empty laundry bag now hung at a slightly different angle, revealing a small watercolour which also hung on the back of the head door. Alvaro lifted the linen bag to see a small, amateur watercolour. It appeared to be of a coat of arms. On the top was an animal carrying an arrow. In the middle of the coat of arms two hands each held a horseshoe. He didn't bother reading the motto, *Te digna sequere*, but he did find it strange that the only picture in the whole boat appeared to hang, invisibly, behind the toilet door.

"Here, mate. This is where we are heading," said Brendan, gesturing with a hand for the Spaniard to join him at the chart table. Alvaro inspected the curved line drawn in an arc around the Bay of Biscay on the chart. It was a rough idea of the course which they would navigate, but Hannah's electronic chart display would do the rest.

"Luarca. Know the place, mate? I did a recce there last year. Me and the wife did a nice little bike tour along the north coast of Spain. Pretty little place."

"Yes, I know it. Important for fishing," said Alvaro.

"That's grand. We decided on this one because the harbour is well protected from the open sea. Easy access too. It was one of several locations suggested to Patrick by his Spanish friend."

"Yes. Where a river called Rio Negro meets sea. No problem. But, in August, too many people. Tourists, you know."

"Really? I was there in October. It was dead quiet, and very wet too! No matter. We'll be tourists too. Perfect cover, mate, hey?"

In a way, thought Alvaro. Perhaps it was a good idea to look like a couple of foreign tourists sailing into the small Luarca harbour. Maybe nobody would suspect. As far as he was concerned, the less attention they brought to themselves, the better. However, to anyone watching, it might look very dodgy observing crates being loaded onto a bright yellow yacht. But these people probably had that sorted, and someone paid to keep their mouth shut. Alvaro's main concern was being caught red-handed with all the contraband, but he knew exactly what he would do the moment he suspected he might be in trouble. He would grab the money, jump ship, and disappear in his own country.

***

Daly spent the next hour showing the trawler captain the Hannah's instruments, the engine, the topped-up fuel and water tanks, the spare outboard, and the sailing gear. It all appeared in order, although it had been a few years since Alvaro had actually sailed. The Spaniard's confidence in the big man began to grow. He evidently knew his stuff and was remarkably nimble for his size, although he did crack his head a couple of times stepping in and out of the wheelhouse.

Two days later, on Tuesday, 9th August, the day they were supposed to sail, the weather turned nasty. It would be suicidal even to motor the short distance between the harbour and the bay. Not even the hardiest fishermen would be out in this. The heavens had opened during the night and gale-force winds thrashed against the Hannah, pounding the wheelhouse with a mix of horizontal rain and hail. There was no way they were going to sail in that weather. Alvaro Cousillas, the tough trawlerman, was grateful. He could do with a couple of days of calmer weather to come to terms with the way the Hannah behaved in the water, especially if he was going to be taking orders from this Brendan fellow, a man he already knew could be very rough indeed.

So the morning was spent making calls. Brendan went to the

telephone box next to the chippie to call Collins.

"Bren? All set then?"

"No, Pat. Have you not seen the weather? It's been lashing it down here since last night and there's a hell of a gale blowing, man. No way we can take her out today."

"That bad?"

The unit commander swore, but he had almost anticipated this might happen. He had been keeping an eye on the weather. He had known Brendan Daly for many years. He was a man of the sea and no chicken. If he wouldn't sail, nobody would. However much Patrick Collins disliked changing a carefully drawn-up plan, common sense had to prevail, and he told Brendan to expect a call back in two hours, at exactly 10.45. As soon as Brendan hung up, Collins telephoned a number in Spain, the number he had dialled on so many occasions over the past few months. It belonged to a man named Gorka Uriburu.

"*Mar celta,*" Collins said, pronouncing the Spanish as best he could.

The coded introduction, Celtic Sea, were the words they had agreed to use whenever they needed to talk. Uriburu picked up the receiver. If the telephone was put down immediately, it meant the coast was not clear. The receiver of the call would telephone back from a call box exactly 30 minutes later. In this case, Gorka was on his own in his *despacho*. In other words, he was sitting behind his office desk at the family law firm in the town of Mondragón, deep in the Basque Country.

Uriburu swivelled the chair around to look out over the grey and red buildings on the other side of the Deba River. Just like Alvaro, the man spoke astoundingly good English, but even better. One could almost say that Gorka's was refined, as if he had received a privileged education, with English language classes as a child far better than Patrick Collins could ever have dreamed of in the depressing chaos of Northern Ireland. Even his accent had that touch of an English private-school education, something that had at first irked and confused the IRA man profoundly. Nevertheless their rationale and ambitions were similar. Whilst Patrick's was a nationalist, political war fed by religious and class divisions, as well as by envy, Gorka's virulent and bitter nationalism was stirred by an inherent hunger for power.

Uriburu could not have sounded calmer. In Spain, last minute changes, even without prior notice, were something quite normal and almost to be expected.

"No problem, Patrick. I shall make other arrangements. Don't worry, my friend. Everything is in position. The merchandise, the men, all under control."

"That's grand, Gorka. I'm sure it is. But, like our Irish weather, some things we can fix, others we can't, hey? Will you be kind and call me back to confirm the details? You know, just to put my boys at ease. Will you now?" Collins, trying not to betray his less smooth ways, was firm in his request. He, unlike his Spanish contact, needed to know that things were going like clockwork.

"Of course, Patrick. I shall telephone you in one hour. OK?"

The man in Mondragon made three other calls almost immediately after swivelling his office chair back to face the wall, where a portrait of his grandfather hung alongside a framed photograph of himself with what looked like a group of students. There must have been about a dozen of them, young men, and women. They stood, fists in the air, behind a blue and black placard with the words *Euskadi Ta Askatasuna.* The words, from which the initials ETA was adopted by what was considered a terrorist organisation, translated as *Basque Country and Freedom.*

Uriburu did not come back to Collins with an agreed modification to the itinerary until close to midday. The lack of perfection always bugged the Irishman, but he had come to expect the more casual approach from his Basque counterpart. The leadership had also assured him the Spanish contact was to be trusted to keep his side of the bargain.

Consequently, back in the Dingle weather, Brendan Daly had been drenched more than once and was feeling miserable after having waited, inside and outside of the telephone box for nearly two hours in the pouring rain, blown across the street by furious gusts of wind. The good thing about the location of the booth was that the fish and chips shop provided welcome shelter, warmth, and a hot meal after the call from Collins finally came through. With him, at the corner table, also devouring two helpings of fish and chips, was Alvaro. He had also used the telephone to make another call to his wife in Galicia. Everything was fine, he said. They were in port waiting for the seas to calm. That is exactly what Brendan told Alvaro.

"Patrick says the weather will clear up in a couple of days. We'll just sit this one out and sail when the wind drops. The weatherman says it should be fine by the end of the week, so I plan to be on our way on Friday."

"OK. Perfect."

"Alvaro, Patrick also informed me there might be a change of plan. It has something to do with Spanish controls at Luarca, but we will know by Friday. Apparently, a mate of yours was caught unloading South American drugs. Do you think you'll be alright on your own for a couple of days? I'll be back on Thursday afternoon. Alright, mate?"

"No problem. I wait here. It's good."

Alvaro attempted to disguise his pleasure at hearing the news that he would be on his own for a couple of days by commenting on the information coming from Luarca.

"By the way, Mr Brendely, I have no friends who traffic with drugs. Please remember that. But, *amigo*, it is good that the attention is on that incident, yes? The police will not expect another boat to risk contraband business in the port for a long time, eh?"

"Nice one, mate. By the way, this is on me, Alvaro," said Brendan, referring to the meal of fish and chips. He also gave up on getting the Spaniard to call him Bren. Perhaps the big Irishman has another side to him, thought, Alvaro.

An hour later, Brendan Daly stepped ashore off the Hannah, leaving Alvaro in charge. The trawlerman decided to lie low on the boat, perhaps only popping out to a pub or to the fish and chips shop in the evenings, if it ever stopped raining. Right now, he didn't really care. It was just so good to be alone.

He also had a couple of books. One was a book his wife had given him, a very Latin, passionate, colloquial story of love in a Caribbean port, by Gabriel García Márquez. The title was *Love in the Time of Cholera.* The other was going to be a massive task, not only because of the sheer size of the book, but because it was in English. He had used a lot of literature in English over the years, simply as an autodidactic method of expanding his knowledge of the language. In this case, however, he was also seeking an external explanation, uncompromised by bitter, one-sided politics at home, about the Spanish Civil War. This mammoth book was by the English historian, Hugh Thomas. It had been recommended to Alvaro by his old school history teacher whom he happened to meet in a café the previous winter. Just as he had done as a schoolboy, Alvaro had questioned his old professor, Don Alberto, about the political situation in Spain and he had been astounded to listen to the teacher's new outlook on life. As a young schoolmaster, Alberto Pérez had been unrelentless in feeding his pupils left-wing propaganda, something he would have been in deep trouble for under the Spanish dictatorship. However, in 1987, when the two discussed politics over a cup of coffee, his old history teacher admitted to having voted for the centre-right party, *Alianza Popular,* in the June municipal elections. The Popular Alliance was led by Manuel Fraga, who had been one of General Franco's ministers during the military dictatorship in the 1960s.

"Spanish history and politics have a different meaning when you look at it from the outside," Don Alberto told him. "The lefties have just as much blood on their hands, possibly more so if you study what happened before the Civil War. There was a reason for the war and the left is to be blamed for that. What happened afterwards, the revenge taken by elements of the right, was equally abominable. But our brothers on the two sides were each as bad as the other. Unfortunately, we will never have true democracy until the Civil War ceases to be a political instrument. If everyone in Spain could read books like this, by a foreign historian with no personal bias, it would make a huge difference to the way we understand each other and our young democracy. It might also help rid us of our stupid, inferiority complex."

Alvaro Cousillas made himself a coffee and began to read *Love in the Time of Cholera*. But it only took him one mug to realise that this was no time for beautiful prose and intriguing love affairs in a book which he imagined was more for a woman than for a man. In any case, he could not concentrate. Don Alberto's words kept coming at him, like the lashings of the rain against the Hannah's wheelhouse. He put down the passionate book, which he knew he would have to read before seeing his wife again, back into the holdall and took out *The Spanish Civil War* as well as his battered Spanish-English dictionary. He then borrowed a pencil from the chart table and sat down, like a student researching for a philosophical essay.

***

A little further south west, in England, and on the following evening, the same kind of weather eventually got the better of Jamie Ryder in Cornwall.

He was never one to let a bit of weather get the better of him, but this was not the kind of gentle exploring of Cornwall he had anticipated. Trained to resist when the going got tough was one thing, but he was no longer in the Army. There was no need to live it rough, however much he enjoyed an adventure, sleeping in the old tent and sharing a field with inquisitive sheep. Even they had turned their backs on him and were sheltering against the stone wall of an old barn at the other side of the field.

The field, in which a few wet puddles had glistened at Jamie when he set up camp in the afternoon sunshine, was now running like a stream. The water began to follow every contour and ripple it could find to get inside the old tent, and Jamie was now desperately trying to keep clothes dry in plastic bags. The sleeping bag was completely soaked through. Worst of all, the earth in the field had quickly become so flooded and muddy that the gale was plucking out the tent pins one by one, as if it were playing a game of Mikado, no matter how many stones he gathered off the adjacent wall to replace the pegs. If he and the water had not been weighing it down, his tent would have become a kite. If only he had done the sensible thing and paid the old girl down the road to stay at her proper camp site.

Jamie followed the sheep's initiative. He shoved all he could into the backpack, plastic bags with dry clothes, whatever biscuits, and food he could save, the portable gas stove and anything else that would fit and made a run for the barn. Before doing so, he loosened the tent poles and lay them inside the tent so that it became like a sheet on the ground. He then picked a couple more larger stones off the wall and threw them onto the flattened tent. Jamie hoped they would keep it from flying away altogether.

As they saw him coming through another downpour, the sheep retreated in unison towards the bottom corner of the field. They would return to the shelter of the barn wall the moment Jamie had gone. He hoped there would be a way into the barn and, as he neared the stone building, Jamie came across a small opening where there might once have been a neat, wooden gate. He ran through the gap and immediately came across the barn's bolted doorway. There did not appear to be a lock and he grabbed at the bolt, but it wouldn't budge. Time had sealed the mechanism. The place looked very abandoned.

Jamie swore. He ran to the other side of the barn. There was a window with broken panes, but it was close to the top of the barn and too high to reach without a ladder. Jamie was becoming more drenched and plastered with mud. There was no option. He would have to try to force the bolt.

It was easier than he thought. A nice stone from the wall which separated the field from the track did the trick. One hard knock and the bolt gave. The barn door swung open on old hinges and Jamie collapsed onto the hard floor after pulling the door closed. He laughed out loud. He had shelter, somewhere dry to spend the night. He would think about what to do next in the morning but, first, he had to get the wet clothes off.

As he pulled off his hiking boots and stripped naked, Jamie got used to the darkness and looked around the interior, making a mental note of what he could use to make himself comfortable. The first thing he noticed, however, as he pulled on his old tracksuit bottom and a jumper, was the smell of oil and damp hay. He soon realised why. At the back of the barn, almost hidden by some kind of tarpaulin, there must be an old tractor or a piece of farm machinery. He might inspect that in the morning.

There were spider webs hanging from every beam, and a few bales of hay stacked untidily against a side wall next to what looked like an old desk. The concrete floor was covered by more hay and tools that had not seen a man for many years. The place reeked of abandon, but the roof didn't leak. The place was perfect, and Jamie's stomach began to ache, telling him it was time to heat up a tin of sausage and beans and to brew himself a mug of tea. The beams were too high to hang his wet clothes on so, after lighting the gas stove, which he used for cooking as well as for heating water for his tea, he went over to the desk, hoping there might be some string or a cable in one of the drawers which he could use as a washing line.

The first drawer was empty and the second just had an old ledger inside but the third, the deeper of the three, contained two old biscuit tins and an oily, plywood box. Inside the box there was a key attached to an interesting keyring. It could be for a tractor although the keyring did seem a bit over-the-top for a farm vehicle, with what looked like a silver, crescent moon attached to it. The first biscuit tin which he opened was full of rusty, old nails but the biggest of the tins had just what he was looking for, a reel of string and a couple of rags. The string was perfect for a washing line and, after Jamie had satisfied his stomach and brewed some tea, he hung up his wet clothes. His next priority was to break up a couple of the straw bales to lay a bed for himself on the concrete floor. The hay was not as damp as it smelt and he built himself a dry, warm enclosure with the remaining bales.

A thunderstorm woke Jamie up once during the night but, by the time he stretched himself awake in the morning, he realised that he must have slept very well. His only problem was that the rain appeared to be as incessant as it had been the previous evening. Until it stopped, he was not going to move. He was pretty well stuck in the barn. Apart from one short spell in the early afternoon, when Jamie left the shelter and went through the gap in the wall to inspect his tent to see what else he could rescue, it kept pouring down. His expedition to the tent had given him reason to chuckle, however. The sheep followed him to the tent and then retreated when he walked back, in perfect formation. They reminded him of cavalry on Guards Parade.

Back inside the barn, Jamie brewed another mug and sat down, notebook in hand on one of the bales of hay, to make some amusing notes about the adventures of the past few hours. As he described the inside of the barn, like an observant journalist but perhaps giving too much poetic detail about how the grey light from a dirty, old window played with cascading spider webs, Jamie remembered that he had still not looked under the tarpaulin. So he put down the notebook, swallowed the last of his tea and crossed the barn to see what it hid.

On closer inspection, it was a bit of old canvas, stained and torn in places where the stitching had come apart along the hem. He lifted it to find that there was no tractor, nor some rusty old piece of farm machinery. Instead Jamie uncovered a bright red, English sports car. Two chrome vertical bumpers required polishing, and the paintwork looked tired, but the letters across the boot, above the number plate, made Jamie's heart race. The car was a real classic. If he was not mistaken the sports car was from the early 1960s or even the 1950s. This one had been lifted off the ground and stood on bricks and blocks of wood. Jamie Ryder could not believe what he had discovered.

Two of the wheels, which had been removed, were untidily stuck inside the topless car, one occupying part of the two front seats. The second was behind the seats, leaning against the soft top cover. He discovered the other two wheels after removing the canvas entirely. They were lying on top of the engine, whose bonnet was being held up by two wooden poles as well as by the vehicle's own bonnet stay. Jamie, impatiently now, inspected the front of the vehicle. It confirmed what he already knew. The red gem was a Triumph TR3. Above the letters, which were spread proudly across the front of the car, separating the open bonnet from the chrome grill and between two large lights, was the classic TR3 badge. The year, though, he wanted to know the year. Removing the wheel from the engine on the driver's side, he revealed the twin carbs which would once have been polished chrome. Above them, to the left of the centrally positioned battery, whose cables had been disconnected, he discovered the identification plate. But the light was too poor. He couldn't make out the letters.

Jamie went to his makeshift camp inside the hay bales and opened one of his backpacks' side pockets. He took out the matches which he kept inside a tightly closed plastic bag and returned to the TR3. He lit a match as close as he could to the plate, taking every precaution not to produce a spark.

The greying identification plate, riveted to the chassis, was not in its best condition but Jamie was able to decipher that this particular motor car was built in 1958 by The Standard Motor Company in Coventry. His head spun. Had this beautiful vehicle been abandoned? Was it owned by a farmer who simply lacked interest in such things and just couldn't be bothered? It couldn't be. If that had been the case it would not have been raised from the ground so carefully to protect the wheels and suspension from years of neglect. Jamie went to the half-open barn doorway where he stood, letting his thoughts soak in like the rain into the earth.

The wind appeared to have dropped but the rain, albeit lighter now, continued to saturate the ground. Anymore and the earth would not be able to take it. But Jamie didn't care. He was eager to find out who the owner of the barn was and why anyone would leave such a gem of a vehicle like this abandoned inside an old barn.

First, however, he decided it was time to rescue the remains of his tent. He might need it again and the barn offered an ideal opportunity to hang it up to dry. Jamie grabbed a plastic bag in which to carry any remaining tins and any tent pegs he could rescue and made a dash through the gap in the wall and across the field. The sheep had gone. He also noticed that the iron gate at the bottom of his field, to the south of his flattened tent, had been opened.

A farmer's work never ceases, he thought to himself. It also gave him an idea. He would speak to the farmer about what was in the old barn.

Jamie did his best to gather up the tent, the poles and as many pegs as he could and returned to his barn. He stripped naked again and began hanging up the tent's sodden layers, including the outer sheet and the guy lines. He then wiped the pegs clean and placed them neatly on one of the hay bales. Everything was going to be fine. If the weather improved, he could pack up and move on the next morning. In the meantime, there was little else to do but wait for the English summer to have a heart. He toyed with the idea of connecting the Triumph's battery, to find out if the engine turned over by trying that key on the keyring in the plywood box but decided his journalistic tendencies had already gone too far. In fact, he put an end to those tempting thoughts by carefully replacing the wheel over the twin carbs and then using the canvas to cover the beautiful red sports car, leaving it just as he had found it. The first thing he would do in the morning, before continuing with his exploratory tour of Cornwall, was to enquire as to whom the barn and the motorcar belonged.

***

Unashamedly, Jamie decided to make his first enquiry at the campsite where he should have pitched his tent instead of borrowing a corner of a farmer's field without permission. The campsite was down the lane on the way to Gwynver Beach. The lady could not have been kinder. The fields, she said, belonged to farmer Bob Bunting.

"You won't find Bob at the farm today. He's on lifeboat duty until day after tomorrow. But I don't reckon he'll be needing any extra hands, love."

"Oh, no. I'm not looking for a job," said Jamie. "I'd just like to ask him something before I catch a bus. I need to get to Mousehole. Lifeboat duty?"

"Oh, I see," she replied with a touch of country suspicion in her look before adding, "Yes, he'll be down at the lifeboat. He is one of the volunteers. Try down there. If there's no emergency call, he'll be at the station."

The campsite lady was disappointed this well-spoken hippie was not going to be a much-needed customer. Nevertheless, she was kind enough to show him a shortcut to the top of the cliff and told him to follow the path above the beaches. It would take him straight to Sennen Cove village and to the RNLI Lifeboat Station.

As Jamie left the campsite behind him, he heard the lady shout to him not to forget the bus left Sennen Cove at just before half past one. He had time to speak to Mr Bunting and get to the bus on time.

It was so good to feel the sun on his face again as he walked towards the cove, and he stopped now and then to admire a surfer doing his best to contend with an erratic wave. The conditions were not the best. The wind was skimming the surface, playing games with the real colour of the water, and preventing any wave from forming into anything surfable. The beach at Sennen Cove was stunning, just like so many beaches around the British Isles, with their long stretches of virgin, yellow sands. If only the water were warmer, this would be yet another corner of paradise.

Bob Bunting was informed that a man wanted to see him. He left the station's common room and went down the steps which were outside the lifeboat station. Jamie Ryder was waiting for him, sitting on one of the smartly painted red benches.

"I understand you are looking for me."

The farmer was probably in his early forties, maybe younger.

"Mr Bunting?"

"Yes."

"I've come to apologise. I've been camping in one of your fields."

"Ah, the tent. Yep, I spotted it yesterday morning when I moved the sheep. Have they done any damage?"

"No, no. If they had, it would be entirely my fault."

"Yes, it would. No need to apologise. I felt sorry for the poor sod who had the bright idea of pitching a tent in my water-logged field."

"Quite. It was a foolish thing to do, but I still wanted to apologise. You see, I also took the liberty of sheltering in your barn. In fact, it was the barn I really wanted to enquire about."

"Bob, the name's Bob. What about the barn?"

"I had to take shelter inside it. I'm afraid there wasn't much option. Everything happened rather fast, and all my stuff was soaked through."

"Oh, aye?"

"Yes. I'm terribly sorry. By the way I'm Jamie Ryder".

"It isn't the barn you've come to ask me about, is it, Mr Ryder?"

Bob Bunting was a good man. He was also patient and recognised Jamie's genuine interest in the abandoned Triumph which was in the barn. He also admitted he only discovered the red sports car months after having bought the farm from the previous owner, Mrs Booth. He hadn't got around to doing anything about it. The car had belonged to Mrs Booth's son, Charlie and it had been Charlie's accident, losing his life on a motorcycle, which had persuaded the old girl to sell up and move to a flat in Sidmouth. It had all been incredibly sad and traumatic.

Jamie quickly concluded Bob Bunting had no interest in the vehicle and decided to enquire if he would be prepared to sell it.

"Well, it would be a shame to let the old crock rot in a barn for another few years. She's yours if you make me a fair offer. The truth is, I could do with clearing out that barn".

"Thank you, Mr Bunting. That's brilliant! If you'll accept a promise that I will buy the Triumph after the summer, I'll find out the going price and take her off your hands in a couple of months".

They sealed the agreement with a shake of hands. There was something more to this meeting between the young backpacker and the farmer than the beautiful sports car in the barn. There was an instant rapport and a warmth between the two. Jamie had not come across it often, but it was something his father always talked about of the old days, old-fashioned trust.

"Whenever you're ready, Mr Ryder. She isn't budging from the barn until I hear from you. By the way, please call me Bob."

"Yes, Bob. Thank you, and please do call me Jamie."

"Here, let me give you my number, Jamie. Call me whenever you want to pick the car up," said the farmer, scribbling down his telephone number on a RNLI leaflet.

As he walked away from the lifeboat station Jamie put the leaflet in his back pocket, but first, he tore off the corner on which Bunting had scribbled down his number and put it into his wallet. Business done; it was time to catch that bus to Mousehole.

As he waited for the bus, Jamie had a beer at a rather beaten-up café in Sennen Cove. He took out his notebook. One thing he jotted down was about how tidy the RNLI lifeboat station appeared to be, how clean and immaculately painted it was in comparison to most of the other buildings at Sennen Cove. It reminded him of the Army, of how order and discipline were the biggest asset to Britain's success as a fighting nation. Thoughts took him back to when he had taken part in NATO manoeuvres in Scandinavia, and to how the Royal Navy assault ship used by his unit as a base had continually been polished and painted, even in the roughest of seas and bitter cold. Another thought made Jamie admire the men who manned the lifeboats even more. He had never realised that some members of the RNLI Lifeboat crews were volunteers, simple farmers like Bob Bunting. There was still an admirable sense of duty in the land.

Chapter 4 – The English Lieutenant's Girl

Late afternoon, on Thursday, 11th August, Alvaro's belly began to tell him it was time he ate something when he felt the Fisher lurch slightly to starboard. The wind had dropped to a gentle breeze and the water in the marina was as still as a duck pond, so he could only assume his days of placid solitude in Dingle were over.

"Fancy going to the chippie, Alvaro, mate? We sail early in the morning before the gulls wake up. Alright, amigo?" asked Brendan Daly as he plonked a bag on the galley deck and two plastic bags on the chart table.

"Sure, Mr Brendely. Sail in the morning. Fish and chips is perfect."

It was their last meal ashore before spending more than two weeks on their sea voyage to Northern Spain and back. Both men ate in silence as they savoured the oily, workman's dish. Brendan was even quieter than usual. Alvaro hardly ever said a word anyway, except when necessary. For a Spaniard, he was remarkably reserved. The only exchange the two men had in the fish and chip shop that evening was about Alvaro's smoking when he lit another fag.

"You should give those up, mate. Smoking will kill you," warned Brendan. Alvaro nodded and shrugged his shoulders.

Neither man had a good night's sleep. Nor did they sail before the seagulls began their relentless squawking, as the Irishman had suggested they would.

When Alvaro went to put on some water for a coffee before going to the head, there was a hint that sunrise was attempting to start a new day, but it was still 04.30 and the light was grey. He noticed his companion was not in his bunk and assumed he would be up on deck or in the wheelhouse making the last checks. He shouted up if Daly wanted a coffee too, but there was no reply. Then he saw the scribbled note on the chart table. *Gone for supplies.*

Why Brendan thought they required more supplies Alvaro

couldn't understand. There was nothing at all they could possibly need, except for good sailing weather. While Brendan had been away over the past couple of days, Alvaro Cousillas had kept himself occupied in between reading. One of the tasks he appointed himself was to do a stock-check and to put some sort of order into their provisions. He was satisfied. The Hannah had more than they would need.

By mid-morning, Alvaro was not only becoming edgy. He was fed to the teeth with all the hanging around, not knowing what the hell was going on. Why was the big man taking so long? Anyway, no store would have been open during the night. What kind of provisions had suddenly become so necessary at this last moment? They should already have been in the North Atlantic and possibly rounding Valentia Island.

It was close to midday when Daly turned up. Alvaro was on deck, tidying and adjusting sailing lines yet again to keep himself busy, but he followed Brendan, who had not acknowledged his polite greeting, into the wheelhouse. In an instant the Spaniard thought he knew the reason why the big man had taken his time. He couldn't avoid noticing the stench of alcohol on the man's breath as he shoved a holdall, one Alvaro had not seen before, under the seating on the starboard side of the wheelhouse. The Spaniard didn't trust people who drank.

Brendan was also in a foul mood, unnervingly quiet but handling every item aboard the yacht with extreme roughness. There had to be some other reason than drink for his explosive temper. Whatever it was, it caused another considerable delay. The Hannah did not leave her berth until mid-afternoon on Friday, 12th August, three days later than planned.

Hijo de puta. This begins well, the Spaniard thought to himself.

The use of the motor helped push the Hannah towards the sea and it wasn't long before they were making good headway south, in spite of a south westerly breeze which had begun to produce an interesting swell. By early evening they had just passed the Kerry Cliffs when Brendan, who had hardly said a word since he took the boat out of the bay, told Alvaro to take over and to round Puffin Island, keeping a good distance and to then follow their charted course south east towards Lambs Head. It looked a treacherous and abrupt coast, and cold, as cold as the prolonged eye contact which Alvaro offered Daly.

Cousillas was happy to be at the wheel but hoped his look of disgust would act as a warning to the big Irishman, that he was not impressed with the day's events. Unfortunately, as the Hannah progressed south, Alvaro understood that his opinion mattered little. In fact, the drinking became a constant during the following hours and the big man's sudden changes of character began to concern Alvaro even more.

Bren Daly, however rough-mannered he might be, whatever chip on his shoulder he had about the English, had been reasonably jovial at times, giving the impression he was at least attempting to be sociable with Alvaro. That was until he came back with those last-minute provisions. The Spaniard thought something must have occurred to trigger this new and lengthy sulk. That is exactly what Alvaro believed it was, a deep, depressive trough into which Brendan had fallen. The man must be taking something very badly. Nevertheless, Alvaro also concluded the mood might only be temporary because Brendan never looked as if he had lost control of his sailing instincts.

***

After settling into his quaint room at the Lobster Pot Hotel, Jamie went for a stroll around the port of Mousehole, like any old tourist. The tide was high enough to begin floating an array of fishing craft and pleasure boats, and he tried to think of what the place must have been like when his parents were young and still learning to explore each other during their honeymoon. He always knew his father had an uninhibited romantic side to him and hoped he too might show the same love his father had for a woman one day. The weather had become glorious again, the colours in the harbour bringing out the unique prettiness of a piece of traditional England.

That evening, Jamie ordered a well-deserved pint of Cornish bitter at the Ship Inn, the pub which overlooked the tiny harbour. He also studied the blackboard above the bar and thought it was time to spoil himself with a good meal after the events of the past three days and the drenching he got whilst foolishly camping like a soldier on exercise. As he waited for his order to arrive, Jamie wondered if his parents had sat at the same window table all those years ago.

***

The quaint luxury Jamie was enjoying at Mousehole contrasted with what was happening on the Hannah, about two hundred miles off the Irish coast. The situation continued to look bleak. It wasn't the gale and the rain which accompanied yet another front, making the sea even greyer in between jets of vapour and eddies which promised that heavier weather was catching them up. It was the big man. Brendan seemed to be drinking less, but his moodiness grew more unpredictable, just like the weather. Twice that morning, he cracked his head stepping down into the saloon from the wheelhouse.

The last time he did, after doing his forenoon watch, was when the Spaniard decided it was time.

"Eh, Brendan?"

"It's alright mate. She's doing fine, but visibility is getting pretty poor again. Keep a close watch on that radar, won't you? One or two big buggers about."

"Yes. Of course. But, please, no more drinking, Mr Brendely."

"Nah, it's only beer or two, amigo. There's one in the locker if you want it."

"No. Thank you. I go on watch. I do not drink."

"Yeah. You never touch alcohol, do you, you bloody dago. Listen, mate, I like a beer. It keeps the soul warm. You have a problem with that?"

"No. No problem. But I think it is not only beer. I see bottles, man."

The Spaniard was too brave. To imply that he had opened the holdall under the seat in the wheelhouse was stupid, and he knew it. However, as far as he was concerned, it was his own wellbeing he needed to think about, not the wrath of an Irishman twice his size. If the Irishman continued to drink on watch, anything could happen. Yes, Alvaro had opened

Brendan's cheap holdall during his morning watch, at just after 05.00. Inside, apart from a couple of cans of Guinness, there were also three bottles of Vodka, one of them more than half empty.

Before the big man could think of a reply, which would undoubtedly be in a state of fury after he had been found out, Alvaro tried the charm.

"It's Ok, my friend. I understand. No worries. But talk to me if you have a problem. No drinking, please."

"No fecking problem, mate. Just keep out of it, alright?"

"We all have problems, Mr Brendely. We all have problems," said Alvaro, trying to put an end to the conversation by stepping up into the wheelhouse. Unfortunately, Alvaro had not only opened the Irishman's bag. He had also opened the hatch to another tirade, or at least that is what Alvaro expected when he realised Brendan had followed him up.

There were no words, however. This time, it was pure, uncontrolled violence. Alvaro was not expecting it to come so soon, and so virulently. He had never been an easy pushover himself and could put up a good fight if he needed to, but Daly took him by surprise. The big man launched himself at him with such speed that Alvaro didn't have time to sidestep away from the wheel. The Irishman used all his weight to slam Alvaro against the bulkhead like a rugby second row. One big hand grabbed him under the collar and the other held his chin and rammed his head hard against the window, almost lifting Alvaro as far as the overhead.

Then, as suddenly as the violence had begun, Brendan let him go and backed away, letting Alvaro slide to his knees on the deck just as the Hannah was rocked by quite a hefty swell that hit them on the starboard side.

"Sorry Alvaro. Sorry mate. Just don't fucking piss me off, will you now? Now, get her on bloody track again. She's moved." This time the words came out like a whispered growl.

"*Hijo de puta!*" swore the Spaniard, pulling himself up and feeling for any sign of blood at the back of his head. Nevertheless, he appeared to remain incredibly calm. Alvaro knew it was best not to retaliate, not yet. The sea was pushing the Hannah all over the place. He needed to keep his head. They both needed to.

"Mr Brendely. Please. No more. It is not good. If it happens again, I quit. You understand? I quit, *hombre*," shouted Alvaro, pointing at the holdall under the seating before grabbing the wheel.

"You're right, amigo. No more. You alright? Sorry, mate. I'm very sorry."

Alvaro didn't bother to look at Brendan this time. Eye contact was the last thing he wanted. He turned the wheel to put the Hannah back on track and the bow reacted by rising nicely over a large wave. It was Brendan who wanted eye contact now and he pressed a hand onto the Spaniard's right shoulder as if that would make a difference and induce some kind of forgiveness. Alvaro just pushed him away and stared straight ahead, his Spanish pride hurting with anger and fear.

"I am really sorry, Alvaro. I don't know what got to me. Bad news back home. The missus, you know. She has left me. Gone to live with her mother." The tough Irishman's voice cracked, and Alvaro could sense the man fighting to prevent himself from breaking down.

"OK, Mr Brendely. You see. Better if we talk. I understand. I am sorry about your wife. Sure you can make it good again when we return. Women are women. But no drink, yes?"

"OK, Alvaro. No more Vodka. Alright mate? But stop calling me Mr Brendely. Just Bren, mate. Just Bren."

"Yes, OK Bren. Thank you. We talk. It is better when we talk, you understand?" Alvaro may have sounded forgiving and calm, but inside he was still trembling with emotion and rage. For a few moments back there he had feared for his life. The man has a problem, Alvaro thought as he turned the wheel even further to starboard. Not just a woman problem. A mental problem.

The Hannah also had a problem. Alvaro wanted the bow to follow the line of the swell, not simply letting the autopilot do its work, but keeping the direction of the incoming waves, which were being formed by a strong south-westerly, to starboard. He might not be able to deal with Brendan for much longer, but he needed to deal with the boat. The Hannah would be his life raft if he had to defend himself, should Brendan lose control again. It took a while, but the Fisher resumed her almost natural passage through the Celtic Sea, once again surfing deep into the troughs before rising again to skim the crests of the waves. As the going became easier again, the yacht pushing forward between the swells, Alvaro had time to think, to consider the situation.

Yes, the Irishman had a big problem and, with it, so did he. Brendan was extremely violent. However, he was also like a spoiled child, needing to be drip-fed praise and affection. Alvaro, the reader of history, came to his own conclusion, like a student of philosophy and politics. As he looked about him, searching the grey horizon for visual evidence of the two larger blips on the radar, he wondered if Brendan's hatred of the English might not betray an inherent inferiority complex, which was something his old history teacher eventually tagged the left-wing nationalist groups with, inside his beloved Spain.

The heart of Brendan's problem wasn't his wife, or his sudden lunge for the bottle to drain his sorrows. It was his mental instability. Alvaro wondered if Patrick Collins knew about this side to the man. Surely, he didn't. He made up his mind. One more episode of drinking and he would turn the Hannah about and head for the nearest coast, to find a cove on which to ground her whilst Brendan slept. Failing that, he would take the Hannah directly towards one of those larger blips and signal for help. The money was rapidly becoming less of a priority. Much more important was to see his beloved little wife again and to play with his grandchildren in the field by the stream.

Nevertheless, Alvaro's next turn on watch was calmer. Daly spent the whole time either sleeping or in the galley. In fact, he seemed to be trying to make amends by cooking something up for them both. The swell was jolting the Hannah too much for his Irish stew, but he tried his best. Perhaps, now that he had got the reason for his mood off his chest, things would improve. They did, and so did the weather when the first blue sky appeared to the south west towards the end of the afternoon watch. Brendan even took Alvaro a mug of coffee to the wheelhouse just before it was time for him to take over at the helm. The radar was scattered with blips. They could now actually see some of the other vessels with their own eyes. Most of them were bigger, container ships and tankers criss-crossing their path on their way to and from the Irish Channel.

Brendan Daly seemed to have behaved himself again when Alvaro returned for another turn at the wheel. There was no smell of alcohol, just coffee. The remains of a plate of beans and sausage suggested Brendan had been down to heat something up for himself while Alvaro took a nap in the bows. Perhaps opening up had indeed done the trick.

The weather front had well and truly moved on too, and the sea sparkled with even crests. The earlier gusts that had pushed the Hannah along at a temperamental, uneven pace, in and out of the swell, had calmed. These were now perfect sailing conditions. Even the shearwaters, decorating the waves with their graceful and effortless gliding, seemed to promise better things to come. Alvaro, during some of his most harrowing trawls over the years, had always taken comfort in these birds. If they could get home to their cliffs after being so far out in the ocean, so could he, even in the toughest conditions.

He had lost many comrades to the sea, in one way or another, and one or two to depression, to that kind of blind state induced by suspicions of what might be going on back home when they were at sea. Perhaps Brendan's complex brain was being tortured by similar suspicions.

That sympathetic thought didn't last very long. Alvaro pushed it away, fearing it would distract him. Instead, he tried to imagine what thoughts, what ambitions, what love affairs those seabirds had. They would soon disappear as the evening light faded, and then, like ghosts in the night, they would torment other creatures with their frightening calls on their return to the cliffs. Shearwaters were so unlike the gulls that floated in and out of the trawlers, accompanying them all the way, knowing that they would be fed scraps from time to time and that the boats would always end up in a port with even more leftovers to scavenge.

***

The Hannah must have looked a pretty, yet curious sight to any observant crew member on vessels she crossed as she ploughed her way, in an arc, towards the English Channel, after frequently modifying her course over the past couple of days of intense weather. All looked well to anyone spying at them through binoculars.

One of those observing the Fisher was Sub-Lieutenant Andy Pringle. He was spending only his second day on the bridge of HMS Ambuscade, one of the Royal Navy's hard-working Type 21 frigates. After a thorough refit, the ship was being put through her paces to make sure everything was in working order before joining a couple of destroyers and an RFA support vessel on a joint NATO anti-submarine exercise with Canadian, US and Dutch vessels in an area between the Azores and Madeira. Andy had been given his first commission and was the happiest guy in the world. He smiled to himself, remembering the last time he went fishing with his old man. The yacht's yellow hull bobbed along like one of his father's eccentric floats.

What Pringle could not have spotted through his binoculars was the expression on Brendan Daly's face, nor the renewed concern stirring silently in Alvaro's mind as he lay in his berth, trying to decipher the implications of information, which nobody ever mentions in Spain, but which were clearly factual, in a chapter of *The Spanish Civil War*.

It was Sunday, 14th August, and what Alvaro had expected to be a second day of relative calm on the Hannah was beginning with another of Brendan's twisting moods. Alvaro Cousillas lay low, as best he could, but it was impossible to concentrate on the fascinating revelations in Thomas' huge work. He tried to sleep instead, but his ears were too alert to the big Irishman's rough handling of everything he touched, and to the man's onslaught of foul language which was directed at an imaginary audience. Brendan's cursing at the English and at bloody women went on all morning. It was as if another kind of civil war was going on inside the man's head.

However, it was what Alvaro smelled in the stuffy air of the enclosed wheelhouse when he went to relieve Brendan at the helm for the middle watch, militarily precise at midnight, that marked the beginning of the end to the brief and impossible entente cordiale between the two men. The big man had been at the bottle again. The absurd thing, as far as Alvaro was concerned, was that Brendan should not realise that it was so obvious, rather like a man who had been told by the doctor to give up smoking for the sake of his health and yet had the audacity to smoke fags in the front toilet, thinking his wife wouldn't notice. The Spaniard had it clear in his mind. Daly was like a spoiled child, unpredictable, self-conscious, and consequently a bully.

If the alcohol didn't make his mind up, the gun certainly did.

Not a word was exchanged when the Irishman clumsily stepped below, but as soon as he began to snore heavily, Alvaro decided to check inside the holdall, which was under the seating, to see how much the man had been drinking this time. He found only two bottles now, one of them half empty. The second, still unopened, had been wrapped up in a thick jersey. It was when Alvaro's hand searched under the jersey, at the very bottom of the bag, for more evidence, that his wedding ring scraped against something hard and metallic. He wrapped his hand around it and pulled it out. It was a gun.

"*Qué coño! Joder!*" swore the Spaniard, almost hurling the Beretta 92 back in the bag. He had no idea what kind of gun it was. The only gun he had ever seen was the small, single barrelled shotgun his old man used for hunting grouse and rabbits in the Galician countryside.

Who the hell are these people? he asked himself.

Madre mía! What the hell am I doing here? he thought.

Alvaro picked the gun up again and shoved it back into the bag as deep as it would go. He was shaking all over but managed to unravel the chart they had been using for that stage of the voyage. By their calculations, the Hannah would be somewhere well south of Land's End, having passed between England and the Isles of Scilly. A glance at the

Furuno course plotter confirmed that they had been reasonably accurate. They were already too far from England for Alvaro to risk heading there before Daly woke up, but he could make it to the Scillies easily. Alvaro did a quick check. The light breeze was still blowing from a south westerly direction but, if he turned her about, he reckoned he could be almost getting the Hannah around the west side of the island of St Mary's in a couple of hours, or even less. He had never been anywhere near the Scilly Islands, but it was the closest bit of land, and the chart told him that the place had a port. With any luck he could bring her alongside a pontoon and make a run for it. There would be no need to tie her up. He would let the bastard drift away.

***

As Alvaro took the Hannah between the isle of St Mary's and the smaller St Agnes to the south, he began to think how he would safely sail her into the bay without starting up the engine. Silence was imperative. Daly might be snoring like a drunk, but anything out of the ordinary would surely stir him. Alvaro had already carefully been down to pack his holdall. One of his options was to jump into the sea if necessary, and to swim into the darkness around another boat at anchor. All he needed was a change of clothes, his passport, cigarettes, and the money, especially the money. He had also shoved his boots in the bag, as well as the book his wife had given him. He could leave *The Spanish Civil War* behind but not something his beloved would quiz him about. As an afterthought, Alvaro grabbed one of two small fruit knives from the drawer in the galley and shoved it into his front, right trouser pocket. He took the precaution of putting the clothes, boots, cigarettes, cash, and passport in three different plastic bags. Trousers rolled up, he was barefoot and ready. Brendan had continued to snore heavily all the time.

Alvaro would reduce the area of sail to a minimum and he hoped the breeze might be sufficient to quietly blow the Hannah towards the harbour. He also prayed there would be no sandbanks. He should be alright. It was close to high tide.

Alvaro had already furled the headsail and he had taken in

the mainsail to a minimum, letting the air stiffen it just enough to push the yacht gently round what he reckoned must be the quay on the starboard beam. In fact, when he turned on the bow searchlight, flicking one of the twelve switches which were in two rows on the wooden control panel, he changed his mind about how to abandon the Hannah. What if someone on the shore saw him jump from the boat and make a run for it, leaving the yacht to the currents? No, there were dozens of small boats in the water. He could take a leap onto one of them as he brought the Hannah alongside.

Alvaro decided he was thinking too much. He had to make the right choice but felt he was being indecisive. He just needed the right boat. Stretching his eyesight to the limit, Alvaro used the searchlight to scan ahead. It would have to be one of the larger boats, at least as high out of the water as the Fisher. With any luck it would also have a tender he could use to row ashore. Perhaps he could even seek out the police and explain the mess he had got himself into, but the water was also a maze of buoys and lines. If he wasn't careful, he would be trawling a fleet of boats as the Hannah drifted amongst them. It was impossible to decide. He should have gone for that pontoon, but it was too late now!

Alvaro had to chance it with the first vessel he came close to. He took another look at the depth gauge before releasing the boom. Breezeless now, the Hannah's momentum still moved her keel slowly ahead, but she also began drifting sideways to starboard, towards what looked like someone's fishing boat. It was now or never. The Hannah was not going to touch the other boat, but her stern would be awfully close to giving one of the fishing boat's fenders a good nudge. Alvaro grabbed his holdall and put it over his shoulder. He then held onto the nearest stanchion and stepped, as quietly as he could, over the stern guardrails. Feeling both his feet firm on the cold gunwale, he leapt.

His right foot landed on the fishing boat's own gunwale, just behind the cabin. Unfortunately for Alvaro, the surface was oily, and wet from the night dew. With no guardrail to hold onto at the stern end of the other boat, his foot slid sideways.

Consequently, Alvaro fell heavily on the fishing boat's deck. He was not as nimble as he used to be. The holdall saved his head from serious injury, but Alvaro grimaced in pain. His left knee got the worst of the bump and his right elbow hurt like hell. Then he felt something warm and sticky and realised he was bleeding profusely. His left arm was torn just above the wrist. He had slashed it on an old, rusting lobster pot.

Never mind the pain and the arm. He could take care of those later, he thought. First, Alvaro needed to check if the noise had woken the Irishman out of his alcohol-affected sleep. He lifted his head very slowly over the stern gunwale so that he could just about get one eye to focus on the Hannah. She was still moving, albeit very slowly now. Alvaro could see that all the other boats were facing him, so the current was moving in the opposite direction and the Fisher's bow was beginning to turn to port, being swung around like a compass needle by the flow of the water. The Hannah was also being dragged to a halt by a spider web of lines in the water attaching boats to buoys, buoys to boats, in what appeared to be a chaotic tangle. Nevertheless, when the Hannah's bow finally rammed another boat firmly on its port side, Alvaro estimated the Hannah was now more than sixty metres away.

He watched, listened, and waited. He rubbed his eyes and watched again. Not a sign of life on the Hannah's deck. No movement in the shadows of the wheelhouse. But Alvaro cursed. He had left the bloody bow searchlight on. If the Hannah turned any more, the light would point directly at his temporary refuge. Perhaps the boat wasn't so old, thought Alvaro, as he tried to bandage his arm with a shirt he had pulled from one of the plastic bags in the holdall in an attempt to stop the bleeding. The robust little boat reminded him of the Rhea Timoniers which were manufactured in La Rochelle, France and which were so popular amongst traditional, Galician coastal fishermen.

He wrapped the shirt as tightly as he could around the wound, using his teeth to tie a knot with the loose sleeves. At the same time, the Spaniard didn't take his eyes off the Hannah. He grabbed one of the lobster pots and pulled it towards him before hauling himself up painfully, using it as a seat from which to watch the Hannah for at least the next half an hour. She seemed to have stopped moving. The good news was that she drifted slightly out of sight between a slim-looking yacht and a smaller speedboat. That, at least, gave Alvaro some respite, for the searchlight beam wasn't going to point at him. Tired and sore as he was, the trawler skipper continued to keep an eye on the Hannah for what felt like an eternity. His situation was desperate, however. It was now just after three in the morning and Daly, however much he had drunk, would undoubtedly be up for his watch at 4 am. There was no time to lose. Alvaro needed to find a way to the shore. A dinghy. He had to find a dinghy.

As far as he could see, there was none aboard the fishing boat nor attached to a line nearby. In fact, by the state of the boat, he didn't think anybody had been aboard for some time. If this one did have a dingy it would be tied to the beach or stored in a corner of the owner's garage. Alvaro tried to look around him. Without the searchlight, it was difficult to make out what other boat close by he could get to, and whether it had anything remotely like a tender on board or attached to one of those lines in the water. He was exhausted, both physically and mentally, but he had to get to the shore somehow. For an instant, leaning over the gunwale and pulling on a line he had hooked out of the water, he thought he had got lucky and that it was pulling a small craft towards him until he realised it was just another buoy. He was going to have to swim for it, from boat to boat, and then maybe haul himself to the beach, using one of the lines that were attached to the shore. He had hoped to get away without anyone knowing where he had come from or who he was, but his arm was going to need attention. He would have to come clean, and maybe even go to the police about what he now suspected the Hannah was all about. Alvaro knew he had broken the law and he would have to face the consequences. He slumped down on the deck of the fishing boat again and tried to gather his thoughts. He was just going to have to make it happen. There was no going back now.

***

Moments later, Alvaro sat back on the lobster pot and took another glance towards the Hannah. The Fischer was now well and truly motionless, almost as if someone or something had tied her up firmly against the starboard side of the slim-looking yacht. Even in the dark, the Spaniard could tell it was an elegant vessel that was partly hiding the Hannah and at the same time providing him with some cover. It was a graceful sight. Then, suddenly, Alvaro fell to his knees.

His breathing all at once became faster. Every intake of air grew shorter, as if he were about to confront his dying moment. He let out a faint cry in response to a new kind of anguish. Alvaro thought he had seen something move amongst the shadows on the deck of the Hannah, which rode higher in the water than the slim yacht between them. Alvaro pushed himself up again to confirm what he thought he had seen. A figure was moving on the Hannah, almost in a frenzy, from bow to stern, from stern to bow. It was the big Irishman.

Alvaro then heard Brendan's shout. More than a shout, it was a roar, like that of a trapped tiger. There was no way he could swim for it now. Again, he let out a faint cry of anguish. What to do? Lie low again and hope Daly thought he had made it to shore? There was nothing else he could do. If he got the chance, he would crawl along the starboard deck of the fishing boat. Alvaro had noticed the way into the wheelhouse was through a sliding door on the starboard side. He hoped it would be open and that he could shelter inside. Right now, however, he had to keep absolutely still. Even though the breeze, playing with a collection of masts around him, was producing a chiming, flapping, and groaning concert, Alvaro could not afford to make a sound. He waited and listened, and occasionally forced himself to look back towards what had become the deadly enemy. Then, quite suddenly, he heard the distinct sound of the Fisher's Yanmar motor starting up.

Alvaro immediately felt relief when he thought he could distinguish a puff of exhaust smoke coming from the Hannah. Brendan Daly was going to sail away. He was going to be alright. Alvaro sat down on the deck again, almost laughing, feeling his breathing becoming slower.

***

Brendan had started, his deep sleep interrupted suddenly, at around 03.30. It was the bump to begin with. Then, as if someone had thrown a bucket of water in his face, it was the total lack of bumps, the lack of movement and the chorus of halyards and lines tinkling in masts around the Hannah that made him leap to his feet. His head throbbed from the violence of a bad hangover and, for a second, he stopped to steady himself. Then he called out.

"Alvaro? Alvaro? Everything alright up there, mate?"

There was no reply. Brendan Daly pulled himself up into the wheelhouse. It was empty. He went out onto the deck. He looked right and left in a state of shock. They were in some sort of bay, surrounded by other craft. The Hannah was rubbing up against the hull of a small sloop, longer beamed than the Hannah but, nevertheless, she was another boat, and they were hull to hull. They should have been somewhere in the English Channel, tossing in and out of the waves, well on their way to the Brest Peninsula. Where the hell were they?

"Jesus, bloody Christ!" he hissed, before running, almost stumbling, to the bow. He peered briefly over the side and then pulled his big legs back again along the guardrail.

"Alvaro. Where the fuck are you? What the hell's going on?" he shouted out. It must have been what Alvaro had heard from his lair on the fishing boat, over a hundred feet across the water to the port side of the sloop.

Brendan was not only out of his mind with rage. He was also in a state of panic. *It was the bloody drink, wasn't it?* The bloody bastard had done what he threatened to do. Alvaro had gone. Brendan looked at the holdall and grabbed it as if he were going to strangle it. He searched inside. Had he really drunk that much?

Shit. You bloody idiot. Jesus Christ! What the hell was he going to tell Patrick? he asked himself.

It was then he realised there was something he needed to do and fast. He had to forget about Collins for now. First, he had to find out where the hell they were and, secondly, he must hunt down the Spaniard.

The gun. Get the gun, he thought out loud. It was still there, wrapped up in the bag. Brendan grabbed it. He was going to kill the bloody Spaniard. If he couldn't find him, he would be in even worse trouble. If only he knew where the hell he was. That's it. He wasn't thinking straight. He needed to look at the radar. He had to check at the electronic course plotter and confirm the information on the charts.

Jesus, bloody Christ! Scilly. Bloody bastard. You won't get far, you bloody, greasy dago! Daly almost laughed out loud. How did the Spanish trawlerman think he was going to get away from this little island? There was only one way. The Penzance ferry. That's right, he would nab him as he went for the ferry. It was now just after 04.00.

Don't panic! Brendan thought to himself. There was plenty of time. He had to think. He needed a plan of action.

Firstly, Brendan switched off the searchlight and turned the mooring light on. Next, he needed to get the Hannah away from the other yacht. Whatever happened, he had to get the boat properly moored and legal. He could not know if anyone was awake and had been watching. The last thing Brendan wanted was the law sniffing about.

From his position, Brendan could see he was in the bay of a place called Hugh Town. There was a thin row of streetlights running from west to east along what was definitely a beach. Slightly northwest, in other words directly in front of the Hannah's bow, looking over rows of pleasure craft and fishing boats in the bay, he could make out the lights of the ferry port. It was a small pontoon, but big enough to cope with a ferry and one or two other craft, small inter-island commuter boats. Brendan started the motor and let it turn over while he went on deck again to inspect the water around the Hannah for possible obstacles. He also switched on the bow searchlight again for a few seconds to help him see what was ahead of him. What he could clearly make out was that the Hannah was rammed up against the starboard side of a sloop and that it was one of several boats moored in a shambolic line. There appeared to be a channel of clean water to starboard in between him and another untidy row of craft. In that line, about thirty metres away to starboard, there was a space. There was also a buoy to tie up to in the middle of that space. With any luck, he could hook up to that one and, if necessary, drop the bower anchor. The depth gauge told Brendan that he was in about five fathoms of water. He had plenty to spare.

Brendan, hungover or not, knew what he was doing. The chill in the dawn air had got all his brain cells working overtime and he was alert to every detail. He moved quickly along the port gunwale, peering over the side to check for anything that might snare him onto the sloop. It looked clear. He then went back to the stern deck along the starboard side, checking one more time for any lines in the water. There were none he could see. A glance behind told him that the water was clear of obstacles. He couldn't understand how the Hannah could have remained attached to the sloop for so long without moving. Surely it couldn't simply be the motion of the current. He would just have to take the chance.

Back in the cockpit Brendan again switched on the bow searchlight and the navigation lights before gently pulling the throttle back. The Hannah at first felt as if she didn't want to budge, as if indeed something was attaching her to the other yacht. Then, suddenly, she lurched astern. As she moved, Brendan turned the wheel and put her into neutral, easing her stern slightly to port. Once he had her at the correct angle, with the searchlight pointing towards that buoy in the gap in the next line of boats, Brendan took her forward very slowly.

***

Alvaro, who had again propped himself up in his temporary refuge to spy on Brendan's movements, watched. He felt more elated by the second. Everything was going to be fine. The Hannah appeared to be making her way now, between a line of moored craft towards the open sea.

Suddenly, however, his stomach felt as if it was going to vomit the turmoil inside and he slumped to the deck again. In horror and fear, he realised what Brendan was actually doing. First it was the change of tone in the motor, a sudden thrust, and a puff of fumes as the Irishman pushed the throttle back again, this time to make her come to a halt in the water as she moved against the tide. Then it was the sight of Brendan moving swiftly along towards the starboard bow with the boat hook. He was going to pick up a buoy. He was going to moor the Hannah. The Irishman had no intention of sailing away. He was bloody staying!

Alvaro pushed himself up again after about twenty minutes. He mustn't just give up. Yes, he was tired and in pain and needed his arm seen to, but he would be safe enough if he just kept calm. With any luck Brendan would assume he had gone ashore. Alvaro's breathing slowed. He had grabbed a hold of himself again. He accepted that there was no option. He had to forget about risking a swim in the dark right now. He would wait and see what happened. He should try to rest. Yes, he needed to rest. He had a clear line of vision to the Hannah between two boats in the next line up, and there was no way Brendan could know where he was hidden, or that he was hurt. He would not find him without hunting from boat to boat. Yes, he would be alright. *Just keep low*, he told himself.

Alvaro grabbed the holdall and pushed it and himself along the deck on the starboard side of the fishing boat. He looked over his shoulder to make certain Brendan was still occupied tying up to the buoy and then stretched his left hand up to the cabin door handle. He held his breath as it turned. Then he felt the latch move and the door slide. It was not locked. Alvaro shoved his bag through the opening and then slid himself inside after it. The place smelt of oil, rubber boots and sweat, but he was safe. He slid the door shut again and put his head onto the holdall. Before he knew it, despite the throbbing pain coming from his arm, he was asleep.

***

Brendan also decided to wait and see. There was little else he could do. After making certain he was nicely attached to the buoy and that the Hannah's bow was facing the same direction as all the other collection of boats in the lines around him, he stepped into the galley and put some water on to boil. After putting a spoonful of coffee and squeezing some condensed milk into a mug, he went to the V-berth to see if there was anything Alvaro had left behind. He was especially interested in the cash. He found trousers, a couple of shirts, underwear, a jersey, and an anorak half strewn on the bunk in an open suitcase. Alvaro's holdall was not there, and nor was the money. Brendan went to the head to empty his bladder and then, as he turned, he noticed the white laundry bag hanging behind the door. He lifted it slightly and felt around it with his hands. There was some laundry in there, not much though. As he anticipated, there were no bundles of pesetas in there, either. He did see a weird picture hung up on the door under the linen bag but thought nothing of it.

The big Irishman then stepped up into the wheelhouse and did something that surprised even himself. He placed the mug of coffee down next to the old, brass compass, put his hands inside his holdall, which was still under the seat on the starboard side, and took out what was left of the vodka. He then stepped out on deck and flung both bottles as far as he could into the water. A moment later, it seemed as if Brendan Daly was an entirely different person, relaxed, confident, and entirely oblivious of anything but the task ahead. Even what had gone on with his wife appeared to be forgotten. He was wide awake, every nerve and every sense in his mind and body alive to the situation. He retrieved the mug, made himself comfortable on the afterdeck seating and sipped at the warm, sweet coffee. The water around him was almost dead calm. Even the chorus in the masts and the creaks of boats moving in the water appeared to be taking a breather. What a beautiful dawn it was going to be, but what the hell was he going to tell Pat Collins?

***

As the sun peeped over the horizon, the colours began to sparkle over the anchorage. While Brendan had slept, keeping his word of warning to his Irish companion, Alvaro had quit. He had sailed the Hannah and abandoned her in what was known as St Mary's Pool, fronting Hugh Town on the largest of the Isles of Scilly.

They had been incredibly lucky not to have run aground on one of the rocks and shoals. It was August, and the place was cluttered with boats of all shapes and sizes. Brendan noticed, as daybreak began to make the flotilla around him glisten, the number of French tricolour flags decorating boats.

Brendan stepped down into the galley to fry himself some bacon and eggs and made himself another mug. He buttered two slices of white bread, prepared himself a juicy sandwich, dripping with fat, and returned to the deck to have his breakfast. If he hadn't been on a mission for the IRA, a failed mission it would now seem, he could live like this forever. After devouring the feast, he reached back for the binoculars, which always hung close at hand in the wheelhouse. It was quite a chilly dawn and his breath steamed almost as much as the coffee.

Just as Brendan was using a big thumb to wipe clean his plate Alvaro rolled over onto his arm and a flash of pain woke him.

"Coño! Joder! Que pesadilla, madre de Dios!" he swore in his native language, crying out for all this to just be some horrible nightmare. He was hungry too. All he had was water and cigarettes. It was better than nothing but, now it was daylight, the first thing on his mind had to be to survive. He needed to make the effort to find out if Brendan was still on the Hannah or if he had gone ashore in search of him.

Alvaro pushed himself up, just managing to get his eyes to one of the rear window panes. It was steamed up and he used a hand to clean it. He grimaced with pain but at least he could see the tender still lying on the Hannah. There was no sign of life, but he knew Brendan was still on the Fisher. Thanks to the alcohol, the Irishman must be out dead again. Alvaro sat down on the wheelhouse deck and grabbed the holdall which he had been using as a pillow. He took a couple of swigs from his bottle of water. He also opened one of the plastic bags and took out a cigarette from a packet. He held the silver lighter which his wife had given him a few years ago and lit up, inhaling the first drag long and deep, feeling the soothing pleasure of smoke filling his lungs. That felt better.

***

Brendan used the binoculars to scan the cove from north to

south. He scanned along the shore, from a rocky mound, where he spotted a stone building with a red garage-like door and a ramp descending to the water, and then inland to some pretty stone houses, before sweeping along the beach, under the frontline houses in Hugh Town. The ramp belonged to the islands' lifeboat station. It had been in existence since the 1850s, but Brendan was only interested in any movement and in any person. He didn't care about the pretty houses or historical buildings. Every time he spotted someone, he focussed in to make sure it was not the trawlerman. There were very few people about at that hour of the morning, except perhaps a fisherman. or someone out walking a dog, or another hard-working, early-riser who depended on the summer tourism for a living. On the surface of the water there was only one small, white rowing boat moving out from the shore towards one of the lines of craft in the harbour.

Brendan took another sip of coffee and began again, this time focussing the binoculars on the end of the mole, where the ferry would be docking in about six hours, close on midday. He took his time, his eyes searching for anything remotely suspicious, even between a stack of pallets. Alvaro would undoubtedly be aiming to take the ferry back to the mainland. It was his only escape. Brendan then brought the binoculars back, doing another sweep, following exactly the same pattern as he had before, but in reverse.

His last sip of coffee was cold, but Brendan would not let up until he found the bloody Spaniard. He had all morning, but his thoughts didn't.

What was he going to tell his unit commander? He could say the man fell overboard in heavy seas. Yes, that would be the only thing he could say. There was no way he was going to own up that he had let Alvaro sail placidly into a harbour packed with pleasure craft while he had been semi-conscious after being on the binge. *What if Alvaro got away and spilled the beans?* No, he had to hunt the man down.

Alvaro, meanwhile, began to clean up the gash in his arm. It wasn't as bad as he first thought when it bled so profusely, but it needed cleaning. If only he had some of Brendan's vodka now, to disinfect the wound. He tried pouring some of his water on the cut, just enough to cleanse the gash a little, but he needed the water to drink.

Is there a botiquín? he asked himself. Did this dirty old vessel have a first aid kit? He doubted it very much but crawled about searching in every corner and in the only locker. Nothing. Alvaro sat back against the bulkhead and lit another cigarette, filling his lungs and exhaling slowly through mouth and nose. He smiled at himself. What a bloody fool he had been. Once again, however, the determination to survive forced him to be positive.

Things could be worse! he thought. He could still be on the Hannah, facing another week and a half of torment and uncertainty. The arm would be alright, and his knee and elbow had recovered reasonably well. Alvaro made up his mind. He would just swim for it, just get himself to the bloody shore. Just one more cigarette and into the water.

***

It seemed incongruous that the Spanish trawlerman could have done with Brendan's vodka to disinfect the wound, and that it was the tobacco, which the Irishman never touched, that eventually brought an end to this nightmare. It was Alvaro's smoking like a chimney which, in its deadly and silent way, broke the tense calm.

Someone on one of the French yachts was also awake. Brendan spotted the movement and used the binoculars to spy. It was a Brigitte Bardot blonde, wearing a man's cream jumper and very little else. She had stunning legs. *Now that's nice*, thought Brendan.

"Come on lass, bend over and show us a little bit more," he said to himself. This cheap voyeurism was fun.

The blonde with the legs disappeared down below and Brendan moved on to the next boat in the line and then to the next, looking for another French flag and more stunners to contemplate in the manner of a crude and perverted character. He skimmed quickly past a speedboat and then over a chunky looking fishing boat before scanning the next. Then, suddenly, he swung the binoculars back to the fishing boat as if there were another pair of legs to focus on. His heartbeat increased with a jolt.

There didn't appear to be anyone aboard the blue-hulled boat and yet all the wheelhouse windows, except the rear one on the starboard side, the one facing him, were steamed up. There was life in that boat's wheelhouse. Someone had been breathing in there and the mix of warm carbon dioxide and moisture had fogged the windows up, reacting with the colder exterior. That someone, whoever it was, had also deliberately wiped one window, the one facing directly at the Hannah.

Brendan lowered the binoculars and looked through the gap in the next line at the blue-hulled boat with the white cabin. He took a deep breath and looked around him before putting the binoculars to his eyes to focus on the fishing boat again. Perhaps it was a pure coincidence. Perhaps it was imagination playing tricks with him. But then Brendan saw it. He saw it through the same window that had been swabbed, a puff of white smoke rising, and then another thinner one twirling up as if the smoker were playing at blowing smoke rings.

"Got you, you bastard!"

Brendan acted with speed. It had to be the Spaniard. He needed to get to that boat and do what he had to do before more *Frogs* and other holidaymakers woke up. It was still very early, there were few people lingering about, but the place would be swarming before long. Now was the time.

Brendan spun down into the saloon, ducking, and missing his head by a fraction. He really was with it now. In half a minute he had put on his boots and was up on deck again. He grabbed the binoculars and pointed them at the small fishing boat again. The man was still smoking away. Brendan grabbed the Beretta 92 and stuck it under his belt. He untied the fibreglass dingy and slid it down over the starboard guardrails into the water. After one more look through the binoculars between the gap in the next line of boats, he stepped slowly into the tender and pushed himself away from the Hannah. He was almost too big for it but used the oars to move the small craft past the stern of the Hannah and along the side of the next boat in the line behind. He then made his way across the channel and between an old, white yacht with a blue canopy and a snazzy speedboat. It was the next line he was aiming for and he rowed across the second, narrow stretch of open water. When he reached that row of boats, he took the dinghy around the stern of two tenders that appeared to be attached together. The target was going to be two or three boats in front, and he kept the next, a fishing boat stacked with lobster pots and fishing rods lined up against the wheelhouse, directly ahead. Rounding this, and still out of sight of the target, he rowed as swiftly as his chunky arms could move the smooth, wooden oars. Brendan kept the tender along the port side of the line until his blue and white target boat came into view again. The moment he saw it, he used the left oar to move the little craft against the hull of a similar fishing boat to the previous one, this one with a smart, red paintwork. She had a playful, blue dolphin painted at the bow, just under the gunwale and above big white letters *SC* and the number *5*. Clearly it was some kind of registration used in the isles.

Brendan was about to row the last few metres, intending to approach the target along its port side, when he suddenly made a grab for an anchor line that dangled invitingly from above the dolphin and pulled the tender hard against the boat's hull. He could not believe what he was seeing only metres ahead. It was Alvaro, and he was sliding into the water from what had been his safe haven for the past few hours.

***

Having taken the decision to swim ashore, Alvaro had sucked one last puff out of his cigarette and stuffed the bloodied shirt into the small holdall with the remains of his water, leaving his gashed arm open to the elements. He had pulled himself up to look across at the Hannah for a few seconds. He had seen no movement, not a sign of the big Irishman. It was safe to go. He had slid open the wheelhouse door and crawled around to the port side. He had unbuckled his belt, pulled the strap round to release it from the loops on his jeans as far as the two at the back. and had fed the end tip through the holdall grips and back again through the loops to the front of his trousers. After buckling the belt again, feeling the bag nicely attached to his rear, Alvaro had sat on the gunwale and had slid, bare feet first, into the water.

It was not nearly as cold as he had expected, but the salt water had stung like hell on his gashed arm as his weight took him under.

When Alvaro surfaced and gulped for air, he trod water for a few seconds. Then he began to swim, very slowly, toward the nearest boat in the last line, the one closest to the white safety of the shore. It was going to be a struggle. Weighed down by the jeans and the bag, which immediately soaked up the water and felt like it was packed with cement blocks, he grimaced in pain with every stroke. The pain, the sheer effort, and the sound of the water being pushed aside, made him completely unaware of what was creeping up behind him, now only an oar's length away.

It was too late now. He was not to know, but if only he had not been a smoker. If only he had noticed that the Hannah's tender was no longer on her deck when he took that last look to see if Brendan was still aboard.

Brendan had been wanting to enjoy seeing terror in Alvaro's eyes. He had looked forward to hearing the man scream for mercy when he pointed the gun at him, seconds before pulling the trigger. However, at the very last moment and with daylight upon them, even in the shadows between the boats, he thought best not to send the seagulls into an even greater frenzy, or to attract attention with the explosion of a gun going off in the middle of the sleepy harbour. Instead, he grabbed one of the oars with both hands, lifted it high in the air and brought the blade down onto the head of the swimmer, like an axe onto a log.

It struck Alvaro just when his head was at its highest out of the water as he swam his way gradually towards the safety of the shore. Brendan knew it had been a heavy blow because he almost lost his grip on the oar. He immediately noticed Alvaro's head go limp in the water and begin to sink, but he needed to make certain of finishing him off, so he grabbed the Spaniard's neck and brought the limp head right up against the dinghy. He then pushed down as hard as he could so that

Alvaro's nose and mouth were well and truly under the surface, making it impossible for him to breath, if he was still at all conscious. Brendan watched the water turning red. The crack on the skull with the oar's blade must have cut a deep groove in the Spaniard's head.

The blow, so sudden and unexpected, had indeed been massive. Alvaro had felt everything go black immediately. He had probably lost consciousness for a few seconds but, after shoving Alvaro's head under the surface, Brendan felt the man's neck twist in his grip. Suddenly there was movement and Alvaro's arms began to fling about in a frenzy under the surface, so wildly that Brendan thought the tender was going to spin around.

Alvaro began to scream. The agonising sound of terror under the surface contrasted with the clatter of freedom in the yacht lines and masts and the comforting groan of creaking boats on the water. With the screams, bubbles burst through the surface. Brendan knew the air in Alvaro's lungs had begun to be replaced with salt water. Alvaro also realised what was happening. He could do little to fight the strength in the big Irishman's arm, so he tried to push himself deeper, using his hands to shove on the bottom of the dinghy. Brendan countered this by gripping harder on Alvaro's neck. Struggle as he could, Alvaro could not release himself. He was going to die. Visions of his wife, of his grandchildren running in the field at home, of his crew on the Lolariz and, oddly enough, of Asturian cider being poured into a slim glass from a great height, flashed through his head. Then, the knife flashed through his head too, the knife in his pocket. It was his last chance before his lungs gave in entirely to the flow of water. He stopped struggling, thinking only of the small fruit knife and slid his right hand down, deep into his right, trouser pocket. Brendan was about to let go, believing the Spaniard drowned.

With true Galician spirit, however, the Spaniard was going to fight to the bitter end. In one quick movement, Alvaro grabbed the handle, lifted the knife as high as he could behind his neck, and stabbed. He felt the small blade hit its target, piercing skin, flesh, and abductor muscles between metacarpals. Immediately he sensed Brendan's hand releasing its tight grip on his neck and instinctively used his legs to push himself up to the surface, where he gulped for air. As he did so, he lost the knife and it spun round and round to the seabed. Alvaro's knife, cutting into Brendan's hand, took the IRA man completely by surprise and offered momentary relief, but Alvaro's vision was too clouded by salt and by his own blood to see what was about to happen. Perhaps it was just as well.

The moment he felt the blade tear into his flesh, Brendan shouted out in pain. Without thinking, he released his grip on the Spaniard's neck and yanked his hand back. But then, stifling expletives and ignoring the pain and the sight of blood pouring out of the neat gash in the back of what was his shooting hand, Brendan felt behind him and pulled out the gun which he had tucked under his belt. The IRA man disengaged the safety catch with his thumb, as he had done so often in routing training. At the same time he grabbed a handful of Alvaro's hair with his left hand and yanked the head upwards again. As he did so, he felt the Spaniard's hands try to get a hold on his wrist, but they had no strength left in them.

Brendan looked into the poor man's eyes, holding the head out of the water for an instant, as if he hoped Alvaro could focus on him and that he might indeed plead for mercy, but then immediately shoved the head under the water with cruel savagery. At the same time he used his other hand to push the Beretta under the surface, ramming the barrel into the side of Alvaro's head.

Strangely, for a man capable of such cruelty, before he pulled the trigger, Brendan Daly turned his head and looked the other way.

The firing pin banged into the bullet and produced a thudding sound. The water dampened what would otherwise have been a detonation loud enough to have been heard by anyone half-awake in St Mary's Pool. The bullet went straight through Alvaro's skull and out the other side. Brendan felt Alvaro's hands release his wrist and slip away into the water. He had gone.

Daly didn't let go of the man's hair. Had he done so, water would replace all the air in Alvaro's lungs and his corpse would slowly submerge itself into the deep. In time, bacteria inside his gut and the cavity in his chest would produce methane, hydrogen sulphide, and carbon dioxide, eventually pushing what remained of the body to the surface like a balloon.

Brendan couldn't just let the evidence disappear to the depths only for it to rise again to condemn him. There would be a murder hunt the moment a torso was spotted floating face down in between the boats, if indeed, it was not washed onto the shore by the currents sooner. He needed to get rid of the body quickly. The Irishman immediately tied a line, like a noose, around Alvaro's neck, his own blood mixing with the Spaniard's, and attached it to the tender. He then began rowing back the way he came, sticking as closely as he could to the line of boats, creeping under their hulls. He kept looking up, back and around him to make certain there were no spying eyes.

Brendan had two options. He could attempt to haul the body onto the Hannah and sail out of the harbour, disposing of it out at sea. The alternative was to attach the body to a weight, perhaps the kedge anchor, and let it sink under the lines of boats in St Mary's, having secured it to the same buoy he had tied the Hannah's bow to. He chose the latter. The water was deep enough, and the weight would take Alvaro's body into the abyss, obscure enough to only attract marauding fish and crabs.

Brendan pulled himself up onto the deck of the Hannah. He attached a line to the little fibreglass dinghy and then unstrapped the spare anchor with its chain. It was not a very heavy kedge anchor, but it would serve its purpose. Before stepping back into the tender with the anchor, he opened the locker behind the wheelhouse and picked out a couple of different-sized shackles, one to connect the chain to a line and the second to attach the other end of the anchor chain around Alvaro's neck. Grimacing every time he put pressure on his right hand, Brendan then used his hands against the hull to move the tender and Alvaro's body around the starboard side of the Hannah, to where the line from the Hannah's bow pulled on the buoy.

There was still some blood oozing from the holes in Alvaro's head, and a trail, like a reddish oil-slick, followed the tender. Strangely enough, it was his own hand that continued to bleed more than Alvaro's head now, although the trace of blood was disappearing quickly in the water. Its meandering patterns were now hardly visible to anyone not aware of the violence that had recently taken place. Brendan's big hands, despite the nasty wound, worked speedily and efficiently, first connecting the line to the buoy and then the chain around the dead man's neck.

Brendan had one more thing to do. The money. If it wasn't on the Hannah, Alvaro must have it in the holdall which was attached to his body. Brendan swore when he realised the bloody thing was belted on to Alvaro's jeans. He looked around again. There was nobody in sight. He struggled to pull Alvaro round so that he was face up and it was even more difficult to lift the man, weighed down with water, high enough to unbuckle the belt.

He managed to release the bag, though, but it weighed a ton, heavy with salt water. Once he had it safely on the tender, Daly took another quick look up and down the lines of boats. When he was quite sure it was safe to do so, he chucked the kedge anchor and the rest of the chain over the side. He waited for the weight to do the rest. In a matter of seconds Alvaro's head disappeared, yanked downwards by the anchor, and his feet swung upwards like the tail of a diving dolphin. Except for a sudden tug on the buoy, like a fisherman's float when the bait is being nibbled at by a tentative fish, all went still on the surface.

Brendan left the tender on the water. He would soon need it to get to the shore, first to make a difficult telephone call to his unit commander, and then to ask the Harbour Master, if there was one, if he could continue using the unoccupied buoy to which he had attached the Hannah in the dark, early hours of the morning. However, first, he needed to dress the stabbed hand.

Before attending to the wound, the big Irishman opened Alvaro's backpack. The money was there, wrapped up in a plastic bag. At least he had that. Brendan put the pesetas in his holdall, which he again placed under the seating in the wheelhouse. At the same time, he proceeded to remove any evidence that there might have been another person on board the Hannah. He began by shoving Alvaro's discarded clothes, shoes, towel, and holdall inside the Spaniard's suitcase.

There was a moment when he actually paused to inspect a book, not because he was interested in reading it, but because it puzzled him. What was a simple Spanish sailor doing reading about the Spanish Civil War in English? Eventually he chucked that in the case too.

Satisfied, Brendan then hunted around for something heavy which he could use to also sink the evidence. He considered using small metal items, like more spare shackles he had noticed in the locker behind the wheelhouse. In the end he went for one of the Hannah's three fire extinguishers and shoved that inside the suitcase, which he left slightly open for water to find its way in. He took it onto the deck. Brendan had a good look around. There were now more people preparing for the day, some on decks, evidently getting ready for a day's sailing or fishing. Hugh Town had also woken up and there was plenty of activity along the seafront and on the quay; but to the west, on the starboard side of the Hannah, whose bow was still pointing at the quay, albeit slightly more towards the centre of the town as the flow altered, there were no eyes to worry about. So, using the wheelhouse for cover, Brendan slipped the case over the guardrail. It took a second for the weight of the fire extinguisher to have an effect. When it did, the Spaniard's suitcase disappeared under the surface, leaving a trail of bubbles.

***

Like any good sailor, despite his hand aching from the pain, Brendan washed down the decks, took a cloth to the windows and began tidying up, flaking the sail on the boom, tying the sail ties, and securing the head of the sail. He then secured the boom, tightened the halyard, and coiled the lines. Next, he stowed away the winch handles and other bits and pieces. He hoped he was being noticed. He wanted to look like any yachting enthusiast who believed he was going to be in the harbour for a spell.

As he carried out the ritual, there was no sign that a few hours earlier the same person had been wrecked on alcohol, or that he had just carried out a violent and grotesque murder. Anyone watching could never have imagined that a body was dangling, headfirst, under the surface, and that the man messing about on the yellow-hulled Fisher was fully aware of it.

However, as innocent as he might appear cleaning up on the deck, Brendan Daly was in deep thought about how to explain to a man called Patrick Collins, back in Ireland, why the Hannah was moored in peaceful St Mary's Pool and not riding the waves off the Brest peninsula.

The man at the desk at the Duchy of Cornwall Harbour Office, situated on the quay, was Dominic Taylor. He loved Ireland. He had been to a wedding there once, in a place called Nenagh. There would be no problem at all. That buoy was available for a fee of seven pounds a night.

"I understand you came in during the early hours and had a bit of a problem finding your way."

"Indeed I did. I had a bit of trouble yesterday evening and then the motor wouldn't start for me until this morning. I had to bring her into the harbour under sail as best I could."

"You ought to get that hand seen to," said Dom Taylor, pointing at Brendan's untidy effort to bandage his hand. Nothing went unnoticed.

"Nah. It's not too bad. There's a good first aid kit aboard."

"Very well, My Daly. Yes, the seas have been rough for the time of year. Will you and your colleague be sailing back to Ireland soon?"

"No, this is a pretty spot. I might stay for a few days. In any case, I can't budge until I get the motor properly checked over. Then I'll be on my way to La Rochelle, in France. I am delivering the boat to a client there. Oh, and it is only me on board."

"Is that so? Well, if you can pay us for the number of days you think you'll be staying for, Sir, that will be fine."

Brendan handed over five £10 notes. It was just as well Collins had issued him with some English bank notes as well as pesetas. He waited for the harbourmaster to give him his change, thanked him, and walked out onto the quay. He didn't think he would need to stay for as long as that, but it would keep the harbourmaster happy.

As soon as Dominic Taylor saw the Irishman walk past the window towards the town, he picked up the telephone and dialled the police station in Garrison Lane. The isles were a peaceful haven. Very little went on to warrant more than the usual community assistance, asking people to be quiet at night, and one or two incidents a year of petty theft, so he thought the two police officers in Hugh Town could do with a bit of gossip, even if there was nothing in it.

"Morning Marcus. Dom here."

"Ah, Dominic. I was about to go down to the quay to sniff out who's coming off the ferry. Put the kettle on for us?"

"Will do, but listen. You might like to tell Shirley to keep an eye on a boat that parked here in the early hours. An Irishman. Seems decent enough but he says he is sailing solo. I was led to believe another man was seen aboard. I could be wrong, but I've a funny feeling about this one. Anyway, it's a bright yellow thing. You never know."

Sergeant Marcus Blyth was the senior policeman on the islands and Constable Shirley Watts was his very pretty assistant and, as it happened, his girlfriend.

"See you in ten minutes. You can fill me in. But there's nothing much we can do unless they break the law or make a nuisance of themselves, Dominic," Sergeant Blyth rightly pointed out.

The Isles of Scilly were that kind of place, peaceful, law-abiding, community-minded, elderly perhaps and, in the main, gentle folk. They were also occasionally the destination for interesting sailors, men and women, on their way to wherever the winds took them.

***

As he walked away from Dominic Taylor's office, Brendan was just in time to see the Scillonian, immaculately white, nudging herself against the quay. It was just after midday and there were a lot of travellers excitedly lining the deck. Most of them were day-travellers. Others intended to stay for a few days.

One of them was Jamie Ryder. He had telephoned Mrs Martin at Annette's Cottage the previous evening, and she was expecting him. She had also given him directions. Even so, Jamie asked the lady in the post office, a stone building of unusual architecture. She was most obliging. All he had to do was follow Hugh Street, and then The Strand, before cutting along the beach, past the lifeboat station, and then straight on as far as Porthloo. There was a second cove to walk around. After that, he would come to Mrs Martin's, on the edge of the wood next to Seaways Farm. Jamie set off, not certain whether he had understood everything, but in the right direction. North, in other words.

Meanwhile, Brendan Daly also walked into Hugh Street and entered the building with the Lloyds bank sign hanging above the door. He and Jamie might well have crossed each other, Brendan striding at a nervous pace, Jamie Ryder taking everything in, the people, the architecture, the smells and, despite it being the high season for tourism, the tranquil nature of the place. The cashier at the bank informed Brendan that there would be no problem exchanging pesetas.

The nearest telephone booth was just around the corner, in Jerusalem Terrace, and Brendan closed the door behind him. He got several coins ready, anticipating a long conversation, and dialled the office number at Cork Whitefish on Dinish Island.

"Hello. Whitefish." It was Abby who answered. She would fetch Pat. He was sorting the new plastic fish boxes that had been delivered. Abby, together with her brother Ray, were not only long-term, trusted employees, but also cousins of Patrick Collins. He liked to keep things in the family. What he didn't like were sudden changes to plans or incompetence, especially when someone did not follow orders precisely. When he stood beside his desk and picked up the receiver, Collins was boiling with rage and almost grey with dread. *What the hell was going on?*

"Brendan!"

"Pat. Bit of a problem mate."

"You're bloody right there's a problem. What the hell are you doing? Why are you bloody calling me? I told you. No calls. Where the fuck are you? You should be halfway to Spain."

"I know, mate. Sorry. We ran into heavy seas."

"So what? You're both bloody good seamen. You'd better tell me you lost a mast or something. Where the hell are you calling from?"

"Scilly. The Scilly Isles."

"The bloody Scilly Isles? Why? Why on earth? You're supposed to be way across the channel. Bloody hell, man!"

"Pat. The boat's fine. We lost Alvaro."

"What? Lost Alvaro? What the hell are you talking about, man?"

"Yes, Pat. We've lost the Spaniard. When I went up for my stint at the watch last night, he was gone."

"What the hell do you mean, gone? He can't have just gone! Do you mean, overboard?"

"Yes, mate. Think so. He must have had an accident. I told you, we ran into big seas approaching the English Channel," lied Brendan Daly.

He lied so well. Like so many people fit for psychiatric investigation, Brendan was very calm in his lying. Every word made perfect sense, and was spoken without a trace of hesitation, although half of his mind was on the vodka, on pushing Alvaro's bleeding head under water and on the weight of the kedge anchor pulling the man, head down, into the depths of the harbour.

There was suddenly a deadly silence. Patrick Collins was obviously taking stock of the new situation. As he did so, beginning to sweat from both anger and a state of panic, Collins closed the office door to the warehouse. He then put down the receiver and unlocked the back door to let air in. Meanwhile, Brendan fed another coin into the box and waited.

Collins sat down at the desk now and rubbed his face with fish-smelling hands before picking up the receiver again. He really did not know what the hell to do, but there was no way he could ask Brendan to sail the Hannah to Spain and back on his own.

"You there, Bren?" He seemed calmer now. It wasn't his friend's fault. The bloody Spaniard! How the hell could a man with his experience just fall overboard? Imagination flashed vivid pictures through his head of the poor man shouting and screaming as the Hannah cut through the water, leaving him to be swallowed up by the white-tipped waves.

"Right, Bren. Listen. There's nothing to be done about Alvaro. Forget the poor, bloody man. He was a good sod, you know. Now we need to sort this out and we bloody shall. I want you to stay where you are. I'll see if I can get someone else over to England to join you as quick as possible. I might even come myself, but not for a few days. We've got to get this job done, one way or another."

"Yes, Pat."

"You have plenty of provisions on the boat to keep you going. Sorry, Brendan, but you'll have to make do with that. Are you tied up to a pontoon? Can you get a cable ashore to plug in to?"

"No, Pat. There's none of that here. I'm tied up to a buoy in the middle of a place called St Mary's."

"I see. Right then, if you need any fresh food and more cash, use some of Alvaro's pesetas. If you must, go to a bank and change some of them. Does the place have a bank?"

It was Brendan's turn to think. He couldn't very well tell Collins that he had already looked for the pesetas and been to the bank. Anyway, he wanted the money for himself.

"Yes. There is a bank. But don't worry, mate. I'll be fine with what's on board. We can stock up again, if necessary, when you get here."

"Right. Good. Now, I'm away tomorrow. Call me on Friday morning on this line and I'll give you an update as to who and when you'll have company."

The call was not as difficult as Brendan Daly had feared. He was quite satisfied, in fact. He almost believed his own story. He also had a bonus in Alvaro's pesetas. He could get them all changed at the bank, or even open an account and get the money transferred to his account in Ireland little by little. He could spin another tale about how Alvaro must have had it on him when he fell overboard in the heavy seas. Yes, that's right. The Spaniard kept the cash with him at all times. He was a cunning, distrustful sort of character, wasn't he?

Brendan, the IRA terrorist, the cold-blooded murderer of the Spanish trawlerman and a handful of other innocent people, felt good as he rowed the tender back to the Hannah. His intention was to return to the bank immediately with some of Alvaro's pesetas. He was going to exchange them for a nice bundle of pounds and enjoy a little holiday while he could. He even eyed up the Mermaid Inn as he pulled away from the shore.

***

Mrs Martin was as Jamie had imagined her, a rounded, small figure of a woman with narrow, smiling eyes. She greeted him enthusiastically. He was her journalist, and she was eager to be his informant. Without a pause to catch breath, and almost before showing Jamie to his very cosy room with a view across St Mary's Pool, Mrs Martin gave Jamie a full introduction to the isles: the permanent artists, the boatmen who ferried people to and from the islands, the traditional export of scented narcissi, the lady who manufactured wool, the fishermen and their old-fashioned ways, the French, the policeman and his girlfriend, the fabulous sunsets he could see from his room.

Jamie explained, as kindly as he could, that he was just a freelance journalist. If he was lucky, he might just find a small space on the travel pages of a travel magazine, but he was so happy to have come to her beautiful island. Yes, unless he told her with plenty of time, he would like an evening meal as well as breakfast. He would probably be out and about during the day. He liked to write in the early mornings or at night. In fact, he was going to explore right away with his notebook, he told her. It was a successful ploy, for Mrs Martin understood that his work must come first. She gave him the sweetest of smiles and left him to it, disappearing down the stairs.

Jamie left unpacking his backpack until later. Mrs Martin had kindly offered to let him use her washing machine, but his priority was to find his way to Trench Lane. He couldn't wait to see the enigmatic woman he had not stopped thinking about since that rainy night in London.

Trench Lane separated one or two small fields on either side, as well as a scattering of whitewashed cottages. In between these, there was evidence that more houses were going up on land belonging to the Duchy of Cornwall. The isle was becoming popular as a growing number of people found the need to find hideaways, as Ruth had called hers. At the end of the lane, past a wooded area, he found, not the small cottage he had imagined, but quite a large property built in stone. The front of the house was adorned by a glorious Virginia ivy and a lady in her fifties, wearing a large straw hat with a blue, silk scarf tied around it, was pruning the rose bushes on either side of the front door.

"Good afternoon," Jamie called out from the lane.

"Hello. Good afternoon," she replied, turning round to see who the greeting had come from.

"I do hope I didn't startle you," apologised Jamie when confronted by the lady's examining look and secateurs at the ready. "I'm looking for a friend."

"No, not at all. Mind you, I don't think you'll find anyone of your age in these parts. Does your friend have a name?"

"Yes, Ruth. Ruth Eaton. She told me she lived at the end of the lane."

"Ruth! That's my daughter! Goodness! Wait a minute, you're not the fellow she met at the school cocktail thing, are you?"

"I think I possibly am. Is she home?"

"No. You've just missed her, but she isn't far. She has just gone down to the vets to take their little girl back. Oh, dear, I do apologise. I must look very peculiar in my tatty, gardening clothes."

"Don't worry. I'm very used to seeing my own mother at the bottom of her garden."

"Why don't you go and meet her? You can both come back for tea. You will most probably find her near the point. She likes going down there. Just follow the lane back the way you came, cross the main road, and then take the path beside the small cove."

Walking down the lane, and then along the path, Jamie wasn't sure what to expect, but as soon as he saw Ruth, he felt a calm returning, like the tiny waves lapping the sandy shore to his right. She was sitting on a flat rock, gazing out to sea as if she were a sailor's woman waiting for him to come back to her. The sea breeze was playing games with her golden locks and she seemed to be letting the salty air redden her cheeks. Jamie left the path and walked quietly over the grass, stopping just a few yards behind her.

"Are you waiting for your French Lieutenant?" he asked, as if he were at Lyme Regis and Ruth were John Fowles' enigmatic Sarah, in the film starring Meryl Streep.

"No, I am waiting for my English Lieutenant," she replied, without turning around. Again, Jamie was struck by that exquisite, childish ring to her voice, and by the teasing and spontaneous response to his greeting. Jamie stood behind her and, as if Ruth were already his, placed his hands on her shoulders and joined her gaze across the sea. It was hypnotic.

"The nights, since we parted company, have been mostly cloudy and starless, but on clear nights I've talked to you through the moon, longing for this moment," he said.

"You're not only a poet. You've grown a beard!" said Ruth when she turned round to look at Jamie.

"I'm afraid I took rambling across Cornwall with a tent to heart. I suppose I look a bit nomadic. Sorry! It will come off with a bit of soap and a razor."

"No, no! I like it. Don't get rid of it," she said, her voice rising to another level.

"Anyway, all those prickles on your cheeks give me something to hold on to."

Ruth stood on her stone and bent her head forwards towards Jamie's. She then put her hands on the sides of his hairy face and very slowly and deliberately tugged at his beard, bringing his face towards hers. What followed took them both by surprise. Ruth pressed her generous lips onto his.

"Oops!" giggled Ruth, looking into Jamie's eyes for forgiveness.

"That was nice," he replied.

It was only brief, but it was an extraordinary thing to have done and to have felt. To kiss and be kissed on the lips by someone Jamie had only chatted to for less than an hour at an old school cocktail party in London was out of the ordinary.

As Jamie would discover as he grew to know her, Ruth was out of the ordinary. Her actions demonstrated an uninhibited, impulsive nerve. Jamie could well have been caught off guard, and yet he wasn't. He wasn't because it was exactly what he had been yearning for, albeit not so soon. He wasn't because he had already sensed Ruth's enticing, almost electric intensity while standing close to her at the Oxford and Cambridge Club.

Jamie took this pretty, teasing, English rose into his arms. Any memories of Olivia, his sensual childhood sweetheart, or the bitterness that had engulfed him only a few weeks ago, were gone. This was a new sensation; beyond anything he had ever felt. It was so sudden, so impulsive and yet, so natural.

Ruth and Jamie clung to each other in silence. Theirs was a long embrace, letting the contours of their bodies blend together. To an outsider, to one who has never believed in love at first sight, that two people could belong to one another without actually knowing each other, this might have seemed improbable and absurd. To a passer-by, however, walking along the coastal path behind them, to someone unaware of the prelude to their love, the image would have been of two young lovers just enjoying a moment together.

The two, young strangers sat down on the flat stone and gazed out to sea until well after teatime. Ruth rested her head on Jamie's shoulder as the shadows began to seduce the evening colours. Not that day, nor for days to come, but very soon, they really would become lovers.

***

On the following afternoon, Ruth and Jamie walked for miles, from Trench Lane down to Ruth's flat rock on the point and around the end of the small airport, where they cut through fields to join the coast again before visiting the vets to say hello to the little daughter. They had tea and scones with Mrs Eaton and, afterwards, Ruth showed Jamie a short-cut through a small wood to Porth Loo Lane and to Annette's Cottage. Ruth knew Mrs Martin. Everyone knew everybody in Scilly.

Ruth and Jamie spent the time learning about each other. Then, as evening promised to gift them with another romantic sunset, they made a picture of happiness, hand in hand, strolling barefoot along the white shore. Occasionally they paused, talked, ran, played, and kissed. Their longing gave way to what they had already anticipated at first sight, that they were helplessly in love.

The Mermaid Inn was situated at the entrance to the harbour quay. That was where Ruth suggested Jamie should invite her to their first evening out together. As Jamie realised, when he ordered drinks at the bar, it must have been the social hub in Hugh Town. It was a typical, English pub, with evident connections to a maritime past. Every corner, every flag draped from the ceilings, every ornament and every framed painting told stories of fishermen, of smugglers and even of murderous pirates.

Jamie would not have known that the big gentleman with the Irish accent, sitting on one of the wooden bar stools, deep in loud conversation with another man, was also a murderous character.

Jamie and Ruth decided to share three different dishes, garlic bread, a more adventurous dish of highly peppered, grilled squid and sliced rump steak, as if they were sampling tapas in Spain. It was nothing like Spanish cuisine, lacking such important ingredients as fine olive oil and spices, but a bottle of Portuguese wine found its own way to foment their relationship even more. It also helped Ruth become slightly tipsy. She had warned him, with half a glass she became dangerously funny. So much so that she began to test Jamie's Spanish, and to compare each other's accents. As each of them repeated a sentence or replied to a series of very serious questions in Spanish, they laughed, and Ruth's giggle grew louder and louder.

Jamie's accent and intonations were evidently from the Canary Islands, a delicious mix of musical highs and lows, with lazy, cut off endings to words. Ruth's was a Spanish learnt in class and refined at university. Despite a very English pronunciation, she betrayed immaculate syntax. Hers was probably more correct than Jamie's, who had grown up with the language but had never been taught the grammatical rules. Occasionally a head turned towards their window table overlooking St Mary's Pool, and once or twice they hushed each other down when their fun became way too loud for a traditional British pub. It was such fun. They were so happy.

"Excuse me. Is that Spanish you are speaking?"

It was Brendan Daly. He had come up to their table and was holding half of a pint glass of ale in one hand. His bear-like figure swayed ever so slightly.

"Yes, it is," replied Jamie.

He was polite but tried to make it quite clear that Brendan's company was not required at that very moment.

"Thought it was. Thank you. Any chance of having a quick word tomorrow sometime? I've got a boat in the harbour. I'm looking for an interpreter."

"Well, yes. Anything I can do to help." Jamie shrugged his shoulders and looked at Ruth before offering a place and a time.

"Here. Tomorrow at twelve?"

"Grand, mate. I'll see you tomorrow then," said Daly, before he drifted back to his stool at the bar.

Much later, when Jamie said goodnight after walking Ruth back to the house in Trench Lane, she called out.

"Come and have lunch with us tomorrow. The forecast is for rain and I can't have you being on your own. Anyway, I'm intrigued to know what that strange man at the Mermaid wanted."

"I'd love to. I'll come straight over the moment I've finished with the guy. Anything I should take your mother?"

"No. Nothing at all. Funny man. I wonder what he wants."

"Don't you worry about that. He said he needed an interpreter, didn't he? Goodnight, my love."

As Jamie made his way to Annette's Cottage, taking the short-cut Ruth had shown him, the moonlight was bright enough to light up the cutting through the woods, but the rustles in the long grass were almost as intriguing as the big fellow at the bar. Despite the renewed happiness in his life, the man's enquiry would make getting to sleep more difficult.

***

The night passed quickly, and Mrs Martin chatted away merrily over breakfast, asking a whole notebook of questions every time she brought Jamie coffee, toast, or scrambled eggs. Until he asked her if she knew of any Irishman on St Mary's, she was the one sounding like a journalist. She didn't know of anybody Irish, but Samantha, the boatman's wife, did mention that a man with an Irish accent had enquired about where he could get a spare anchor. Jamie, the apprentice journalist, could never keep up with how news travelled so quickly in this place. He would have to be careful, or Mrs Martin would soon discover that her bearded young journalist was an impostor.

Jamie was at the Mermaid earlier than agreed. He ordered a half a pint and took up position at a window, which had a panoramic view of the harbour, towards the lifeboat station, and across the Mermaid lounge to the front door. The wind had picked up over the bay. Ruth and the weatherman had been correct. There was a grey mass approaching with rain from the west. A small, white boat was being rowed ashore from the same direction, rather clumsily in Jamie's opinion. It was his Irish friend and, before long, he was sitting opposite Jamie with a full pint in his hand.

After introductions, which had been absent the night before, Brendan shot a series of questions. To Jamie, it felt like an interrogation.

"Can you sail?"

"I have sailed, but not much. I am more accustomed to boats

with a motor."

"Do you live here?"

"No. I'm only here for a week or so." Jamie nearly told the man the same story which he had told Mrs Martin, that he was a journalist, but he thought better of it.

"On holiday then, mate?"

"More or less".

"Are you staying for long?"

"Look, Mr Daly. What is this?" Jamie put up the shield. He did not like being questioned.

"Sorry. I'll get to the point."

"Please do."

"From what I understood last night, you speak Spanish. I don't speak the lingo myself, but I've been to Lanzarote a couple of times with the wife. You sounded just like one of them, if I may say so."

"Well, I suppose I do. But I don't see what that has to do with this."

"Yes. Well, I've got a little problem, you see, and I need help. If you can, God bless you. If you can't, no problem."

"How can I assist you?"

"You see that bright yellow boat in the bay?" asked Brendan, inviting Jamie to look through the window.

"I do. Can't miss her. Ah, here comes the promised rain."

The rain did indeed come. Suddenly huge raindrops began spitting against the pub window, as gusts of wind brought in the front.

"More bloody rain. What a summer. The problem is actually with the boat, you see."

"Wouldn't you be better trying one of the local fishermen or the boat supplies store?"

"No. The boat's in perfect nick. The thing is, I am sailing her to a place in northern Spain, where the new owner of the boat is waiting to take delivery. My colleague was taken ill and has gone back to Ireland. He spoke Spanish, and I need someone to come with me to interpret with the buyer. Otherwise I'll lose the sale."

"I see. You mean, actually sail to Spain?"

"That's why I asked if you could sail."

"Good grief! Look, I'm terribly sorry. I would help you if I could, but I've only just arrived on the island and I'm here to spend a few days with my girlfriend. I'll be in real trouble if I just went off to do a bit of sailing. I'm sure you understand. Anyway, Mr Daly, I already told you, I am alright with motorboats, but I've only sailed two or three times, and that was awfully long ago."

"Never mind. Beautiful girl, if I may say so. Aye, I wouldn't leave her out of my sight for a moment. Well, if you change your mind, you know where to find me. She's a good sea boat and she can find her own way. You'd soon get the hang of it."

"I really am terribly sorry."

"Nah. No problem mate. I can hang around for a few days. I'm sure I'll find someone else, even if I can't get anyone so familiar with Spanish. Anyway, you know where I am. You'd take a good cut from the sale, of course."

With that, the Irishman swallowed the rest of his bitter, stood up and went up to the bar. Brendan didn't want to hang around, of course, not with a dangling corpse under his buoy. The sooner a substitute arrived from Ireland, the better.

As he was poured another pint, he winked back at an astonished Jamie Ryder. The ex-Army man's impression of Brendan Daly remained much as it was the previous evening. Jamie did not care for the man, and his offer to give him a *cut* only made him find Mr Daly even less trustworthy. Perhaps if Jamie had needed a penny or two. Perhaps if the most important ambition in his life right now was not Ruth. He did feel for the Irishman, though. It must be tough for the guy, however uncouth he seemed. Jamie also stood up, went to the bar, and paid for both their drinks.

"These are on me," he said, shaking Brendan's huge, rather sweaty hand.

"You're going to get wet, Mr Ryder."

"No matter. There's something warm waiting for me," replied Jamie before he pushed open the pub door, zipping up his windcheater as he did so, and disappeared into the blustery rain."

***

Jamie's jeans and boots were drenched by the time he got to the house in Trench Lane. He felt almost as he had in that field near Sennen Cove. Ruth opened the door.

"You are not coming in like that!" she said, laughing mercilessly at the sight of him. "Go round the back of the house. I'll open up the boiler room," she added, pointing to her left.

"Kiss me!" growled Jamie as she stood at arm's length in front of him in the back room. It was indeed the boiler room. It was also the boot room, the garden tool room, and the laundry room.

"I shall when you stop looking like a soggy rag. Here's a towel, and take those boots off before you catch something," she said, throwing a towel in his face.

Before he could reply with another request for her lips, Ruth disappeared. Jamie untied the laces on his boots and kicked them off before placing them neatly on the stone floor. Then he took off his windcheater, hung that on a peg and pulled his socks off. He was squeezing water out of them into a drain when Ruth returned. She was carrying a pair of pink corduroys and a cream shirt.

"These were Dad's. Sorry about the faded cords, but they should fit you. You are about the same height," she said, turning to leave him to it.

"Kiss me!"

"You are dripping wet, for goodness sake!"

"I refuse to wear pink trousers unless you kiss me!"

Ruth pretended to give in to his threat and stood inches away from the new man in her life. She then put both hands on his hairy cheeks, looked into his beckoning eyes and closed hers. She stood on tiptoes to reach as high as she could, before letting her generous red, red lips meet his. Unlike the previous speculative pecks, this time the touch of her lips lingered on Jamie's rain-wet mouth and he pulled her firmly against him, feeling her mouth open for his tongue to explore. That was Ruth's point of no return. A flame suddenly lit and burst through her defensive barriers when she felt Jamie's warmth growing against her tummy. She pulled away slightly and began tearing at Jamie's shirt buttons, undoing them, and tugging at his shirt to come out of his jeans. Her hand gripped Jamie's belt and began to unbuckle it. Ruth, so demure by the window at the cocktail party in London, looked up into Jamie's eyes again. This time her look was hungry with passion. Her movements became slow and deliberate, and her eyes shone with wickedness, as if she knew she were doing something forbidden, but nice. Jamie shook his head, pretending to want her to stop, but he was captivated again by the sensuality of her next searching kiss.

Suddenly, a voice, like that of a soprano right up against the boiler room door, broke the spell.

"Ruthy. Do they fit, darling?"

"Yes, they do. Coming, mummy," she replied in between giggles, releasing Jamie's belt, and placing both her hands on her cheeks. Eyes wide open and shining with pleasure, Ruth pleaded with him not to say a word. The moment of play was over, but it was a prelude to what would occur sooner or later. They were dying for each other.

"You had better make sure they do fit, Mr Ryder, because I shall love you in pink!" Ruth teased. She then turned to open the boiler room door into the kitchen and blew him a kiss.

The shirt was a bit tight around his broad shoulders and the corduroys felt loose around the middle, but Jamie felt good.

***

While Brendan Daly saw out the first band of rain in the Mermaid, treating himself to a generous helping of pub food and a couple more pints, Frances Eaton prepared a light summer's lunch of leek soup, followed by selection of cheeses, slices of ham and coleslaw. To drink, there was a choice of lemonade or plain water. Jamie liked Ruth's mother and she approved of him. It was clear to see. She was so much younger than his own mother and yet she looked frail, something Jamie put down to depression after losing her husband. They took coffee in the drawing room. It looked out into a small, wild garden, bordered by the wood at the rear of the house which her father had bought when the Duchy of

Cornwall, to which most of Scilly belongs, began to sell off some of the freeholds of several properties. The rain had ceased but it was time to be still, to take in their new situation, to talk and even to feel a drowsy after-lunch doze coming on as Ruth and her mother sat in front of the television watching some kind of equestrian event.

It was when Frances Eaton said she was going into the garden to take advantage of the lull in the weather that the subject of the Irishman at the Mermaid cropped up. Jamie had more or less put the matter out of his mind. He was so enjoying the sense of belonging, feeling Ruth curled up on the sofa, pressed up against him as if they had been together, as young people in love, for months, when she suddenly sat up with a jump and her eager eyes focussed on his.

"Oh, yes! Tell me what the man at the pub wanted!"

"Nothing really. I told him I couldn't help."

"Come on, he must have wanted something, the strange man," she insisted.

"Well, the poor guy is a bit stuck. The man he was sailing with was taken ill."

"So? What's that got to do with him barging in on us and asking if we were speaking Spanish? I thought he was a bit drunk, actually."

"Yes, he'd had a drink or two. No, it was rather odd, actually. Apparently, they were on their way to deliver a yacht in northern Spain. He is looking for someone to replace his mate, and it seems, someone who can speak Spanish. That's why he came over to talk to us. He heard us fooling around."

"Yes, but why did he want to speak to you? Oh, wait a minute. I know. He wants you to go with him. Gosh!"

"Exactly. But I'm not going to. I told him I couldn't possibly. Anyway, I've not sailed for years."

"Wow! It would be such an adventure! Tell him I'll go instead!" she teased.

"Ruth, my lovely. The only thing I want in the world right now, is you. You are my adventure."

"Is that all I am, an adventure?" she said, dropping her eyes in fake contempt.

"Yes. You have already proved to me in the boiler room that you are the most adventurous, delicious creature I have ever set eyes upon," he said, before drawing her close to kiss her once more.

"Well, I think you should go!" insisted Ruth, cheeks flushing as she pushed him away.

"But I don't want to. I've only just found *you*, right here, in your secret hideaway. I don't want to let you out of sight for a moment."

"My love, I'm afraid you're going to have to anyway, just for a few days. That is, if you are still here, Jamie. I've got to go back to London with Mummy and I'll be staying with her for a few days. She's got an appointment with her specialist."

"Oh, dear. Is she alright?"

"Yes, nothing to worry about. She would normally stay in London, but this time she wants to come back to St Mary's until December. My sister is going to be on a month's trip to Australia and it can be a bit lonely in her flat, although she has so many friends. Anyway, that's not the point. I'll be away for at least ten days. I don't know what on earth you are going to do here on your own for so long. Unless, of course, you've got to go back to Lymington."

"I could write an article about the adventurous, wicked, and delicious women of the isles of Scilly," Jamie said, raising an eyebrow and grinning roguishly. "No, I intend to stay for a bit longer, at least until you have to start work. If you can stand me, that is."

"Oh, please, I beg you not to go to Lymington just yet. Please stay until term starts. I don't know what I'm going to do without you. But, seriously now, Jamie. Why don't you help that man? Yes, do it. Do it while I am away with Mummy. Help the Irishman deliver his boat. Then come back to me and our boiler room!"

That wicked smile and a furtive cuddle on the sofa brought some sense back to their lives, until Ruth again sat up and shrieked.

"I've got it! If you don't go with that strange Irishman, why don't you stay here. Yes, that's it. Stay here and look after the house while we are away in London. Oh, yes. Will you? Will you, please?"

"I'd like to, but what about your mother?"

"She would love you to stay. You've seen how happy she is about us. In fact, I haven't seen Mummy so excited and with it for months. You've not only come to save my heart. You've jerked Mummy up. She's stopped thinking about herself. You simply have no idea how different she has been since you knocked on the door on Monday afternoon. I'm almost jealous!"

No more was said about the man at the Mermaid for the rest of the day. Jamie stayed for supper and Frances Eaton accepted his invitation to a pub lunch, weather-permitting, on the following day. Ruth was astonished her mother had agreed to go out for lunch. They also agreed Jamie should move in the following Tuesday and that, if he could, he would stay until they returned from London.

***

Jamie was able to tell Mrs Martin over breakfast on the Thursday morning that he was following the scent of what could be an interesting story involving a boat, and that he would tell her all about it, even if he had nothing published, sometime in September. But it was all a bit hush-hush, he said, so she must not mention it to anyone. Jamie knew he was being mischievous, but he had to keep up appearances. There was no harm in making his landlady's life more interesting. Indeed, Mrs Martin was thrilled to be part of the conspiracy and spent the rest of the morning humming like a bee, even though Jamie also informed her that Monday, 22nd would be his last night at Annette's Cottage.

What Jamie did not reveal was that he was going to inform Brendan Daly that he would accept the proposal to help him deliver the yellow boat.

Jamie told Brendan Daly that very morning after spotting the Irishman tying up the tender to the shore at Town beach. It was Brendan who opened his mouth first, with a snide remark.

"Girlfriend's kicked you out already, has she?"

"Good morning, Mr Daly. No, you assume wrong."

"Well, I was only guessing the reason why you have come to see me."

"You're wrong about the lady, but you are right that I've come to speak to you. I see you've no longer got the bandage around your hand."

It was something he had noticed when the man had come up to their table at the Mermaid to enquire about their Spanish. He had noticed it because it was not a very professionally tied bandage. He could see the hand was red and there were signs of a gash, but that is not what he had come to talk about.

"Yes, mate. I had a bit of an accident with a knife. It's alright now. Go on then, what do you want?"

"If your offer still stands, I'll sail to Spain with you. With one condition."

"Oh, now that's grand news. And what is that condition?" Brendan asked, with a sly grin on his face.

"No money involved. I shall treat our trip as a pleasant few days of summer sailing, and it had better be pleasant, Mr Daly."

"Ah, but that's so very good of you, Mr…"

"Jamie. Jamie Ryder."

"Well, that's just grand, Jamie. But I insist. Meals and drinks on me. I'm off to the bank just now, but we can get down to the nitty gritty later."

"How about if I come aboard tomorrow morning? You can show me around and we can talk about a schedule."

"Perfect. Weather permitting, I'll bring the dinghy across tomorrow. Same time. Alright by you?"

They went their separate ways, Jamie to Trench Lane and Brendan to the telephone booth. Collins had told him to call on Friday, in other words the following day. But this couldn't wait.

"You've done it again, Bren. I told you, call me on Friday. That's tomorrow, mate."

"Yes, but…"

"Don't you bloody but me, Brendan. I'm beginning to worry about you, chum. How long have we known each other? Everything needs to work like clockwork. This bloody job looks like it's getting too big for you."

"Patrick, will you just let me talk, man!" Brendan had never dared raise his voice to his unit commander before.

After a chilly silence on the line, Collins spoke again, this time in a calmed, almost understanding manner.

"I heard about you and the wife, Bren. Sorry about that."

"This has nothing to do with her, Pat. Don't worry about her. I'll sort her out when I get home. No, Pat. I'm calling a day earlier than you said because I have news."

"Go on."

"If you are OK with it, I've found a replacement for Alvaro, right here in the Scillies. He knows about boats and speaks Spanish. Strong, young guy in his twenties. He's our man, Patrick. He's our man, I swear it. That is, if you are good with that." The last thing Daly wanted was for his boss to come over.

It took a good bit of explaining and questioning, as well as numerous coins swallowed up by the telephone, but Collins eventually concluded that he would have to trust Daly's judgement. He didn't have much choice, actually. He hadn't found anyone else yet to replace Alvaro Cousillas, and he was keen to stay on the side lines, in the shadows, as he had always been instructed to.

"OK Brendan. Go ahead. We can deal with your young English friend when you get yourselves back home. Don't forget your destination is not going to be Dingle. You'll be sailing her to Lawrence Cove again."

"Grand, mate. You won't regret it. I'll get the stuff."

"You better had, my friend. You better had. One more thing. I have made new arrangements with our Spanish contact. Plan to sail from Scilly no later than 24th. That's Wednesday, next week. We've still got the berth in Luarca for as long as it takes, but they'll do the job on the night of 30th or 31st. You might have to stick around a bit. Now, I trust you. Alright, mate?"

There were no more calls. Brendan and Collins never spoke again. Brendan Daly showed Jamie Ryder around the Hannah the next morning. They also agreed, Jamie having been spurred on by Ruth's adventurous spirit, that they would depart from St. Mary's Harbour at midday on Wednesday 24th, all being well.

Jamie did move into the house in Trench Lane, which he discovered was actually called *The Ferns* because of the giant tree ferns growing in a lush corner of the garden, but he stayed for only the one night. He and Ruth were quieter than usual over dinner. There was no visit to the boiler room, nor any furtive passion. Their adieu was a walk around the fields to Peninnis Head, to catch the last glimmer of orange glow as the sun set, and then a rug on the grass bank until even the stars began to close their eyes. It was not a goodbye. It was a promise of things to come.

Jamie would have to return, if only to pick up his backpack, the old tent, and the camping gear, before Ruth resumed her teacher's job. He also promised Ruth he would come as often as possible for long weekends on St Mary's, and Ruth accepted his invitation to dine at Le Lutèce, in Blandford Street, when she returned to London at Christmas. They yearned to be together.

Chapter 5 – Infiltrator

Gorka Uriburu, the ETA lawyer, was to be present during the operation in the Luarca harbour, which nestles under the Asturian hills in the municipality of Valdés. In fact, his trusted assistant, Mikel, had already driven him to Luarca from his hometown of Mondragón, in Gipuzkoa, a province in the Basque Country. It had been a risk, and Gorka had employed all the usual methods, disappearing through the back door of his favourite tavern to avoid the remote chance of being followed by Spanish agents.

However, his presence at Luarca was now required, especially when the bag with the English pounds, which Collins had informed him was hidden inside the hull, was extracted. Given how the deal had been hanging by a thread in the last couple of weeks, with his Irish counterparts forcing changes to the itinerary on two occasions, his ETA bosses had decided it was imperative for him to personally ensure the last pieces in the puzzle came together smoothly.

Gorka and two colleagues had taken rooms, independently posing as ordinary men on business, or just travelling through, at a small hotel which overlooked a corner of the port. It was situated on the inner section of the purpose-built marina, where the fishing vessels tied up. Gorka's room also had a good view of the fish market. The three men had arrived at different times, and by separate means of transport, on 28th and 29th August, and had spent the hours examining every detail, every routine, and every movement in the port. They had especially nosed around the fish market and across the water, on the opposite side of the harbour, where an empty berth was waiting for the yellow-hulled Hannah to innocently tie up.

The berth had been acquired with a simple bit of bribery. The white Ford refrigerated van, disguised with the logos of an inoffensive Asturian fish-supplier, was obtained by extortion in Gipuzkoa. Both methods were habitually used by the organisation and, as far as ETA was concerned, justifiable.

The operation was quite straightforward. Although it sounded complicated to an outsider, as long as all sides stuck to the plan, and to precise timing, there would be no difficulty. The main impediment might be a natural one, the condition of the sea. That is why the months of August or September had been marked for the transfer, precisely because conditions were usually at their most favourable. Even so, the north of Spain very often received the same kind of weather fronts that had been tearing over the British Isles in 1988.

The business had been made possible with a little help from the same individual at the Valdés Town Hall who made the berth available. The weapons, which were hidden in wooden and plastic fishmonger's crates and boxes inside the refrigerated fish van, were to be transferred, like ordinary boxes and crates, onto one of Luarca's longline fishing boats in the early hours of the morning on 30th August, long before the market began to receive the fresh catch. Conveniently, the security lights around that corner of the harbour would fail for a couple of hours. There was nothing unusual in power failures and electrical faults occurring in Spain. Nobody would care. The boat would be parked alongside the west wharf, coinciding with the narrow loading steps which were parallel to the main entrance to the fish market.

The moment the last box had been safely loaded onto the fishing boat, Gorka Uriburu and his two companions intended to climb aboard, posing as crew members. The boat would then chug gently out of the harbour, innocently passing the *salvamento marítimo* ocean rescue vessel on its port side, as if they were departing for a few days of fishing. They would then round the narrow pier, to the west of the hillock and lighthouse on the starboard side and make for the open sea between the two outer breakwaters. Once clear of the port, the fishing boat would steer north into deeper seas and then east towards Cape Busto. The meeting point with the Hannah, scheduled for around 04.30, was to be exactly one nautical mile directly north of the Busto lighthouse. The Spanish fishing boat was to develop a faulty green navigation light at precisely 04.30. It was the agreed recognition signal for

Brendan Daly. The IRA man, whose turn on watch it would be as they approached their destination, would have set a course to approach from the east. His instructions were that the moment he spotted the intermittently flashing green navigation light on the fishing boat, he was to offer three flashes with his bow searchlight, one short, one long and another short one. In return, the fishing boat was to acknowledge with one prolonged beam from one of its own searchlights.

Once the encounter had taken place, the Hannah would follow the Spanish boat into the calmer waters of a sheltered cove. They would decide on the day which particular cove to head for, but it would be either on the west or east side of the remote Busto peninsula, depending on the direction of the wind. Wherever the fishing boat skipper decided was safest, the Hannah would then be brought alongside and the boxes and crates containing the merchandise would be swiftly transferred from the fishing boat to the yellow yacht. Gorka and his two colleagues, Andoni, and Seba, would also transfer to the Hannah. They would then escort the Irish boat, hugging the coast, to her berth at Luarca. During that short passage, sails furled and moving only under the power of the motor, Jamie would begin his job as interpreter. The Spanish long liner would, by then, have disappeared into the Bay of Biscay.

After tying up in the harbour, Gorka would remain aboard the Hannah whilst his two colleagues slipped off and returned with another, smaller craft, to park it at the stern of the yellow Fisher 30. To any onlooker across the water, it should look like a couple of guys carrying out minor repairs at the rear of the Hannah, but the two men's prime objective was to unscrew the nicely carved, wooden piece carrying the boat's false name. They would hand the bag containing the cash up to Gorka, as well as two canisters of fuel for the Hannah's motor, even if it were not required. Lastly, they would replace the carved, wooden piece, and return the small craft to its original position in the marina. Gorka, before stepping off the Hannah and strolling along the pontoon to the vehicle which would be parked opposite the Mont Blanc bar on the harbour promenade, would go below decks to make certain the Irish had kept their part of the deal, by counting the cash. Brendan Daly would not hang around for long, and nor would the ETA man want him to. The sooner the weapons were away from Spain and on the high seas, the better. The quicker Gorka could get back to Gipuzkoa, the easier it would be to melt away into his profession again as an honest, law-abiding lawyer.

***

A wide high-pressure area had at last established itself just east of the Azores. Sailing conditions were now perfect, as the Hannah made headway around the Bay of Biscay, from north to south, making use of a strong north easterly. She really was a good sea-going craft and Jamie had very soon got the hang of using sail. Brendan Daly was impressed with the Englishman's enthusiasm, strength, and quick learning. He also took credit by assuming he was not a bad instructor either. It was something Jamie was also prepared to acknowledge. Brendan was equally struck by Jamie's knowledge of first aid, for it was his young crewman who had nursed his hand and got it almost back to its right colour again within a couple of days.

Jamie not only got the hang of the boat very soon. Brendan also noted that he was also a competent team member, mucking into every task, big or small. Although they were just two, it was obvious to him that Jamie was accustomed to working in a team. That aspect, as well as the lad's solid shape and body language, did strike similarities with someone in the armed forces, but Jamie told Brendan he worked in the City and played rugby. As far as the Irishman was concerned, he had picked his crew member well.

Jamie, despite knowing he was on a totally different wavelength to Brendan, as well as being instinctively wary of the man, enjoyed every moment. As Ruth had suggested, he should treat the trip as an adventure. That is exactly what he did, knowing he would grab a hike to Santander and catch the first Brittany ferry to Portsmouth the moment he reached Spanish soil. He would be back with his new girl in no time at all, before the school term began.

Jamie especially enjoyed being on watch during the starlit nights, when he imagined talking to his Ruth through the moon. On one overcast night, whilst on the middle watch, he was fascinated by the lights of a Spanish trawler fleet, dipping, and rising on the horizon to the rocking motion of the Hannah. The gleaming dots looked like unidentified flying objects. Jamie was thrilled with the whole experience until the fifth and final night before reaching their destination.

It was his turn to come off watch for a deserved rest when he noticed it. Jamie had begun to feel fatigue setting in, unused to being at sea for days on end, and he was about to collapse in his berth; but he needed to visit the head. It was not the first time he had closed the door behind him, but this time his father's old watch, which he wore on his right wrist, caught a loose thread on the laundry bag which hung on the back of the door. The bag moved a little when he jerked to release the watch, but it moved enough for a picture, which hung on the door behind the bag, to catch his eye.

Jamie was curious and lifted the bag to one side to have a closer look. What he found was a nicely framed, amateur watercolour. But it wasn't just any old watercolour.

Images and thoughts immediately began flashing though his head because he knew what the picture represented. It was a coat of arms, and he had seen it before.

It wasn't so much the coat of arms, or the colours and the symbolic hands grabbing the horseshoe, or the leopard-like creature holding the golden arrow in its jaw. It was the motto, *Te digna sequere,* the same Latin words his father had repeated and repeated to him throughout his life. *Follow things worthy of you*, it meant. Follow things worthy of you, his old man would always say whenever they parted company, whenever Jamie was packed off back to school, and the day he went to Sandhurst. It was advice Jamie always kept at the back of his mind and which he had not always followed.

The coat of arms hanging on the back of the head door belonged to his father's old school, Sir William Borlase's School, in Buckinghamshire. To begin with, Jamie felt a pleasant tingle running up his arms. What a find! What fond memories! Then, quite suddenly, he felt mystified. What was something like that doing on a boat piloted by a rough Irishman?

Jamie's feeling of fatigue, or his desire to catch some sleep disappeared instantly when he turned the framed picture around to see if there was any reference to his father's old school. He froze when he read the words Peter Rennie, the boat's previous and legitimate owner, had written after suspecting something bad might be about to happen: *If you read this, SOS. Please call Anthony Rennie Tel: 0189620186.*

Any sense of joy and adventure drained away. Jamie turned around and bent over, feeling he was going to be sick. He remained in that position for some time, until his skin stopped sweating and his mind took control again. He looked at himself in the mirror. God, he looked awful! It wasn't the fact that his ginger beard had outgrown its charm, hiding all trace of his handsome looks. It was the look of someone mentally exhausted and concerned.

What the bloody hell is going on? Who are these people? He asked himself repeatedly after taking note of Anthony Rennie's telephone number.

When he stepped into the forward berth and lay down on his back, it was 00.30 on 30th August. He should have fallen asleep instantly. He desperately needed sleep, especially as he would be in the wheelhouse again for the morning watch at 04.00. However, there was no way he was going to close his eyes, a gut feeling telling him he was unwittingly helping some criminal organisation.

After nearly two hours lying awake, at one moment believing fatigue might be playing with his imagination, he decided the best thing to do would be to question the Irishman, to confront him. Brendan Daly would not be expecting it, but Jamie was going to have to be extremely careful. In the early hours of the morning, in the wheelhouse of the Hannah, and skimming the waters of the Bay of Biscay, the direct question Jamie had in mind would either have Brendan plead indignantly that he was totally unaware of where the yacht may have come from, and that he was just a delivery man, or make him react like a cornered bear. The latter could be extremely dangerous indeed.

On his way through the galley, Jamie opened the cutlery drawer and took out the potato peeler. It was the sharpest thing he could find. He slid it into the back of the boot on his right foot, making sure the bottom of his trouser leg covered it. There was no harm in taking precautions, even if Brendan turned out to be perfectly innocent.

Jamie was about to step up into the wheelhouse when he heard the Hannah's motor cough into life. He looked at his watch. Surely, they couldn't be so close to port yet! Whatever reason there was for running the motor, Jamie decided to make himself a mug of coffee. It would give the impression that he was relaxed about things, and totally ignorant of what might be going on when he began to ask questions. He also made sure the coffee was a strong one. He might need it.

Brendan was not in the wheelhouse. Jamie peeped out behind. He was not there either. It was only when he stood at the wheel and peered ahead that Jamie noticed that the jib had been furled. Jamie also saw that Brendan had slackened the mainsail. It was luffing and Brendan was speedily lowering it.

"Need a hand?" shouted Jamie.

Brendan did not appear to hear at first, probably because they were moving into the wind, but he heard Jamie's second, louder shout, and turned around with a start. He was not expecting company. It took him half a minute to gather himself and signal to the young Englishman that he was OK. Jamie looked around and across the sea in every direction. There were lights flickering in and out of view on the horizon to port and nothing else. Then, directly to starboard, he saw the flash of a lighthouse. Five seconds later, it flashed again, and then he counted five more seconds before its white beam came round again. Further away to stern, he spotted another flash. It was also a lighthouse, and it also emitted a signal every five seconds.

Jamie looked at the electronic chart plotter and at the radar. He also glanced at the old, brass compass to confirm what he thought, that the Hannah's bow was pointing east, and not west as it should have been. It was actually the first time he had looked at the instrument closely. Once again, the shock and the tingling sensation. It was that motto. The compass was inscribed with those same words, *Te digna sequere*. His father, or something, was trying to tell him he needed to be careful.

Jamie stepped down into the saloon to look at the chart. He followed the pencilled plot and then searched for the names of lighthouses along the coast where the chart plotter told him they were. The first lighthouse, directly to starboard and to the south of their position, was on a point called Cape Vidio. The second, the one closest to Luarca, was on another bit of land jutting out on the wild Asturian coast. It was Cape Busto. Nearing the latter would have been a more suitable time to furl the sails, so why had Brendan started up the motor up so soon?

"Did I wake you, mate? Sorry," shouted Brendan, poking his head down from the wheelhouse. Jamie turned abruptly on full alert, but he managed to disguise his thoughts.

"I heard the motor. Everything alright, Brendan? We can't already be nearing Luarca, surely? Want a coffee?" Jamie tried to hide his concern with a fake yawn when he offered to get the man a coffee.

"No, thanks, mate. If you can't sleep, come up. There's something I want to explain, Jamie."

As he spoke, Brendan reached into his holdall under the seating and pulled out the Beretta. He tucked it into the back of his trousers and covered it with his baggy sailor's jumper. The moment had come to tell Alvaro's replacement part of the truth. There was no option. Jamie Ryder would go along with it or maybe he wouldn't. If this Englishman didn't, then he would get a bullet through the back of the head. It was as simple as that.

"Why are we pointing east?" asked Jamie when he joined Daly next to the wheel.

"We're not any longer. I had to get her into the wind to lower the sails. We are on a westerly course again. You were looking at the chart just now. You must have seen that lighthouse," said Brendan, pointing to the south.

"I did."

"Well, we're aiming for the next one, not far ahead. Then, if you look even further west, you should then make out another light. That will be the Luarca lighthouse. We're almost there, mate."

"Yes. I more or less gathered that, but why the rush to lower the sails and motor her when we've still got a fair way to go?"

"I'm about to tell you, Mr Ryder," replied Brendan, with what Jamie considered was almost menace.

"What are we really doing in Spain, Brendan?" asked Jamie. He was not going to wait.

"Nothing for you to concern yourself about, sonny," said Brendan, standing square to Jamie, who had positioned himself with one foot on the deck.

"It certainly does concern me. What are we doing?" insisted Jamie, firmly.

"Just a little bit of business on the side. Sorry, mate. But I needed you. You just play along, and you'll come to no harm, I swear."

"We are not here to deliver the boat, then?"

"No mate. We're here to pick up a little merchandise."

This is where Jamie played his own card. He was thinking fast and clearly, like the Lieutenant on patrol in enemy territory. The menace in Daly's look, the cold and rather arrogant tone, and his thuggish stance. They indicated that one wrong move might be his last. So, he counter attacked with his own deceit.

"In that case, Mr Daly, I shall accept a bit of the cut you mentioned," said Jamie, with a hint of a smile appearing on one side of his mouth, half despising, half arrogant. In his gut, Jamie was scared as hell but ready for whatever might come, but a new look in Daly's eye, together with his body language, shuffling his feet closer together, indicated to Jamie that the big Irishman had fallen for it.

"That's my man. Good on you, Jamie," said Brendan, apparently relieved, before going on to explain what was about to occur. Just as Collins had done with Alvaro, no mention was made of weapons. Just a little bit of contraband, that's all it was. There was no need for Jamie to know what would be in those boxes. In fact, it would be better for him not to know. However, Jamie already suspected what he might have got himself into. The big man was Irish. Brendan must be IRA. It had to be weapons. What else could it be?

***

At precisely 04.30, they saw three lights approaching dead ahead of them. In fact it was Jamie who first spotted them. One white at the top of a mast, a red, and an intermittently, flashing green. It was their fishing boat, and it was moving towards them at quite a rate. Brendan immediately flicked the switch to the left of the wheel three times, using the bow search light to signal with one short, one long and another short flash. Seconds later, the approaching vessel replied. Just one, drawn out beam. Then it turned about. The faulty green light was now on its starboard side and had miraculously stopped flickering.

The Hannah was very soon following the other vessel towards the Busto peninsula. The wind was not too strong, but it was gusting from the east, so the fishing boat skipper rounded the cape to the more sheltered waters in a patch of sea known as the Altar. Above the cliffs, and beyond the little beach Jamie could make out, there was only farmland. It was most unlikely there would be spying eyes to witness the two vessels nudging alongside each other, and how rapidly the merchandise was moved onto the Hannah. Three of the fishing boat crew helped with the transfer. Brendan told Jamie to lend a hand shoving the two longer, wooden crates into the forward berth, which had had the port-side bunk removed in Dingle. They were heavy. Two plastic fish containers were placed onto the bunk Jamie had been sleeping on and a couple more, smaller wooden boxes, fitted neatly where the galley table and part of the seating would have been. The last two containers were placed on each side of the stern deck and immediately covered with tarpaulins and strapped down by Brendan.

Jamie stayed below deck to reorganise his own stuff, so he didn't see, seconds before the long liner pulled away and headed at full steam further out into the Bay of Biscay, how Brendan Daly helped Gorka Uriburu and his two younger colleagues step over the guardrails and onto the Hannah. One of the young Basques was Andoni, a slim and fragile-looking individual. The other, as chunky as Gorka, but two or three inches taller, was Seba. He wore a flat cap and dark glasses, even in the dark of the dawn.

Brendan shouted down for Jamie to come up to begin his interpreting job. Uriburu immediately gestured to his men to go below. Brendan assumed he wanted them to check things out. As they stepped down, Jamie was making his way through the galley.

"*Buenos días,*" he said, cheerfully. They nodded, but their faces remained expressionless. They followed Jamie up to the wheelhouse.

Brendan, who was at the wheel keeping the Hannah well away from the rocky coastline as they made for Luarca, indicated that the man to talk to was out in the dark. When Jamie stepped out on deck, one of the two younger men followed and stood in the doorway, immediately behind him. The other, the slimmer and taller of the two, sat down on the seating in the wheelhouse. He looked as if the motion of the boats, when they had sat still in the water for the transfer of the goods, had affected him badly.

Gorka Uriburu was standing with a foot on one of the boxes which Brendan had covered with tarpaulins. He was looking back over the water with both hands on the guardrail. When he heard Jamie's greeting, he turned around and accepted the Englishman's handshake.

"*Dígame usted,*" said Jamie, offering his services for whatever the Spaniard required.

"*Ya veremos si todo sale bien,*" replied Gorka slily, insinuating that all would depend on how things went. Then he pulled out a packet of cigarettes and offered one to Jamie.

"*Gracias. No fumo,*" said Jamie, telling the stocky, wide-shouldered man that he did not smoke.

There were two initial sparks from Gorka's lighter, as he protected it from the draft against the back of the wheelhouse. A third produced a flame good enough to light up the Spaniard's face with a warm, orange glow as he sucked on the fag. It revealed a very ugly, deathly pale appearance, with what Jamie thought were very nasty little eyes looking sideways at him.

Once again, Jamie momentarily turned to ice. It wasn't Gorka's eyes, or his ugliness, poor man, with scars of acne forming little craters all over his cheeks. It was the brown, hairy birthmark above his right eyebrow. Jamie recognised him immediately. Gorka Uriburu was the man who had sat next to John Palmer, together with four others, at Alonso's table at Rosie's Cantina in Tenerife. It was a night and a face he would never forget.

He always knew Olivia's father was a bloody crook. This confirmed it.

What a bastard! thought Jamie.

For an instant, Jamie felt a pang of sadness. It didn't last, though. The man's same ruthless stare pierced through any melancholic thought, never losing eye contact, as if it were his way of paralysing a prey. Nevertheless, Jamie felt certain Gorka had not recognised him, possibly because his face was now covered with a thick beard. He played the same game he had done with Brendan, acting as if all was well, and that he was a total stranger.

"Seguro que todo sale como previsto," said Jamie, turning his face away from Gorka's stare, but attempting to sound as if he were trying to reassure the Basque, suggesting that everything would go to plan.

"Sure it will," replied Gorka, surprising Jamie Ryder in the most perfect English.

"You speak English?"

"Of course. Does it surprise you?"

"Only because I was chosen to come to Luarca to help in the exchange because I speak Spanish."

"You speak it well. You were in South America? The accent is not from Spain."

"Yes. A lot of English students go to Peru to perfect their Spanish," replied Jamie, trying not to reveal his Canary Islands connection.

"And your English is not Irish," pressed Gorka.

"No. Nor is it from Scotland, the land of my father. My accent is more like yours, in fact," acknowledged Jamie, suspecting what might be going through the shadowy man's head. Jamie was sparring with words and trying to get out of the corner Gorka's questions were pushing him into.

It seemed to do the trick. Uriburu turned away to look towards the Busto lighthouse. No more words were exchanged as the Hannah chugged slowly onwards, Brendan taking her through a wide arc around Encoronada Point and in between the outer breakwaters of the well-protected Luarca harbour. There were still two hours to go before the sun rose but the harbour, even the corner near the fish market, was sufficiently lit up for them to take every precaution.

One of Gorka's men, Seba, the one with the flat cap and shades, slunk off along the pontoon after making absolutely certain it was all clear. He would be joined, when it was daylight, by the second man. In the meantime, it was time for Brendan to inspect the merchandise, especially what was in the forward berth. He began to do so, with Gorka observing his every movement. Jamie was dispatched to begin tidying up the decks and preparing halyards and lines, making sure winches were in good shape and ensuring the sails were ready to unfurl at a moment's notice for the return voyage. Although Brendan imagined Jamie would have guessed what was inside the boxes, he instinctively wanted to keep him as ignorant as possible.

***

The sun began to peep through broken clouds towards 08.00, and the port had suddenly become a hive of activity. There were three or four small trawlers parked alongside the wharf, just north of the fish market. The car park across the water, to the stern of the Hannah, was now packed with vehicles of all shapes and sizes. Jamie had more or less finished on deck when he smelled the familiar perfume of bacon being fried in the galley. Minutes later, Brendan brought him up a bacon butty and a steaming mug of tea. He was followed by Gorka, who had refused Brendan's hospitality.

Jamie was starving and polished off the dripping butty like a hungry tiger. Although Gorka had revealed that he spoke the most polished English, for some reason the ETA man still wished Jamie to interpret between himself and the big Irishman. It was almost as if the Basque considered Brendan unworthy of being treated as an equal. This amused Jamie. At the same time, he believed the gingery growth on his face might not disguise his own identity forever. In fact, whilst he did his best to portray total collaboration in this clandestine operation, his every sense and muscle were on full alert. Jamie was aware that one false move, or a loose word, would put his life in danger.

There really was not much for Daly and Uriburu to talk about, however. The weapons were on the Hannah. All that was required, as far as the Irishman was concerned, was for the cash to be counted, for Gorka to be satisfied, and for him to clear off.

The low cloud melted away completely by 09.00 and the sun promised a warm end to the month. Gorka informed Brendan, and Jamie translated for the Irishman, that he was nipping off across the road to the Mont Blanc café for a proper coffee, and that his colleague would remain on board until he returned. The cold-eyed colleague, slimmer and younger, the one Jamie understood to be called Andoni, did remain on board. He stood halfway between the wheelhouse and the galley, with one hand in a jacket pocket. They were taking no chances.

What neither Jamie nor Brendan could have been aware of was that Gorka Uriburu had begun to smell a rat, and it was all to do with Jamie, the interpreter.

To begin with, it had been Jamie's English accent as the Hannah motored towards Luarca. It was simply too English, too private school. It just didn't go with the Irish lot his people were doing a deal with. In his experience, just like his own people, who detested anything smelling of Spanish imperialism, Collins and his people despised anybody remotely poisoned with English blood. His presence on the Hannah just didn't add up. There was something odd going on. Therefore, as far as Gorka was concerned, Jamie must be considered a possible threat, not only to this operation, but also to his organisation.

Then, when the sun became bright enough to reveal the mullet, sucking at scraps on the surface of the water in and around the Hannah and between the boats parked alongside, Gorka's suspicions were confirmed. Jamie's bushy, ginger beard no longer disguised him enough and he saw through it. At the same time, the more he heard Jamie speak, the more he remembered the voice. Gorka had a good memory for voices and the Englishman's was the same strong, calm tone of voice that had bid them an enjoyable evening, almost mockingly, at Rosie's Cantina. He remembered Jamie's arrogant, self-assured presence, and his defiant look. Above all, the Basque with the hideously marked face remembered the veiled apology which Alonso had made to Mr Palmer and to the others at his table about the interruptions, first by his tearful daughter, and then by the English army lout who had been accosting Olivia.

With Gorka's suspicions about the identity of the Englishman confirmed, his mind also began to spin conspiracy theories, especially with the added factor Alonso had hinted at, that Jamie Ryder was in the British forces. Gorka's organisation had a self-destructive habit of suspecting everyone to be *on the other side*. In other words, anyone not sworn to be an ETA supporter must be treated as the enemy, perhaps even as a Spanish agent. It was one of the habitual symptoms of any organisation which is founded upon, and nourished, by an inferiority complex based, like so many nationalist movements, upon feeling hard-done-by.

In his years within the separatist organisation there had been several infiltrators. Some had got away with it and provided valuable information which helped lead to the terrorist organisation's demise; others were discovered and brutally murdered in some remote wood or gully.

Gorka Uriburu now believed Jamie Ryder must be an infiltrated English agent. Perhaps the big Irishman was part of an undercover plot too, designed by British intelligence and assisted by Spanish counterparts in the Basque region, to undermine both of their organisations. Suspicion confused him to an extreme and blurred his judgement. After all, Brendan was as faithful to the IRA as Gorka was to his own separatist group. Nor was the younger Englishman a conspiring member of Her Majesty's Secret Service. He had simply been an innocent onlooker who had come along for the ride.

Unfortunately for Gorka, and for Brendan too, Jamie Ryder was a man of duty and his duty as an ex-serviceman was to do his bit for Queen and country.

***

Gorka's proper coffee at the Mont Blanc included a telephone call from the café's old-fashioned telephone booth. It was behind a wooden partition, which the barman indicated to after he had sipped and enjoyed his strong *cafecito*. His call was to a secret number at a safe house in the French town of Pau, on the other side of the Pyrenees mountains. Once again, a password was given before any conversation took place.

The man he spoke to was Francisco Mujika, alias *Pakito*, the leader of ETA's military operations. The conversation ended with clear instructions. By no means should the Hannah be permitted to sail until new orders were received. Gorka should telephone Mujika again at 11.00 from a street telephone booth. He would then be told how to proceed. In the meantime, to delay the Hannah's departure without raising suspicions, Gorka was to count the cash and then insist that it fell well short of the stipulated amount, and that he would need to retain the Hannah, and the weapons, until the misunderstanding was cleared up.

When he returned to the Hannah, his breath perfumed with strong coffee, Gorka Uriburu dispatched the slimmer colleague whom he had left on guard and waited. He did not have anything to say except to tell Brendan and Jamie that they were on no account to go ashore.

Brendan was happy with that. He just wanted to get the bloody hell out of the Spanish harbour as fast as possible. Jamie, on the other hand, was eager to find any excuse to walk along the pontoon to see if he could get some pounds changed. His intention was not to do a bunk and to save his skin. He wanted some coins to make a call. He fully intended to do all he could to save the lives of British soldiers and citizens by alerting someone about what he believed was going on. He had thought of making a fuss right there in Luarca, attracting the attention of the Spanish police. However, his mind was thinking further ahead; if the Hannah could get safely back to Ireland, it would give British intelligence the chance to pick up a trail and do considerable damage to the IRA. In the circumstances, he would have to wait until the wretched man with the horrendous birthmark on his face decided the Hannah could sail. He would then persuade Brendan to let him go ashore to buy his girlfriend a souvenir. However, if things turned sour and he felt his life was in danger, Jamie decided he would just jump ship and run like hell to wherever he could.

As he pretended to make even more preparations for sailing, Jamie saw Gorka's colleague, Andoni, go up the steps from the pontoon to the avenue. He watched him walk almost as far as the fish market. The man then appeared to stop for a moment before retracing his steps for about fifty yards to the entrance to another pontoon, where numerous smaller boats were parked. One of these, a small speedboat, was letting out a plume of exhaust fumes. At the ready, in the driver's seat, Jamie noticed the other member of Gorka's team. It was Seba. As soon as the slim one was aboard, the boat reversed, and then moved slowly in their direction. Jamie wasn't sure what was going on, but he decided it was time to arm himself with something more than just the potato peeler which was still hidden in his boot. The only thing he could think of was the wooden pole hook. It could be pretty nasty if it was used like a pick and aimed at somebody's neck or face. He grabbed the pole hook and concealed it by sliding it under the windows in front of the wheelhouse. While fiddling around with lines and the boom, on which the mainsail was folded, Jamie kept an eye on proceedings.

As the speedboat nudged up behind the rounded stern of the Hannah, both Brendan and Gorka stood on the deck. Brendan appeared to point something out to the two men in the smaller craft while Gorka looked around nervously. Brendan then handed over two lines. From where he was standing, Jamie could not see exactly what they were doing, but one of the men handed the wooden board with the Hannah's name on it up to Brendan. Jamie still wasn't certain where all this was leading until he saw what looked like something in a black bin bag being passed up, this time into Gorka's reaching hands. Only then did Jamie think he understood. It was payment in exchange for the goods.

Immediately afterwards, the Basque went into the wheelhouse and disappeared below. At the same time, Brendan handed the men in the speedboat the Hannah's carved wooden identity board, which they proceeded to screw back into place again before handing up what looked like two Jerry cans. Five minutes later, the speedboat moved away and back to its position on the pontoon on the inner side of the harbour. Jamie noticed one of the men, Andoni, the tall one, walk in the direction of the fish market. He then cut back along the very edge of the wharf and into the car park on the north side of the market. There, Jamie watched him get into a van and drive away. The other colleague crossed the road and made his way back to the Hannah on the opposite side of the road. He was very soon back on the Hannah to await further instructions from Uriburu.

Seba's presence gave Gorka the security he required before announcing the bad news. Once again, Gorka refused to speak directly to Brendan Daly, the big Irishman, in his perfect English. Jamie's presence was required in the saloon.

As Jamie made his way through the wheelhouse and down below, he grabbed the binoculars which had been hung untidily on the wheel and stuck them into one of his windcheater pockets. It was an instinctive move. He might need them.

Jamie listened as Gorka spoke slowly and calmly, always directing his look at Brendan. When the Basque said what he had to say, which was very brief, he turned to look at Jamie, almost challenging him to be careful what he told Brendan. Jamie translated, word for word, only raising a hand to stop the big Irishman from interrupting. It was clear Brendan was working himself into a state and Jamie was eager to prevent the man's temper putting them in immediate danger.

"There's a little problem," began Jamie. "But it can be sorted out," he added, as Brendan's face reddened, and his fists tightened at his side.

"Brendan, it appears the cash in the bag which the gentleman has counted is not the agreed amount," continued Jamie.

"Mr Gorka will not let us sail until the mistake has been rectified. Mr Gorka is sure it will be. We are not to leave the boat. Once a solution has been found, we will be free to sail. In the meantime, Mr Gorka will be going ashore to make the necessary telephone calls and he will return to inform us."

"*¿Alguna pregunta?*" asked Uriburu as soon as Jamie had done his bit.

"Mr Gorka asks if you have any questions, Brendan. Personally, I think he has made it quite clear. I would leave it at that if I were you."

"Would you now? I'll decide that, if you don't mind, Mr Ryder," replied Brendan, almost reprimanding the Englishman, trying to reassert his position. "Yes, tell the gentleman to bloody get on with whatever he has to do. Don't forget we've got a stack of bloody weapons on board ready to get us into a whole lot of trouble." It was the first time Brendan had admitted what he assumed Jamie already knew, that the boxes contained weapons.

Just to put Brendan even more on edge, Seba stuck his head down from the wheelhouse with chilling information.

"*Policía. Guardia Civil!*"

It wasn't just the police. It was the Civil Guard, the most efficient, feared, and worst paid police force in Spain. The Guardia Civil were also the natural and ruthless hunters of ETA's military wing, of those who, like the IRA, had perpetrated dozens of murders of innocent people. For an instant, Gorka Uriburu gave signs of being even more on edge than the Irishman. Jamie, on the other hand, felt a kind of pleasing relief. He might be arrested, but he could prove his stupidity.

"*Se fueron al bar,*" informed the younger ETA man from the wheelhouse. The Guardia Civil officers had gone into the bar.

Gorka shoved Jamie to one side and grabbed the bag with the cash in it from the galley deck. He then pulled out a pistol from his windcheater pocket and used it to urge both Brendan and Jamie to sit. As he waved it about, Jamie recognised the weapon as a Browning GP-35. It was one of the many semi-automatics he had seen and handled during his spell in the Army.

The tension mounted. Five minutes passed. Jamie and Brendan remained in total silence. They could even hear the water lapping the Hannah's hull as a vessel passed behind her, sending small waves against the pontoon. Ten minutes. Twenty minutes. It was quite common for the Guardia Civil to stop off at a bar when on duty to have their *desayuno*. Very few public servants have breakfast at home in Spain, and Guardia Civil officers prefer a mid-morning bite and a coffee. It breaks the monotony. It also provides an opportunity, something the general public is unaware of, to make acquaintances. They might also be onto a trail. Whatever the circumstances of their visit to the Mont Blanc bar, they would also sniff around.

The tension was broken when Gorka's colleague stuck his head down again.

"*Ya se van,*" he said. The policemen were leaving.

"*Y aquí llega Andoni,*" he added, sticking his head into the galley again to inform Gorka that his other colleague, Andoni, was returning.

Gorka Uriburu gestured to the two boatmen to remain where they were, put the pistol back into his pocket and went on deck clutching the bag with the money. Jamie and Brendan looked at each other. The Irishman was perspiring, beads of sweat trickled down his forehead, and his hands were clasped together in front of his face. Jamie broke the silence.

"IRA, Mr Daly?" he asked quietly, standing up to peer through one of the starboard portholes.

"You guessed right, Jamie. I'm bloody sorry to get you into this, mate." The man sounded genuinely sorry, but he wasn't going to fool Jamie again.

"No, Mr Daly. I'm sorry for you. Now look, we've got to get

the hell out of here somehow. You will either die here, at the hands of your so-called chums, or you'll end up in a British high security jail."

"Shut your bloody mouth, will you? He said he was going to sort it out, so no false bloody heroics from you, son."

Before Jamie could reply, Gorka stepped down into the saloon again. This time he spoke to both of them in his perfect, highly polished English.

"Please remain on the boat. You may eat or go onto the deck to prepare for sailing, if necessary. But do not try to leave the boat. Both my men will be here to see that you do not try anything stupid. Andoni will wait inside and Seba will be in the wheelhouse. Do you understand?"

Both Jamie and Brendan nodded.

"In fact, it is better if you take it in turns on the deck. Look occupied preparing the sails or something. That would be more realistic, perhaps. I shall leave you in the good hands of my friends while I make an important call to your Mr Collins. For your sakes, I hope he can clarify the error." Again, Jamie and Brendan nodded, even though there was little more they could do on deck. The Hannah was more than ready to sail. All she needed was for someone to start the motor and cast off the lines.

Gorka turned and left them. They felt and heard him step over the guardrail on the starboard side. Half a minute later, the one called Andoni joined them below. He spoke to Jamie in Spanish, generously suggesting he got himself a mug of coffee before ordering him to go on deck. Jamie did not wait for a better offer, hurried up into the wheelhouse, and then onto the deck where he moved along the port gunwale. He stopped between the wheelhouse and the main mast and looked all around him. Astern he saw the ocean rescue vessel parked across the water. If only he could attract a crew member's attention, but it looked totally unmanned. Out of the corner of his eye he saw the other younger ETA man's face glaring at him through one of the wheelhouse windows. Jamie moved himself further forward to the bow, where he acted as if he was checking rigging and other items.

The next hour and a half passed without incident. Jamie relieved his unlikely friend below deck twice and, on the second occasion, he put the kettle on to make himself a mug of tea.

"*¿Le apetece?*" He asked Andoni if he would like a mug of coffee. Jamie played the friendly game, but he knew the slim man would decline the offer. He didn't fool his kidnapper. In fact, Jamie felt that he was someone's prisoner, like a foreign spy waiting to be exchanged.

***

Half an hour later, shortly after midday, when he had just begun his next stint on deck, Jamie toyed with the idea that it was time to attract someone's attention. Once again, however, he pulled himself back from the edge. He had to stick this out. His last thought coincided with a blue Mercedes pulling up just past the Mont Blanc bar. Jamie swore under his breath when one of the rear doors opened and Gorka stepped out. Jamie instinctively stiffened in anticipation but Gorka didn't come straight along the narrow pontoon. Instead, he entered the café after a quick glance towards the Hannah.

Five minutes later, just after the Mercedes did a three-point turn and pulled away, Gorka appeared again. This time he strode across the avenue and returned to the Hannah. He called out for Jamie to follow him down to the saloon. Once again, he addressed the two foreigners in English.

"Gentlemen!" he said without removing his sunglasses. "I have good news for you. You will be pleased to know that your friends have accepted there was a mistake in their accounts. The problem has been solved very quickly indeed. A telex notification has confirmed that a bank transfer has been ordered for the missing funds to be deposited into our account at a Swiss bank. Everything is in order."

It was all a pack of lies, of course, but Gorka and his people needed to keep up the pretence. Jamie didn't trust the ugly one for one second but managed to produce a gesture with his hands to imply that he was relieved. It was Brendan who didn't seem to understand. He was a man who took orders. He had never been paid to think too hard.

"In that case, Mr Gorka, are we free to go? I'm sure you realise that the sooner we make for the open sea, the better."

"Well, not exactly, I regret to inform you. There is nothing for you to worry about but, as you know, the police were looking around this morning. We feel it best if you wait until dark before you sail, you know, when there is not much activity in the harbour."

"Surely, if the police are sniffing about, the last thing we want to do is to stay here any longer," Brendan pointed out.

The man does think, after all, thought Jamie. In fact he nodded in agreement and pressed Gorka to realise that it made perfect sense.

"I agree. It is time we shook hands and went our separate ways, Gorka."

"No, my friend. As I said, you are not to leave. But listen, don't look so sad*, amigo*. You should be happy. We should celebrate. Yes, we should celebrate! I invite you both to drink some good Asturian cider with me this evening. It is the best cider in the world, you know. Indeed, you cannot leave without trying this cider and perhaps a *tapa* or two."

"I don't think that would be necessary," said Jamie, but Gorka realised, by the change of expression in Brendan's face, that the Irishman found the idea harmless enough. He was not going to say no to a drink.

"It is indeed necessary, Mr Ryder. I shall return to collect you this evening at seven o-clock. I know where they serve the best cider in town."

"At what time do shops close, Gorka?" asked Jamie.

Realising there was nothing else he could do except go with the flow, Jamie surprised the Basque with what appeared to be such a trivial question, so casual and so unrelated to their predicament. Gorka looked back into the Englishman's eyes as he was about to step out into the wheelhouse from the saloon. His glare invited Jamie to expand on his query.

"My girlfriend. I promised to buy her a souvenir."

Gorka Uriburu did not bother with a reply. He just shrugged his shoulders and disappeared. A moment later, Jamie and Brendan heard the Basque's cigarette lighter click into action as he talked to one of his men on the deck. It was Andoni.

"Souvenirs? How the bloody hell can you think of buying a bloody souvenir at a time like this?" asked Brendan, half mocking the stupid Englishman. He was about to add a not very pleasant and unnecessary comment about Ruth when Gorka stepped down into the saloon again. The Basque didn't like, or believe Jamie, but he was confused enough to decide to play along. He offered a jeering grin before pretending to play the compassionate card.

"Very well, my friend. I have to go to do some business, but Andoni will accompany you to the nearest shop. Just one shop, please, Mr Ryder. Please do not mess with my colleague. Well, let's say, I would not if I were you. He is not a nice man. Do you understand?"

"I shall need to go to a bank first, to change some pounds, but thank you," Jamie pointed out.

Brendan groaned in disbelief next to him. What happened next was not expected, but it placed Jamie and Brendan further into the toying hands of the sneering Spaniard who hated Spain.

"No banks. Here, this should be enough, don't you think?" said Gorka, placing two green, thousand peseta notes on the chart table. Before Jamie could politely object, the Basque continued, this time in Spanish.

"*Me caes bien, inglés. No te ofendas, hombre, pero las mujeres nos pueden matar. Esta tarde nos tomamos un par de culines y me cuentas como es tu mujercita, eh?*"

He then spoke in English to a very confused Brendan Daly.

"Mr Daly, after I have gone, in about fifteen minutes, Jamie will be going ashore with Andoni. You will not be alone. Seba will remain on board to keep you company. Please do not try anything foolish. I expect Jamie to return within one hour. If he does not, it is because I have given Andoni instructions to shoot Mr Ryder if he tries anything his girlfriend would regret."

This time, there was no reply from either Brendan or Jamie, and their captor disappeared. One or two words were exchanged on the deck in the extraordinary Basque language before Gorka was heard to step off the Hannah once again.

"You're not going to use those, I hope, Jamie," said Brendan, pointing a large, brown finger at the bank notes on the chart table.

"I am, Brendan. I most certainly am. It would be very rude of me not to accept such generosity from your friend," he said, as he picked the notes and put them in a back pocket of his jeans.

Before Brendan could utter another word, Seba stepped into the saloon and indicated with his head that Jamie should go up on deck. Jamie did not wait for another hint and brushed quickly past the ETA man, who then sat himself down, uncomfortably on the top step, between the saloon and the wheelhouse. Andoni, Gorka's slimmer friend, was waiting for Jamie. The moment Jamie stepped onto the deck, Andoni put his left finger up to his eye and deliberately placed his right hand behind his back and slightly under the baggy jumper he was wearing. He was merely telling the Englishman to be fully aware that he was armed. Jamie nodded in response. The Basque immediately put a hand forward, indicating that Jamie should walk ahead.

Both men walked along the pontoon and up the steps onto the avenue pavement, which separated parked vehicles from the water's edge. They turned right towards the town centre. Jamie managed to have a quick look at the Mont Blanc café. It was typically Spanish and had obviously been converted from what must have originally been a front-line house. The ground floor, which housed the small bar, was nicely painted, and decorated outside with beer barrels, tables and one or two potted plants. It was also remarkably busy with almost every table occupied by clients. Most were locals, talking in customary, loud Spanish fashion. Others, more discreetly, conversed in a variety of languages. Jamie had noticed one or two yachts in the marina displaying French and Dutch flags, but he also heard the distinct, bubbling chatter of a group of elderly British gentlemen who were seated around one of the tables.

If only I could speak to them, thought Jamie, as he looked back towards their table. He noticed that the Mont Blanc's second storey was in a bad state of repair, with greying white paint peeling off and windows that looked as if they had not been opened for several seasons. In fact, although most of the port walkway was a merry scattering of cafes, bars, and restaurants, all of which had attracted the usual midday crowd, Jamie couldn't help thinking that Luarca must become quite a miserable place in winter.

The thought took him to Hugh Town in Scilly. That too, must be quite dull and lifeless after the summer visitors departed. He must get back to Ruth. She was so full of character and overflowed with enthusiasm for what she most loved, which was looking after children, but she was also so fragile and alone.

Jamie, followed closely behind by Andoni, walked all the way along the harbour. There were no shops, just cafes, restaurants, and closed doors. So, just under a blue sign with the words *Hotel Báltico* on it, Jamie turned round and shrugged his shoulders, as if to ask Andoni for help. The Basque used a nod of the head and two fingers to indicate that Jamie should continue walking , implying that he would find a more commercial zone a couple of streets ahead. As they walked behind the fish market Jamie wondered how people could stand living with such a strong smell at their back door. He was making mental notes of every detail. He crossed over a ridiculous roundabout, which would be impossible for a bus to navigate without going straight across the middle, and then followed the main road round to the left. It hugged grander buildings lining the left side of the road. Across a river, which he came to on his right, there was some more attractive architecture on the opposite bank. It was the Rio Negro river.

Two minutes later, just past a sign for a Sabadell bank, Andoni told Jamie to enter the second street. There it was, a small, brightly painted shop, selling almost everything tourists could hope to find. He expected Andoni would wait outside, but there was no way he was going to let Jamie out of his sight, and the Basque pretended to nose about inside. While hunting for a souvenir, Jamie looked for a back door. He could make a run for it. It wouldn't matter, even if he didn't get anywhere. Surely Andoni would not start shooting in the middle of a shop full of customers and two middle-aged ladies behind the counter. Once again, however, Jamie remembered his duty, that he fully intended to do his bit. There was no way he was going to run for it. He wanted to get back to the Hannah and to sail away with Brendan. He needed to give the British authorities a chance to make a big dent in the IRA's leadership. He had to stay with it all the way. He must make that call. He needed to remain calm and just get himself some coins.

Jamie bought the first thing that caught his eye. It was a cheap, handcrafted, blue necklace with a crescent moon and three stars engraved on it. It only cost him 835 pesetas, but it was rather pretty, he thought. He got some change, but decided it probably wouldn't be enough, so he asked one of the ladies if she could change the other thousand pesetas note..

"*Lo siento mucho, joven. Necesito todas las monedas que tengo. Le puedo dar una o dos de cincuenta, pero no más.*" The lady was truly kind, but she could maybe offer him a couple of fifties, but no more.

"*Para hacer una llamada a mi novia en Inglaterra,*" he whispered. He was on a boat and needed to make a call to his girlfriend in England, he told her.

The lady hummed and hawed, but her compassion shone through like the sun warming those faces on the café terraces. She surrendered to Jamie's charm and to his reason, and took the thousand peseta note, exchanging it for five one hundred peseta notes and a mix of 25 and 50 peseta coins with the image of King Juan Carlos I inscribed on them. She did not have these in the till but handed them over after disappearing for a couple of minutes behind a lace curtain. Jamie thanked her most graciously and stepped out of the shop, closely followed by Andoni.

"*Eh, inglés. Por qué tanta moneda?*" asked Andoni, coming up behind Jamie much closer than he had been instructed to. Why so many coins?

"*Quiero llamar a mi novia*", Jamie replied, hoping that a

wish to call his girl would soften the Basque, and that he would feel the same compassion demonstrated by the shopkeeper. But it was not to be. He was having none of that.

"*Ni hablar, amigo. De eso nada. Directo al barco,*" he growled, warning Jamie to head straight back the way they had come to the boat, once again pointing a finger to his eye.

The Hannah smelled of baked beans and Brendan, after asking Jamie what had taken him so bloody long, told him there was still some left in the pot. Jamie showed the Irishman the pendant with the moon and the stars on it and then cracked a couple of eggs, which he dropped into the remains of the baked beans. That was his lunch, a late one and not much, but it would provide enough energy for his next move. Jamie's plan, his immediate priority, was to make a call or two. He would have to wait until the night. Perhaps he would have a chance to get away from his shadows whilst they drank their ciders. If not, he would just have to hold back until he was back in Ireland and make a big enough fuss to attract the Irish police, the Garda Síochána, if necessary.

Chapter 6 – Cider with the enemy

Shadows and the glistening water were beginning to blend together in the Luarca marina, as the sun dipped at the end of the day, and it was at 19.30, an hour before darkness fell, that Gorka returned. He immediately gave instructions, in Spanish.

Seba and Andoni were to walk with Jamie to the car park on the other side of the water, next to the fish market. They were to use their second vehicle, a red Skoda, to drive to *Casa Luis*. Brendan, he said, would wait for five minutes more on the Hannah before they too followed. The blue Mercedes was waiting for Gorka and the Irishman about a hundred yards along from the Mont Blanc. Jamie translated for Brendan. This time, the IRA man didn't utter a word.

Jamie was told to sit in the driver's seat next to Seba. Andoni sat immediately behind him, placing a hand on his shoulder. It was to remind the Englishman not to do anything stupid. As the red Skoda turned out of the car park onto the Oviedo road, Jamie noticed the blue Mercedes a hundred yards ahead on the same road.

Soon after passing the same street where he had bought Ruth's pendant, Jamie again began to take mental notes of the surroundings, of reference points he might need later. A police station flashed past them on their left. Seba turned the car sharply right onto a bridge over the Negro river. They came to a fork in the road. The road was split by a very slim building, almost as if someone had shrunk it to make room for two streets. A road sign indicating the way to La Coruña, to the west, to the region where a family were waiting for poor Alvaro, the trawler skipper, still unaware that they would never see him again. The Skoda stopped to let another vehicle pass in front. Jamie noticed the plaque on the old, stone wall to the right suggesting they were in a square called *Plaza de los Pachorros*.

It isn't much of a square, thought Jamie, as the Skoda sped up a narrow, cobbled lane immediately to the right of the slim building. He thought the lane would never end. It meandered steeply up a hill and the vehicle's tyres screeched round three or four very sharp curves. Then, suddenly, the hill came to an end, and Seba pulled up on a grass verge on the right-hand side, just past a row of tired-looking buildings. Outside one of these, an inviting sign hung from an iron balcony. The name on it was *Casa Luis*. They had arrived at the drinking hole.

Before being escorted into the tavern, Jamie carried out a quick, panoramic inspection. The light was fading quickly but the views were still superb. Inland, Jamie could just make out fields, some green and others parched yellow during the hot summer, and small woods stretching in between small valleys towards distant hills. Much closer, an old railway bridge straddled the river. Below, the red rooftops of Luarca gave the impression that there must once have been great wealth. Back towards the sea, a corner of the marina was just visible. That is where Jamie would prefer to have been, setting off on the return voyage with Brendan, retreating from one enemy and with plenty of time to confront the next.

Seba and Andoni ushered Jamie across the tavern. It was already buzzing with customers, some of them sitting at tables and being served generous helpings of *fabada*, the region's famous bean stew, flavoured with highly seasoned pork, black pudding, and chunks of bacon. Despite tension pulling his guts this way and that, the sight and the smells inside the tavern, a blend of garlic, spices, steaming stews and a strong aroma of spilled cider, also tore into his hunger.

Gorka Uriburu was waiting for him halfway along the bar. Jamie thought it was like the scene from a wild west movie. From a distance and in the haze of cigarette smoke, Gorka Uriburu painted a diminutive figure, dwarfed by the big Irishman. He beckoned Jamie and his men to join him, and told the lanky barman waiting for his order that he wanted five. In other words, five green bottles of cider, which the thin figure placed in a line on the bar with the speed of a gunslinger. The barman then put five, wide-rimmed glasses, in a similar row on the bar, each one coinciding with one of the bottles. What followed was something Jamie had heard of but had never witnessed. Gorka was the first to be served, eager to show his guests how it was done.

The barman lifted one of the bottles high above his head with his right hand and then tilted it around the back of his neck, as if he were performing some strange kind of circus act. As he did so, a river of golden liquid fell, like rainwater cascading down a narrow waterfall, into Gorka's glass, which the barman held at arm's length just above his knee with his other hand. As soon as the bottom of the glass had received a mere *culín*, in other words, when only two or three centimetres of the glass had been filled, the barman gave the glass to Gorka. He did likewise with Brendan's bottle and glass, once again filling just the bottom of the glass with the cider. Gorka swallowed the contents of his glass with one gulp and emptied any remaining drop, with a flick of his wrist, onto the stone floor, which was covered in sawdust.

What both Jamie and Brendan had just observed and partaken in was the ritual of drinking cider in Asturias. The act of delivering the cider to the glass from such a height, and in such small quantities at a time, had the effect of making it taste even flatter than it already was. Each small quantity of the liquid in the glass was what the Basque had referred to as a *culín*, the bottom of the glass, when he had invited them to sample the best cider in the world. Jamie found he preferred it to the English ciders his mother so enjoyed before a summer day's lunch. Brendan, a pint of bitter man himself, was not so impressed, but then he was not accustomed to understanding different cultures and tastes.

"Bit flat for my liking," he said, speaking to Jamie out of the side of his mouth before chucking the remains of his *culín* on the floor. With that action, he did as the locals did. Gorka had heard Brendan Daly's remark, however, and spat out an immediate response, making a mocking and cynical reference to the bible and to the absurdity of religious conflict in Ireland.

"You, in Ireland, have too much pride in your crosses, but here, in Asturias, is where the world began. Didn't you know? This is where Adam and Eve tasted the first apple. Yes, believe me, it was their descendants who told your God, whose son died for nothing on a cross, how to produce this exquisite drink from the fruit. However, as you know, Mr Ryder," he added, turning to Jamie, "we, in my country, kept the serpent that tempted Eve."

Brendan looked even more bewildered than he already had been after watching the barman pour the cider into the glass from such a great height. Jamie, however, knew exactly what the ETA man was referring to with his reference to the serpent. One of the most symbolic features on ETA's emblem of terror, designed by a Basque left-wing anarchist who fought against General Franco's Nationalists during the Spanish Civil War, was that of a snake slithering up an axe's handle.

***

During this initiation ritual into the drinking of cider at Casa Luis, Jamie noticed that, after the first *culín,* Gorka and his colleagues wasted most of the liquid by flicking their glasses over the sawdust which covered the stone floor. They just pretended to swallow each pour, whereas Brendan began to have more respect for the flat drink and swallowed every drop. Jamie was doing the same as Gorka. Most of the liquid in his glass also ended up adding to the slushy mess on the floor. Gorka, whose eyes caught every movement around him and beyond, was aware of the fact. There was no doubt in his mind now that Jamie was a highly trained professional. But, first, there was time for something to eat.

"Our table is ready, gentlemen. It is in the corner," he said, gesturing with his head for Seba and Andoni to accompany the two foreign men towards the rear of the tavern.

He ordered *fabada* and another Asturian speciality, a kind of battered beef steak stuffed with ham and cheese, known locally as a *cachopo*. A waiter also placed a jug of water and another brimming with wine in the middle of the table.

"You must try the wine, Mr Ryder," he said, in his exquisite English so that Brendan could also understand.

"You did not like our cider, I noticed," continued Gorka, pouring Jamie a glass of a deep burgundy, which he announced was from the *Ribera del Duero* region of northern Spain.

"I did. I liked it very much, actually."

"That is not what I observed, *amigo*. Or was that piss under your feet?"

The man really was the epitome of evil, as slimy as the serpent on ETA's emblem, thought Jamie, who also understood that the Basque was trying his utmost to tempt him into squirming with fear. That was perhaps Gorka's weakest point, his constant desire to ridicule an opponent. Jamie didn't cringe. In fact, he smiled, almost convincing everybody around the table, except Gorka, that he was totally unaware of the Basque's intentions.

"No, really. The cider here is delicious. I far prefer it to the stuff back home. But I have to be careful, you know. I shall be on first watch when we sail tonight, and cider has a habit of going to my head," said Jamie, looking across at Brendan for complicity.

Brendan was oblivious, however. He had already swallowed one glass of wine and was spooning bean stew into his mouth as if he would never eat anything more delicious again.

"Ah, but you need not worry yourself anymore, dear Jamie, about such trivial matters. You are going to be my guest for a few days. Yes, indeed! Until I hear from Mr Collins that your boat is safely back where she belongs, you will remain in Spain."

"I beg your pardon? I'm not sure I understand," said Jamie. Suddenly he did lose some of his composure. Even Brendan had understood, though, and he looked over the table at Jamie with what can only be described as eyes filled with panic.

"Yes. I have a man arriving tomorrow morning. He is a good sailor and one who spent many years as a waiter in Miami, so he speaks English well enough for you to get along perfectly, Mr Brendan. You will appreciate his sense of humour, too. Yes, my friend, his name is Jon, easy for you to remember. He will be accompanying you on your trip back to Ireland, but you, Mr Ryder," he said with that sniggering smile of his, "will be my guest."

Jamie made to stand up but was immediately hauled down again with Gorka gripping his left arm tightly and Seba, on his right, grabbing the other.

"Relax, Jamie. Please. Please do enjoy this excellent wine. You will see that it tastes far better than the vinegar produced by the vineyards in Tenerife," said Gorka, with his small eyes and false smile aimed directly at his English guest.

Jamie offered Gorka an equally contemptuous smile from the corner of his mouth. He now realised that he was really in a worse fix than he thought. This Basque bastard was even more despicable than Olivia's father. He had probably known all along that, under his gingery growth, Jamie was that impudent boyfriend who was so despised by Alonso. What Jamie hadn't begun to consider, because it defied all logic, was that Gorka Uriburu had marked him down as an imposter, as a British agent.

"In that case, Sir, if I am your guest, at least permit me to visit the gents, or there really will be piss on the floor," pleaded Jamie, with words that were a mix of anger and submission.

Gorka used a bit of bread to push some stew onto his spoon and shoved it into his mouth. He was thinking. He then sipped at his wine and used a paper napkin to dry his lips.

"*Andoni. Vete al baño y mira lo que hay.*" Andoni immediately stood up and walked through a doorway to the left of the bar. He was doing what Gorka had ordered, going to check out the lavatories. When he returned, he did not sit down, but leant over Gorka's shoulder and whispered something in his left ear. Jamie had no chance of knowing what he had said because he had whispered in *euskera*, the unique Basque language. Gorka's first order, to inspect the toilets, had been in Spanish for Jamie to understand that he should not attempt anything stupid.

"*Acompáñale.*" With that order for Andoni to accompany Jamie to the gents, the slim one with the dark glasses put a hand on the Englishman's shoulder and made him walk ahead to the narrow passage which was to the left of the bar.

Jamie looked right along the bar. Not one barman caught his eye. They were too busy pouring *culines*. There were no signs to gents or ladies. In fact, it was something Jamie noticed when he entered the tavern. There was not a single woman. At the end of the passage, there was a curtain hanging down from the nicotine-yellowed ceiling. Jamie caught the glint of glass through a tear in its worn fabric. A window, perhaps.

Andoni followed Jamie into the gents. It was a filthy dungeon, reeking of everything a man's body can possibly evacuate. Andoni pointed at a long, stainless steel urinal trough. Jamie could plainly see was bunged up with dozens of spent cigarettes, preventing gallons of men's urine to flow out freely, so he looked at Andoni and shook his head. Before his shadow could object, he entered the closest of the two independent cubicles and closed the latch which was barely held in place by a couple of loose screws. Jamie unbuckled his belt and pretended to roll down his trousers, assuming Andoni would do what one sees in films, which was to get down on all fours and peep under the gap of the cubicle door. He did just that and seemed satisfied because Jamie heard him stand up again and open a tap, presumably to wash his hands.

"*Venga, hombre. Que sea rápido!*" he growled, urging Jamie to get on with it.

However, Jamie had other plans. He quietly did his trousers up again and grabbed the potato peeler which he still had tucked in the back of his boot.

"*Eh, Andoni. Papel. No tengo papel,*" Jamie called out, informing Andoni, the slim Basque, that there was no paper in the cubicle. After a couple of cynical suggestions, Andoni accepted Jamie's misfortune and agreed to pass him some paper, if there was any, through the gap under the cubicle door.

Jamie acted as silently and swiftly as a wild cat. He had to be quick, before anyone else came to use the lavatory. The moment he heard Andoni go into the next cubicle in search of a toilet roll, he unlatched the door and spun round like a gymnast to place himself behind the Basque. In two explosive and flowing movements, Jamie doubled his right knee and gave one of Andoni's slim legs a savage kick behind the knee. As the man crumpled in pain and shock, Jamie put his left arm around Andoni's neck and twisted it back, using his right hand to shove the point of the potato peeler under the man's chin. He could have jabbed it through the neck and killed the Spaniard there and then but, if he had, he would not only have Basque terrorists after him. He would also have the Spanish law hunt him down for murdering a Spanish citizen in cold blood, whether they recognised the victim as a member of ETA or not.

"Una palabra y te rajo," growled Jamie, warning the man that he would slit his throat if he made a sound.

He didn't slash Andoni's throat, but he did use extreme violence. Jamie was not a violent man. He was a warm-hearted, generous, fun-loving guy, but he had been trained in the British Army to fight and, if necessary, to kill to defend himself and his fellow soldiers.

Before Andoni could even put his hands up in a sign of defeat, Jamie twisted the man's neck, yanking it even further back, pulling it towards his waist and then, in the same movement, used all his muscle power to punch Andoni's head hard against the toilet bowl. Andoni's arms fell loose and drops of blood began to decorate the floor. Jamie hadn't killed him, but he was out cold.

Jamie searched in Andoni's pockets and pulled out his pistol. It was another Browning. He then spun the man around and sat him on the toilet seat, propping him up as best he could. He closed the cubicle door behind and listened for ten seconds. There was no sound of anyone coming towards the toilets. Jamie opened the door to the passage and poked his face round. The coast was clear, and he exited, turning left towards the curtain at the end of the narrow passage. He looked behind him to make sure he was still alone and pulled the fabric to one side. There was glass, but it wasn't a window. Better still, the glass he had seen through the tear in the curtain was one of six panes of glass on the top half of a doorway. He tried the handle. It was locked. Once again, he turned around to look along the narrow passage towards the bar. Still nobody. He looked to the ground behind the curtain and then used his left hand to feel along the top of the door frame head for a key. There was nothing there.

At that moment, two men appeared from the bar end of the passage, laughing loudly. Jamie walked towards them, as if he were returning to the bar. That he was coming at them from the end of the passage, and not from the toilet, did not seem to concern the two friends in the least. But Jamie needed to act fast. Too much time had been wasted and Gorka would be sending Seba to see what was going on in no time. Jamie knew he would have to smash his way through the glass panes, and he ran towards the door with the intention of doing just that. Then, as he was about to use the old curtain to muffle a kick at the glass panes, he noticed a key hanging on a hook on the wall just to the left of the door. Why the hell hadn't he seen it before? He took it off the hook and fed it into the keyhole. It worked.

Jamie opened the door without further ado and stepped out. It was now well after sunset and it was becoming quite dark, but he could make out that he was in a narrow alley, with the rear of the tavern on one side, billowing steam and smoke through the kitchen windows and funnels, and a high stone wall on the other. There seemed to be no way out to the right, where there were a couple of overflowing, black rubbish containers stacked against a brick wall. To the left, however, about ten yards away, he realised the alley led around the tavern. Like a workman's entrance, it took him outside of the building to the lane they had sped up earlier. Not only that, but the Mercedes Gorka had been driven in was the nearest vehicle parked in a small, private car park which obviously belonged to the tavern.

When he crept alongside the vehicle only one thing entered Jamie's mind. He still had Andoni's Browning in his right hand, but he moved it to his left and took out the potato peeler from his boot again.. He stabbed the right front tyre of the Mercedes. For a simple potato peeler, the instrument had a remarkably sharp point. Air immediately began to hiss out. He was about to do the same with the rear when he heard a shout from the far side of the small car park, from behind another vehicle. Someone had spotted him.

Jamie suddenly realised that he had forgotten all about

179

Gorka's driver. Perhaps he was also in the tavern, keeping guard at one end of the bar. Or perhaps that was him running towards him between the parked vehicles. Whoever the man was, Jamie was not going to hang around and ran as fast as he could down the lane, in the same direction he had been driven up in the red Skoda. As he sprinted down the cobbles, past the same Skoda on his left, he glanced back to see the man in the carpark stop and push through the tavern doorway. They would be after him in no time. He had to get away. But first, instinct in retreat told Jamie to cause more havoc and he ran back to the Skoda. This time he hurriedly stuck the peeler into both front tyres. Jamie chuckled. He was almost enjoying this. Nevertheless, his rapid breathing and pounding heart betrayed the fact that he was in a high state of alert, risking his life skirmishing with the enemy.

As he ran down the slope towards Luarca's town centre, towards the plaza that wasn't much of a plaza, to the bridge that would take him across the river and, if necessary, to that police station which he had spotted, thoughts flashed through his head.

Would Gorka and his mates get into their cars to give chase before realising their tyres were slashed, and that their vehicles had been put out of immediate action? How fast could they get the wheels changed? Did Gorka have another friend with a third vehicle? Jamie looked over his shoulder again and again. There was no sign that anyone was running down the lane after him. Not yet anyway.

He must make that phone call. He carried on running downhill, every now and again stopping at what he hoped might be a short cut but wasn't. He glanced back, panting, groaning and at times uttering a faint cry, like a fox being chased by a pack of hounds. It wasn't fear. Or was it? Perhaps it was, together with the fact that he wasn't nearly as fit as he was a few months ago, but he had to keep going.

Then he saw it, the end of the lane. That was better. At least there was some traffic on the road to La Coruña, albeit very little. He was almost there, into the town. They would not dare make a move for him in view of other pedestrians, even though they were few and far between at this late hour. Jamie suddenly realised he had a bloody gun in his hand for all to see and shoved it into one of his windcheater pockets. The weight almost balanced the one on the left, which still had the binoculars in it. Now, he had to find a phone box. He stopped to look around. There were none in sight. He looked up the cobbled lane. No, there was still nobody running down after him. Why? They had to be after him, surely? Never mind that. He had to get across the river. He began to run again, this time not making it so obvious that he was fleeing, attempting to look more like a man going to miss the next bus. He could not keep this up much longer, though. Anxiety was beginning to play tricks with him. One of the few cars that passed him on the bridge might be the one to stop with thugs to haul him in. However, none stopped; most were late commuters on their way home.

Sticking the potato peeler in those wheels must have delayed them long enough for him to make it all this way; and yet, it had not actually been very long at all. It seemed like an eternity, but he had only been running, stopping and starting, for a little more than fifteen minutes at the most. Even so, it surprised him that there was no sign of either Seba or the Mercedes driver giving chase on foot. He might have been lucky, and someone had called the police to the tavern, after a man had been found beaten up in the toilets. Perhaps Gorka and his men had been detained. But that couldn't really be the case. He had not heard any sirens, nor had he met any police vehicle speeding up the cobbled lane.

Jamie decided to play it safe, whatever happened. Instead of walking down the same road to the port on the banks of the Negro River, he turned right after two hundred yards, into the same street where he had bought Ruth's pendant, with the Sabadell bank on the corner. He discovered it was a cul-de-sac, but he followed a very narrow alleyway at the back, on the left side of the souvenir shop. He guessed it would run parallel to the harbour, and it did. Every now and then it crossed another narrow lane connecting it to the harbour. On the corner of one of these he found what he was looking for, a telephone booth.

***

It was close to 23.30 on Tuesday, 30th September. It might be a bit late for his friend and ex-Platoon Commander, Colonel Smith, but Jamie couldn't think of anyone else. Smith would surely get the ball rolling, immediately advising a relevant member of British security forces of what was going on. Jamie was also anxious to pass on the telephone number he had discovered scribbled on the back of the picture in the Hannah's head. The SOS message behind the coat of arms was as clear as it was pleading. It urged the finder to telephone someone called Anthony Rennie.

Jamie had absolutely no doubt in his mind as to what Smith would advise him to do in the situation. He would tell him to get the hell out of there and not to try and be a hero. Jamie also knew he would not heed that advice, however wise it was. He was well and truly involved in this business now and wanted to get that boatload of weapons, and Brendan Daly, out of the place and into the hands of the British authorities. Come what may, he was going to get that yellow tub out to sea.

Jamie put a coin into the slot and dialled the number he knew by heart. It was Colonel Smith's private number in Exmouth. A very sleepy woman's voice replied that her husband was away on exercise. She was not in bed, because Jamie heard her tell one of her kids to turn off the television, so he asked her if she could get a message to her husband. She couldn't. The colonel was on overseas deployment with his unit. She did not expect to hear from him until the middle of September.

"*You're on your bloody own, mate!*" Jamie swore to himself.

For a moment he thought about telephoning his mother in Tenerife. He could ask her to give him Henry Clark's number. She would still be up. She was a night owl. Uncle Henry was getting on, but as she had said, his godfather was still very well connected. But he didn't call her. She would only worry and ask questions he couldn't answer. Nor was he in a fit state to make pleasant conversation with his beloved mama.

Ironically, in the middle of this night of tension, Jamie

182

suddenly felt guilty. He felt guilty because he didn't even know his godfather's telephone number. Clearly, he didn't speak to him enough and would have to make amends one day. All he honestly remembered about Henry Clark was that he was very close to his mother, and that his father had always joked about his old friend spending most of his days at the Travellers Club in London.

Jamie stepped out of the telephone booth and looked about him for any sign of the enemy. There was none. In fact, except for the sound of a television with its volume far too high in an apartment above him, the place was dead. He considered making a dash for the Hannah again, and was about to start running, when a name shone in his head, like a lighthouse. *Farmer Bob!* It was a long shot, but it was worth a try. Who was to know? That man might just be the person to run to when in trouble and he had his number on a torn corner of a RNLI leaflet in his wallet.

Bloody hell, it's late, he thought. He had to give it a go.

Jamie looked around again. When he was absolutely certain that nobody was aware of his presence, he opened the booth door and slipped in again. He felt for the Browning in his windcheater pocket to make sure it was still there, then pulled the wallet out of his pocket, this time not only for a few more coins but also the piece of lifeboat brochure. He found it. It was a bit crumpled, but the numbers were legible enough.

Once again, the English dialling tone offered some comfort. It was the only familiar sound he had heard in days and it kind of settled his mind.

"Bunting," replied the voice at the other end after a few rings.

"Bob. Very sorry to bother you so late."

"No problem. Just come in from the chickens. Who is this?"

"Jamie Ryder, Mr Bunting. I don't know if you remember me. I camped in your soggy field," said Jamie.

"Yes, I bloody well do. Look, it is a bit late, come to think of it. Give me a call in the morning, will you? I'll be up at five before seeing to the cows." He did sound a little miffed this time, as if he suddenly realised that no decent person would make a call at that hour of the night.

"Sorry, Bob. It can't wait until the morning. This is urgent. I am calling you because I need your help and I need it right now. I wouldn't bother you if I didn't think you were the right man to call in the circumstances."

"Better be important. An apology for sleeping with my sheep again will not do, Jamie."

"Thank you, Bob. I knew I could count on you. Now look, I've not much time and I want you to listen very carefully. You must contact someone about rescuing a boat."

"Well, that is my business, son," interrupted Bob Bunting, almost with a chuckle.

"Please let me finish, Bob. This is not your usual emergency. But lives are at stake. My life too," said Jamie firmly.

"OK. Where is your boat?"

"The boat is too far out to sea for you, I reckon. But you can help. I know you can, and I know you will."

"Go on," said Bunting.

"The point is, Bob, that this particular boat is mixed up with IRA terrorist activity and so am I. This is not a hoax. I repeat, this is not a hoax. I am ex-Army and right now in a heck of a lot of trouble. I need your assistance. Are you in?"

"Shit, mate. I knew you were no hippie. Count on me. What can I do?" Bob replied, with a serious tone appearing in his voice. As he heard Jamie out, a thought stirred in and out of his head. Was the man who had pitched the tent on his land actually some sort of field agent? Perhaps he had read too many thrillers during those long hours at the station waiting for something to happen.

The farmer listened intently to what Jamie had to say and to what he proposed. Firstly, Jamie explained about the Hannah, describing the kind of vessel she was and, very importantly, her colour scheme. If he was going to be spotted, her yellow hull might be the best thing to look out for in the middle of the waves. Jamie then told Bob about the SOS message on the Hannah. Bob took down Rennie's name and number. Jamie told him that on no account should he call the number himself. That call to Anthony Rennie had to be left to someone experienced in dealing with a possible kidnap situation. It may well be a pretty painful conversation. Jamie told Bob Bunting he feared the worst, considering in whose hands the Hannah was now.

Jamie put another coin into the slot. They were disappearing too fast, but thanks to the lady in the shop, he still had a few left. He didn't bother explaining what the hell he was doing on a boat being used to smuggle arms by the IRA, but he needed Bob to get cracking. He had to inform someone. If not the police, Bob must contact someone closer to home. There was no use in asking the man to get in touch with the Ministry of Defence or MI6, but there had to be some kind of communication between the RNLI and other services on a regular basis. He or his superior at Sennen Cove must be able to alert the proper authorities.

"My brother is an engineer at Culdrose," interrupted Bob.

"What? Brilliant! That's splendid. That's a bloody good start, anyway" replied Jamie. He was well aware that Culdrose, known in the Royal Navy as HMS Seahawk, was a major naval air base on the Lizard Peninsula. In fact, it was the largest helicopter base in Europe. If Bob Bunting could persuade them that his story was totally accurate and that Bob wasn't pulling his brother's leg, then it would be all go. The base was owned and controlled by the Ministry of Defence.

"Now look, I know this is going to sound bloody crazy, but I fully intend to sail the boat across the Bay of Biscay and to get it as close to home as I possibly can. With any luck, I'll have an Irish fellow with me as well as a stash of weapons, but if I have to do it alone, I shall," continued Jamie, to Bunting's utter astonishment. In fact Bob was about to interrupt when Jamie added, with a slightly muffled and emotional voice all of a sudden, "I consider it my duty, Bob".

"Of course, mate. You do your bit. I give you my word that I'll do mine."

"I know you will, Bob. I know you will. Thanks. Now listen. This is very important. If you manage to get things moving over there, and I expect you will because this could become a very big catch for our people, I will assume strings will be pulled so that every ship in the Bay of Biscay and beyond will be on the lookout for a yellow tub floating about in the water. However, if things go wrong my end, and if I can't get out of here within 72 hours from midnight tonight, the Brits must inform the Spanish authorities that there is a yellow boat sitting in Luarca Harbour with a whole lot of weapons in it. Is that clear, Bob?"

"Bloody hell! Bloody hell!" was all Bob Bunting could say and then, "Can you spell that for me?"

"L-U-A-R-C-A".

"Got it. But, how the hell did you get into this?"

"Listen, Bob. Just let me finish and then get the lines buzzing," said Jamie, not bothering to reply.

"I will not be calling again, and I might not make it out of here. But you must get this message transmitted at once. Whether I can pull this off or not, I repeat, I fully intend to take the yellow Fisher out of here within the next three days. If I get out of Luarca alive, I shall be steering a compass course of approximately 300°, northwest by west, for around six hours. That should take me towards the Atlantic, and maybe into shipping lanes crossing the Bay of Biscay. With any luck a friendly ship will pick me up. If none does, I shall then set another course north northeast. That will be six hours after leaving port, and I'll be heading straight for the Brest Peninsula in France. Got that? Yellow boat with a daft Englishman in a lot of trouble?"

"Got it. You're too bloody right, I've got it. God knows you must be out of your mind but count on me Jamie."

Before Bob could say another word, Jamie cut him off and quietly put the receiver down. He ducked under the advertisement panel, which was on the outside of the booth. Out of the corner of his eye he had noticed a tall, slim figure in black slinking along the street, sticking to the buildings too closely for his liking. Jamie thought it might be Gorka's driver, Mikel. He held his breath. However, whoever it was, the figure did not seem to notice him in the telephone booth, nor took the slightest interest. The man just turned left towards the harbour, hugging the walls of each building as if he were drawn into them by magnets. Jamie only began to understand when a plump woman came running along the same street and went down the alley after the figure in black. When she caught up with the man, she grabbed his arm, gave him two almighty slaps across the head and tugged him in the direction they had come. As they passed alongside the telephone booth and under the streetlamp on the corner, Jamie realised that the poor fellow had a kind of haunted, lost look in his eyes. He had seen something similar in Tenerife, where the man next to his father's barber had been diagnosed with symptoms related to schizophrenia.

If he didn't get some shut eye soon, thought Jamie, he would end up like that too. He had to get on. He also had to find somewhere to lie down, to grab a couple of hours of sleep. He had not slept for twenty-four hours and he needed to be completely alert for what he was going to do. He remained, crouching in the telephone booth, thinking out his next move. Yes, he had to find a dark corner somewhere, just to close his eyes. If a tramp could, he could. His mind was made up. He would carry on down the same alley. It still seemed to run parallel to the port avenue. It was late. Nobody was going to bother him. He would take a rest and then work out what to do next. He had some cash left over to get himself a bite in the morning. He would then recce for a vantage point from which to keep an eye on movements in and around the harbour. He knew those binoculars would come in handy when he took them from the wheelhouse.

Unfortunately, the end of the alley took him down again to the harbour, precisely to the Báltico Hotel. He could not have known it was the hotel used by Gorka and his chums, but he cut back along another very narrow lane which took him to an area of trees and overgrown grass, behind lines of buildings. On the other side, Jamie came to a road which he decided to follow round to the left, between apartment blocks and a small car park, until he came to a curve in the road. On the right, there was a large tree at the entrance to what looked like a school. To his left, there was a patch of earth with a large earthmover parked to one side, up against a hedge. At least the ground was dry this time, and not a waterlogged field in Cornwall. Jamie crawled under the earthmover and tucked himself up against one of its huge tyres, after ripping out a few handfuls of grass from under the hedge to use as a pillow. Jamie had slept on more uncomfortable ground in the Army. He was asleep within minutes. He didn't even have the energy to imagine what might have happened after he made a run for it from Casa Luis, or why nobody had pursued him down the lane.

***

Although it had become evident that his life was in grave danger, Jamie could not have known that Gorka Uriburu's cynical invitation to drink cider and to eat fabada at Casa Luis was just part of the man's psychopathic game, and that he had intended it to be Jamie's last supper. Gorka had not only made up his mind that the Englishman was an impostor, but also that he was surplus to their needs. He got a kick out of sharing a table with someone he planned to execute.

Nor could Jamie have guessed that Gorka had decided to give Brendan Daly the benefit of the doubt. Gorka simply didn't see the Irishman having the same cool professionalism as the English infiltrator. He was just a pawn in the deal, and he would still be required to sail the Hannah back to Ireland with the new colleague Gorka had summoned to replace Ryder.

While Jamie was being escorted to the toilets, Gorka's face had continued to flash smooth and ugly smiles. The spectacle of Brendan Daly spooning himself with more helpings of *fabada,* and gulping glass after glass of wine, amused him. Nevertheless, his body language around the table suddenly changed, and he began to look anxiously towards the door to the passage leading to the gents. He swore angrily every time a waiter rushed between tables, impairing his vision. Jamie and his shadow, Andoni, were taking too long.

It was only when the two jovial men Jamie had encountered in the passage returned to the bar that Gorka stood up. Something was not right. He ordered Seba to go and find out what the hell was holding Andoni and the Englishman up for so long. Meanwhile, Brendan Daly appeared to be oblivious to the commotion.

Seba was about to disappear through the door at the side of the bar when Mikel, Gorka's driver, charged into the tavern and shoved his way through a growing number of customers towards Gorka's table in the corner. The frantic look on the driver's face immediately told Uriburu that something was indeed very wrong.

"Go with Mikel. Now!" Gorka growled at Brendan. When the big man failed to respond immediately, Gorka grabbed him roughly by the collar and hauled him out of his chair.

"*Sartu kotxean!*" Gorka ordered Mikel, in Basque, to get Brendan into the car. At the same time, he used his eyes to indicate that he would follow Seba to the gents. As Mikel put a hand hard on Brendan's shoulder, and moved him towards the entrance, Gorka followed Seba along the passage to the lavatories. Just before pushing open the gent's door, he pulled out the Browning from under his jacket.

"Andoni. Andoni," he shouted. The gents were empty but one of the cubicle doors was pulled to. A faint cry came from inside that cubicle and Gorka booted the door open. Andoni was as Jamie had left him, sat on the throne, and propped up against the lead pipe on the wall that came from a cistern above. He was semi-conscious and a nasty gash on a very swollen forehead told Gorka exactly what had just happened.

"*Ama izorratua!*" growled the ugly Basque. Son of a whore!

"*Que no entre nadie!*" he ordered Seba. He didn't want anyone coming through that door.

Gorka ripped out several pieces of paper from the roll lying on the floor and soaked the bundle with water from one of the sink taps. He then quickly swabbed the wound and did his best to clean the blood off Andoni's cheek and nose. He took more paper, dry this time, and held it against Andoni's wound. The man was fully conscious now and cried out in pain.

"*Cállate, hombre!*" said Gorka, telling Andoni to shut up. Gorka was evidently furious that his man had let the Englishman escape. In fact, he was far angrier with himself for allowing Jamie to deceive him with such ease. Gorka became even more enraged when he put his hands into Andoni's pockets and found nothing in them.

"*Tu pistola. Tu maldita pistola, joder. Dónde coño está?*" Of course, Gorka knew exactly where the bloody pistol was. Jamie had it. He shouted at Seba to hand over his cap and those shades that stuck to him as if they were part of his flesh. Seba did so, but only after a few reluctant seconds, when he fully understood why Gorka insisted on having them. The boss shoved the cap onto Andoni's head. It was far too big for him, but the paper stuffed over the gash in his forehead made it a tight fit, and the sunglasses hid the rest. Gorka told Seba to open the door and to check the end of the passage for another way out, for the same exit the Englishman had made his escape through.

Gorka's table in the corner at Casa Luis became available. To begin with, it appeared the five men had hastily left without paying the bill. But that was not the case; minutes later, Gorka pushed his way back into the tavern through the front door. First, he asked for the bill. Then, very politely, he requested if he could use the telephone.

Gorka and his men would indeed have left without paying the bill if Gorka's driver hadn't realised that his front right tyre had no air in it. Mikel had already reversed the Mercedes and had got the two rear tyres onto the cobbled lane. It was only when he pushed his foot down and began to turn the wheel that he became aware of the problem. At the same time, Seba came running past the front of the tavern to tell his boss that the Skoda had two flats and had been rendered useless. There was no option. Whilst he left Seba, Mikel, and the big Irishman to push the Merc into the carpark again, Gorka, beside himself with rage, went to pay the bill. However, the main reason for entering the tavern again was to inform his superiors about the mess he had made of the whole operation, with a little help from his inept colleagues and an English infiltrator.

In the dark, it took almost half an hour for Mikel to get the spare wheel out and make the car driveable again on the uneven ground. It took almost as long for Gorka and his chums in Gipuzkoa and Pau to come to a decision during the telephone call from a noisy, Spanish tavern.

The Irish deal would have to be called off. They could not risk remaining in Asturias for a minute longer. They concluded there were two likely scenarios. One was that the Englishman may have already reported the incident, and that the Guardia Civil would be onto them in no time. The other was that Ryder would also have called a halt to his own mission. In either case, the assumption was that they would not see the infiltrator again. Gorka received orders that on no account should they go hunting for Jamie Ryder. Who cared? They had the cash. They could now keep the weapons too.

One would think Gorka might have been disappointed not to be given permission to pursue the bugger there and then, but he wasn't. He was a patient man. The moment for retribution would come sooner or later. Ryder had a home and a mother on the island of Tenerife. Gorka knew that from the conversation around the dining table at Rosie's Cantina back in July. His friend, Alonso, owed him a few favours. Life could be made exceedingly difficult indeed for Jamie and his family.

Collins would be given a reason of sorts for the messed-up operation. His man, Brendan Daly, would be blamed for the fracas. In the meantime, the man who was to accompany Brendan back to Ireland, with the Hannah and the weapons, would be given fresh orders. On his arrival at Luarca in the morning, Jon would indeed go aboard the Hannah, not to sail her, but to be her guardian until further notice.

Gorka Uriburu and his colleagues had to get out of the place immediately, and they did. However, first, they had to switch vehicles. It was close to midnight. If only Gorka had known that his English agent was not an agent at all, but that it was just a figment of his twisted imagination, and that he had just been in a public telephone booth across the river, making a call to a man called Bunting. The Basque might also have risked an encounter with the Guardia Civil, had he been aware that, just three or four kilometres away, Jamie had collapsed, exhausted, under an earthmover. However, he didn't, and the priority now for Gorka Uriburu and his men, was to get the hell out of Luarca and Asturias, without leaving a trace of evidence.

The main evidence, of course, was the yellow-hulled boat which was sitting peacefully in the borrowed berth down at the marina. She was a big problem, and she would be dealt with presently. The friendly contact at the Valdés Town Hall could be bribed again to extend the loan of the berth if necessary. He might also be persuaded to arrange for the same, friendly, long-liner fisherman to provide his vessel once more, this time for a reverse operation. If bribery didn't work this time, or if too much compensation was requested, ETA would revert to its other methods of persuasion.

Mikel drove them to the abandoned warehouse inside the industrial estate, five kilometres from the port of Luarca. He stopped the vehicle in front of the corrugated doorway and, when Seba pushed it open, Mikel drove the Mercedes into the middle of the empty building and chucked the car key to Gorka, who caught it in mid-air. The warehouse was empty, except for the fish delivery truck which they had previously used to transport the weapons from the Basque Country to the fish market car park in the tranquil Luarca harbour. It was at the back of the warehouse, in amongst stacks of old pallets.

The truck would be their getaway vehicle and, as always, Mikel would be doing the driving. Seba and Gorka would sit alongside Mikel in the fish delivery vehicle's cabin. Andoni, who had recovered enough, but was feeling extremely sorry for himself, was told to lie down in the truck's refrigeration compartment. Gorka handed him a dirty old rug. A wooden pallet was then shoved in beside him to stop him being flung about. It might be a rough ride.

Brendan could easily have gone in behind with Andoni, but that was not to be. When ETA decided that the deal with the Irish was off, they meant it.

Gorka ordered Brendan to take his sailor's pullover off. Confused and terrified, the Irishman did what he was told and handed Gorka his pullover. Before giving Brendan an explanation, Gorka chucked it at Andoni in the back of the truck and told him to use it as a pillow.

"You won't be needing that, my friend", Gorka Uriburu informed Brendan. "Your next journey will be in the comfort of the Mercedes Benz. You'll be nice and warm in there". The ETA man's tone was remarkably soft, almost comforting, considering what had happened in the last hour.

"Where are we going? I'll need the jersey on the boat," whined Brendan, desperately fishing for answers.

"You may go wherever the car takes you, Mr Brendan. Here, it's all yours," Gorka said, handing Daly the car key.

"But the steering wheel is on the left, and it's automatic. I've never handled one of these," complained Daly, as he was unceremoniously shoved into the driver's seat.

"Just put the key in the ignition", growled Uriburu.

Brendan never said another word. He just put his hands on the wheel. He had never had anything so posh in his hands before. The smooth, leather-bound steering wheel felt so pleasant to touch. It could have been so soothing for him. However, his hands were shaking too much to feel anything except dread when Gorka got into the Mercedes and sat in the rear behind him.

"Now, my dear, before you depart, tell me about your English friend. Who is he? Your Patrick Collins informed me there would be a Spanish man crewing the boat with you."

"Yes. There was. We lost Alvaro on the way from Ireland. He fell into the sea. I don't know who Jamie is. Just an English lad I picked up in Scilly. I had to. We wouldn't have come, otherwise," pleaded Brendan.

"Ah, but we think you do know who Mr Ryder is."

"How the hell should I know?"

"That's alright, Brendan. Suppose I believe you. Maybe you are telling me the truth and you really don't know."

"I don't. I tell you; I never saw him before. Please believe me," cried Brendan.

"You certainly don't understand the implications, do you? Whether I believe you or not, you really should learn to pick your friends better, don't you think, Mr Daly?" growled Gorka, with his face so close to the back of the big Irishman's head that Brendan could feel his breath, and spittle bombarding his neck.

"Gorka! *Déjalo ya, hombre. Hay que irse!*" It was Gorka's right-hand man, Mikel, and he was urging his boss that they really had to get on with it fast.

Mikel was right and Gorka nodded. He gestured impatiently with his hand for Mikel to get into the truck and then leaned back in the seat, staring at the rear of Daly's head for a few seconds. There were no more questions. There was no point. The Basque acted swiftly now. He pulled out his Browning and put the barrel up close behind Brendan's left ear.

"Enjoy the trip, my friend. Goodbye."

It was a short and painless farewell, but Gorka sighed just before pulling the trigger, as if the whole matter had become too tedious for words. The Irishman, the same Brendan who had so brutally murdered the innocent Spanish trawler captain in St Mary's pool, died instantly. His head slumped forward in slow motion.

Mikel let the delivery truck move gently through the doorway and into the darkness. Seba began to push the door closed again, leaving just a small gap for Gorka to slip out. It was enough of a gap to allow him watch Gorka pour a whole lot of petrol from a red container into the Mercedes, over Brendan's body and around each tyre. Satisfied, he walked nonchalantly towards the warehouse entrance, leaving a trail of fuel behind him. Gorka then bent over, flicked his lighter and let the flame touch the inflammable liquid on the ground. The fuel burst into flames and a funnel of blue began to shoot towards the Mercedes. Gorka Uriburu immediately got into the truck, while Seba pushed the warehouse door closed.

They did not wait for the Mercedes to catch fire, but it did. Half an hour later, the fire brigade and police were on the scene. A murder investigation began the following morning. The first indications were that it had most probably been another act of revenge perpetrated by the many drug gangs, whose boats ran their errands in and out of ports all along Spain's coastline. By the time the press got hold of the information, the refrigerated fish truck was well past Gijón, the old industrial city in that part of the world, where the capitalist steel and ship-building industry had once provided so many jobs. Gorka and his ETA thugs were on their way, innocent as hell, towards their beloved Basque Country.

Chapter 7 – The Journalist

The other man, Jon, was also a Basque. He was more French-looking, with a streaky mass of blond hair. Shortly after 10.00, he stepped aboard the Hannah. Jamie Ryder, who had been using the binoculars to keep watch on the harbour since before 07.00, observed his every move.

Jamie was starving but refreshed and alert. He must have slept on and off for four hours, awakened now and then by an occasional vehicle passing by the rough piece of land on which he had laid himself down against the giant wheel of the earthmover. He had also heard two or three police sirens followed by the dreaded sound of fire engines in the middle of the night. Nevertheless, he had soon been rocked to sleep again by the soothing sound of waves lapping a shore.

When he had pulled himself from under the earthmover and dusted himself down, it had been light enough to see that he was above a small cove, and that the road he had walked along from the town centre followed the shore around to the north. It circled under the imposing Luarca lighthouse, which was on the point separating the cove from the entrance to the harbour.

Jamie decided to continue along the same road after it narrowed into a single lane. Just beyond the lighthouse, he came across the sloping, town cemetery. There was a wrought iron gate which he pushed open, not because he wanted to find the grave of an ancient navigator, but because he felt there must be a tap somewhere inside for him to drink from. He found one, conveniently placed beside a beautiful marble cross. It was there for relatives to fill watering cans to water the flowers of their dead, but Jamie put his head under the tap, feeling the freshwater soak into his head before drinking, like a camel, to quench his thirst. As he drank, he realised that he smelled like a tramp and that the clothes he had not changed for a couple of days had the aroma of salt, sweat, and cider blended into the fabric.

Jamie pushed the gate closed behind him as he stepped out

of the cemetery. He wondered how much history lay under those immaculately maintained tombstones. He also thought the dead must be in paradise. They were blessed with such magnificent views over the sea.

Jamie continued under the holy place and walked down the hill. The narrow road took him where he anticipated it might, back towards the harbour. It had looped all the way round the point and now led back to the marina. Just past a large ochre-coloured building with official emblems on it, Jamie found what he was looking for, a perfect vantage point from which to view the Hannah and the whole port. It is where he decided to make use of the binoculars which had been weighing down one side of his windcheater, and he sat down on a low ledge at the top of stone steps which led down to the east mole. It was also from there, peering between trees, that he first saw the man with the streaky blond hair walk along the pontoon and onto the yellow boat. He was carrying a brown bag in one hand and had a small, amber-coloured backpack over his shoulders. The action had begun.

It was Wednesday, 31st August, and it was going to be a warm day. Jamie was already feeling the heat of the sun on his back and moved into the shade. At some stage he was going to need to go back to the cemetery for some more water, but right now, he dared not take his eye off the marina.

Jamie pointed the binoculars at the Hannah again the moment he noticed the man with blond hair step out of the wheelhouse onto the deck. He followed his every move, occasionally pointing the binoculars in the direction of the man's gaze. Not once did the blond man look up towards Jamie's lookout. The man only appeared to be interested in the town. Now and then, Jamie did the same as he had done on several occasions since positioning himself at dawn, pointing the binoculars along the avenue and beyond, towards the fish market. The place seemed to be buzzing with activity but there was no sign of a blue Mercedes, a red Skoda, or of the fish delivery van he had seen Andoni drive off in the day before. Jamie asked himself who this new man on the Hannah could be. He also wondered where Gorka and his buddies were. Why hadn't they shown up, and where the heck was Brendan Daly?

Jamie asked himself the same questions repeatedly. He tried to imagine what might have happened after he escaped through the rear of the tavern, his mind turning over different scenarios. He also began to plan what to do next, weighing up several options. He discounted a few of them but, for the time being, his best bet was to be patient, to wait on the enemy's next move.

***

Plans were also afoot, and lines were buzzing in the British Isles, where two emergency situations had begun to be discussed and dealt with. The first, which was well underway since Bob Bunting managed to contact his brother at Culdrose, was at the Ministry of Defence. The second was in the peaceful bay at St Mary's, in the Isles of Scilly.

The telephone and walkie talkie lines in both arenas had not ceased exchanging information for the past hour. Captain Jimmy Barratt, Commanding Officer at RNAS Culdrose, had immediately put the information received from Petty Officer Bunting into the hands of the Ministry of Defence. Bunting was a good man and Barratt had no doubt that the message he had received from his brother, the lifeboat volunteer, had to be taken seriously. The Ministry, understanding that the information, if true, might be more of a matter for British Intelligence, consulted the Foreign Office.

Sir Geoffrey Howe, who was still one of Margaret Thatcher's faithful allies, had just arrived for his morning briefing at King Charles Street, when his private secretary suggested there was a call which might be out of the ordinary. As he sipped his first cup of coffee of the day, he listened in his usual, quiet, thoughtful manner. When the call ended, Sir Geoffrey immediately asked to be put through to Christopher Curwen, head of British Security. It might not be anything at all, but it was better to be safe than sorry, he said.

Christopher Curwen ordered that someone should investigate the information received, and to establish if there was any reason to pursue the matter, although he also referred the matter to MI5. There had been so many hoaxes, so he was hesitant at first. Nevertheless, he knew how much interest the Prime Minister placed on anything which might have the slightest relevance to damaging the IRA, and therefore decided to place the matter in the tray marked for priority attention. The first task was to find out all there was to know about an ex-Army Lieutenant called Jamie Ryder, and about the volunteer staff at the Sennen Cove lifeboat station. Half an hour later, he received a report on Lieutenant Ryder. He was described as a fine, young officer with a cracking record. He had been marked down as one to watch in the future. The Regiment had been extremely disappointed to lose him.

As information began to confirm the facts, Curwen asked to be put through to the Foreign Secretary.

"Yes, Christopher. What do you think? Shall we tell Madrid?"

"Um, not yet Sir Geoffrey. As the lad said, let's give him a bit longer. He requested 72 hours and I am prepared to put a bet on it that this Ryder chappie is really on to something. By all means inform our Embassy in Madrid, but I beg you to keep this one strictly to ourselves for the time being. Oh, one more thing. I gather the yellow boat in question, which has apparently been in IRA hands, may well have belonged to one of our retired Army chaps. He and his wife went missing earlier this year. If what this Ryder fellow says is true, an SOS note was left on the boat with a next of kin to contact. The MOD should handle that, but I suggest no calls are made to any family members until the whole thing is sorted out."

"Quite," replied the Foreign Secretary and then casually asked, "Is Ryder one of yours, by the way?" He knew very well that MI6 had a habit of picking up strays.

"No. But if this turns out to be what I suspect, I'll wish he were."

"Oh, really? Are you thinking what I'm thinking?"

"What I am thinking is that this could be another Gibraltar. So, whatever we do, it must be kept absolutely hush. I would not even tell our dear lady until we have to," replied the Security chief. By mentioning Gibraltar, he was referring to Operation Flavius, when three members of the Provisional

IRA were shot dead on the isthmus by members of the SAS just six months earlier, in March 1988.

"Right, Christopher. Two days. No more. Keep me informed. By the way, what do you propose to do immediately?"

"My people tell me three of our ships are in the Atlantic, returning from a joint naval exercise. They should be ploughing past the Bay of Biscay tomorrow. We have already made contact. They could make a small detour into Spanish waters."

"Oh, lord. Do they have to? Any excuse for them to snipe at us about the Rock. I had a meeting with their chaps only last week. It was embarrassing, to say the least."

"Sir Geoffrey, I believe it happens all the time. There is a well and tried reason for altering course unexpectedly when the Spaniards are in the equation. It happens in the Mediterranean. It happens in the Bay of Cadiz and it happens closer to home, in the Irish Channel. Our seamen are always having to change course to avoid Spanish fishermen and their precious nets, especially our subs."

"Very well. Goodbye." There was a sacred trust within the old network.

***

The second incident, which nobody could have suspected might relate to the first, involved the gruesome discovery of a body in St Mary's Harbour.

It had been planned for some time, in fact for over a year, and the work should have been carried out before the high summer season. St Mary's Pool was a mess. Not only was the seabed becoming littered with objects ecologists would be up in arms about. It was also a tangle of lines, some discarded and others creating a spider's web of cables and ropes, both on the surface and under the water, as sailors used otherwise neat rows of mooring buoys selfishly and haphazardly, with an almost first come, first serve attitude. The locals were getting very fed up, although it was the French who had complained most about the dangers to their propellers getting caught up in the web.

As a result, a team of six divers had come over from the mainland. Two of them were experts, and the other four were using the opportunity to get some experience as part of their diving course. They had begun cleaning up the seabed and cutting away lines and ropes that were simply not being used by any boat. One of the local craft had been seconded to accompany them, as a surface boat, to collect any small debris which the divers lifted and handed up to them. The vessel also had the job of marking any objects the divers could not move without a crane, like a discarded fridge and lost anchors. They had been diving for three or four days in the early mornings, before the happy sailing community began to play about in their boats, working outwards, using one line of boats and buoys at a time to measure and to mark their progress.

It was on their last programmed sweep of the harbour, halfway through their session, when one of the less experienced divers appeared to panic and surfaced in an uncontrolled ascent. Recognising the symptoms, the two experienced divers swam to his aid. One of them signalled to the other three amateurs that the clean-up was finished for the time being, and that they should surface. The other trod water about six feet from the diver who was in trouble. He put his hands up, in an effort to calm the diver who was shouting incomprehensible words, choking and flinging his arms about on the water. Once or twice, the diver's head sank below the surface, but minutes later it was all over when strong hands hauled him onto the surface boat.

When the reason for the diver's panic was discovered the whole team of divers got out of the water, as if they were being pursued by a monstrous fish. They had spent some thoroughly enjoyable days working in such a beautiful setting and, even more so, getting to know many of the charming islanders. Now, however, they were horrified and couldn't wait to get out of the place. In fact, the whole Isles of Scilly community fell into a strange state of horror and shock when the news spread. A corpse had been found, feet up under the surface, with its neck chained to an anchor. If Jamie had still been on the island, and not in his own kind of predicament, he would have been thankful that Ruth and her mother were not in Scilly to witness the horror.

Islanders were not to know it for weeks, but the body was of a Spanish trawler skipper named Alvaro Cousillas. He had been brutally murdered, right there in their pretty little harbour. When the corpse was disentangled and brought ashore, it was horribly bloated and its skin, which had turned a greenish, black colour, was blistered all over. Fish or other sea creatures, like crabs, had evidently already been feeding on the man's softer parts, especially the eyes and lips. In fact, a small, grey crustacean was seen to crawl out of the man's mouth just when Dominic Taylor, the Harbour Master, came along to see what all the fuss was about. What he witnessed was horrendous, like something out of a cheap horror movie.

"Jesus Christ!" was all he said, turning away immediately. As he did, he spotted Marcus Blyth, the islands' police sergeant. The poor man was bent over, thirty yards away. He had one hand against the harbour wall, at the top of the beach, and he was vomiting his breakfast.

A few minutes later, after Marcus moved along the wall a yard or two and was using a white handkerchief to wipe his mouth, Dominic Taylor thought it safe enough to go up to the policeman. Totally unaccustomed to dealing with crime, let alone anything so abominable, he was not his cheerful self.

"I told you there was something fishy about that Irishman on the yellow boat," said Dom Taylor. "Look, I'll pop over later and help you make your report. You'll need to get the guys in Penzance to come over for this one, Marcus."

"Yes mate. I'll get on to them. They'll have to send a chopper. I'll see you up in Garrison Lane. If you get there before me, not a word to Shirley, alright Dom? I've got to get the body covered up and put this end of the beach out of bounds. See you in a bit."

"Right you are Marcus. Do you want me to make any calls?"

"No, that's OK mate. This isn't my usual stuff, but it had to happen sooner or later. I was trained for this, you know," he said, trying to make light of the fact that he had just puked at the sight of Alvaro's corpse.

***

From his vantage point above Luarca harbour, Jamie Ryder kept a close watch on the Hannah for the rest of the morning. If anyone asked questions as to what he was doing spying on the port, he would say he was an English birdwatcher trying to spot one of Spain's unique species of gull. Nobody asked any questions. They were not that kind of people in this part of the world.

It became monotonous, but he was making a mental note of the other man's movements, and of the coming and going of an occasional police vehicle. He should keep open the option of attracting attention to himself if things got out of hand. From the moment he had first arrived in the middle of the morning, the man had spent most of the time sitting on one of the tarpaulins covering the boxes on the aft deck or walking to the bow and back. One Guardia Civil vehicle, a four-wheel drive Toyota, stopped once outside the Mont Blanc for the men in green to have their *desayunos*. A while later, a pair of local policemen in their dark blue uniforms also walked, very casually, back and forth along the edge of the harbour before disappearing behind the fish market. Jamie also noted that almost on the hour, every hour, the other man stepped off the Hannah, walked along the pontoon, hopped up the steps to the road and disappeared into the Mont Blanc café, across the way. Jamie's stomach was grinding away at his mind all the time, telling him it could do with some nourishment. If only he had a ration pack now.

His chance came at two o-clock. The tall, blond man went ashore again. This time, however, he did not go into the café. The man turned right and went all the way along the waterfront as far as the Báltico Hotel. There, Jamie watched him go in through the main entrance. He was carrying the brown bag, which Jamie had seen him arrive with at 10.00, but he did not have the small backpack over his shoulders. Jamie deduced from that that he would be returning to the Hannah. It had taken the man four and a half minutes to walk from the Hannah to the hotel. It didn't give Jamie much time, but he decided he had to take the risk. He needed energising desperately for whatever might occur later. Consequently, keeping his eyes peeled on the other end of the marina, on the Báltico Hotel, and for any sign of a blue Mercedes or the red Skoda, Jamie ran down to the café and went inside.

The place was bigger than he thought it might be. He went to the far end of the bar and ordered a coffee and two large cheese and salami *bocadillos* to take away, as well as a couple of bottles of drinking water. He also asked for the key to the *caballeros*. He paid the gents a very much needed visit and was pleased to find that these at least were kept clean. He didn't take long in the café, in spite of asking for a second coffee while he tucked into half of one of the baguettes. He had given himself ten minutes, and it had taken him twelve.

The moment he was back on his perch, Jamie trained the binoculars on the Báltico Hotel, scanned along the front as far as the Hannah, and then focused on the hotel once more. It was not until 15.45 that the other man came out of the hotel and made his way back to the boat in the marina. He had obviously enjoyed a good lunch. What Jamie was still unaware of was that Gorka Uriburu had also booked the boat's watchman a room at the Báltico, and that Jon had also needed to pay some extras which Gorka had failed to attend to in his haste to flee back to Gipuzkoa. Gorka had also left a bag in his room. Jon was to apologise pleasantly for the mess-up, pay what was owed, and retrieve the bag from Gorka's room. In fact, the blond Basque had to pay an extra night because the limit set for guests to leave their rooms was eleven o-clock. As far as Seba and Andoni's bills and belongings were concerned, they were unnecessary. No mention was made about them.

Jamie, still observing everything that was happening around the Hannah and in the port, was also racking his brains trying to understand what was going on. There was a strange kind of apathy in the blond man's body language. There was no apparent sense of urgency. It was almost as if he was not expecting company.

By 16.30, Jamie Ryder began to understand that there might be only two scenarios. One was that he had managed to make people so nervous the night before at Casa Luis that nobody was going to come near the Hannah until it was after dark, bringing along Brendan to sail the boat away with the man who was now its custodian. And yet, although Jamie knew the Hannah was ready to leave her berth at any time, the man didn't seem to be checking lines, sails, or any other on-deck equipment for an imminent departure.

The other scenario which Jamie began to consider was that nobody else was going to show up at all, not even the Irishman, and that the blond fellow was now simply the Hannah's custodian until an alternative plan had been worked out. Suddenly Jamie also began to believe that Brendan Daly might be in serious trouble because of his own actions. The thought didn't bother the young ex-Army man too much, though. After all, Brendan Daly was IRA. If anything happened to him, it would be collateral damage, as the Americans so liked to describe their errors in war.

Jamie's feeling, that the blond man's attitude looked far too casual for anything imminent to be about to happen, increased when Jon walked to the Hannah's bow with what looked like a couple of the cushions from the berth under the chart table. He placed them on the deck, just in front of the cabin top, and lay down with his head on the cushions. He had made himself very comfortable indeed and looked as if he had every intention of making the most of the afternoon sunlight for a siesta.

An hour later, the man got up and went below decks with the cushions, only to appear again after a couple of minutes. Once again, the man's relaxed manner and the calmness with which he went about his business, was remarkable and confusing. Jamie watched him again make his way along the pontoon and then across the road to the café. He was only indoors for a few minutes before he came out again, this time with what looked like a folded newspaper in his hand. He sat lazily at one of the tables which were outside on the pavement. He didn't even look towards the Hannah. Seconds later a waiter came out with a tray carrying a coffee for the blond man. As this was happening, Jamie noticed a sudden gust of wind and he looked across the water to the west. The surface was no longer as still as a pond. It had begun to ripple. The sun, which had given a gentle warmth all day, was being swallowed up by dark-looking clouds which had formed against the green hillsides. The weather was changing, and Jamie smelled rain. If he was right, he might need to find shelter before too long.

**

Enjoying the warmth and shelter of the bridge aboard HMS Ambuscade, the Captain, Commander Jeremy Neville, had been making Sub-Lieutenant Andy Pringle put into practice what he had done so often during his spell at Britannia Royal Naval College. He had him exchanging signals with one of the destroyers which was sailing parallel to them on the port side. It was a rather cruel thing to make the new lad do because it was lashing down with rain, as it had been since they began cutting through the waves past the Azores island of Porta Delgada, on their way to the English Channel.

They were making good progress, and Cape Finisterre was about three hundred miles almost directly east. The exercise with their NATO partners had been short and swift, but a great success, especially in terms of perfecting new technology for submarine search and destroy tactics. However, it had been all go, and every member of the ship's company was looking forward to a short breather back in Portsmouth, before their next deployment to the eastern Mediterranean.

"Message from Captain Ambrose, Sir," said a dripping-wet Sub-Lieutenant Pringle, after stepping onto the bridge and saluting. "He said to inform you to expect new orders at 19.00."

Captain Ambrose, on HMS Exeter, a Type-42 destroyer, was commanding this particular British flotilla. He had just received a direct order from home. Two of his ships were not to maintain their present course for the English Channel. Instead, for reasons to be disclosed in a further communication, they were to steer a course into the Bay of Biscay. Two ships were to penetrate 150 and 200 nautical miles, respectively, into the bay, on a course parallel to the Spanish coast, maintaining a distance of approximately 100 miles from the Iberian Peninsula. The RFA support ship and the second destroyer should continue back to the UK, as scheduled. Once into the Bay of Biscay and beyond the normal shipping lanes, the two RN ships were to cruise at no more than ten knots, unless approached by a Spanish naval vessel. If that occurred, they were to swiftly turn for home after providing an explanation, if one was requested, that another Royal Navy Harrier may have been lost, presumably in the Bay of Biscay. Memories were still fresh about how, in 1983, a British Harrier pilot had lost his bearings and had landed on a Spanish cargo ship to save the aircraft, just before he ran out of fuel.

It seemed a strange order, as well as an irritating one. However, the more enigmatic the communication, the more interesting it was, and Ambrose was eager to learn more. He also fully intended that his should be one of the ships to enter the Bay of Biscay. When further information and orders came through, at 18.37, he told his communications officer to transmit his own orders to the other ships.

At precisely 19.00, Neville, on the Ambuscade, received his. They were sent up to him from CIC, the Combat Information Centre. He was still on the bridge and would be handing over to the officer of the watch at 20.00. He was also accompanied, along with a Petty Officer and a young rating, by a now dry Sub-Lieutenant Pringle.

"Good grief! Good grief!" said Commander Neville out loud, after reading the text a couple of times. "Whatever next!"

"Pringle. Get Lieutenant Allfrey up here, will you? Oh, and extend my sincere apologies. I know he's not on for an hour, but I need him to see this."

"Aye, Sir," Andy Pringle replied, before shooting off, eager to discover what had made his Captain remark with such enthusiasm and surprise.

When both Allfrey and Pringle arrived back on the bridge, Neville briefed them. They were being diverted to intercept a yacht. No, it was not an Admiral's private yacht. This one was suspected of transporting weapons for the IRA. With any luck, their new heading was going to take them somewhere close enough to intercept the arms boat. The ship's Wasp helicopter and Ambrose's Sea King Mk5 would be sent to make quick sweeps of the seas in an area where British intelligence believed the yacht might be during the following afternoon. The course was also going to steer them, as fleetingly as possible, just inside Spain's exclusive economic zone. That is why the mission was to be swift, and action stations would be called when the time came. Although they would still be in international waters, Spain, as a major fishing nation, did have a touchy problem with any shipping that could not be classified as pleasure craft, cruise liners or commercial vessels, such as tankers and container ships. Foreign fishing fleets and military vessels, other than those belonging to their immediate neighbours, France, and Portugal, tended to hurt Spanish pride. Gibraltar and its waters were a constant topic of discussion between British diplomats in Madrid and the Spanish Government.

"London's having kittens about this, so the plan is to do a quick dash and hover and get out before we get Spain sending a friendly aircraft to ask us if we have lost our way. However, gentlemen, I do not intend to flee for home until we have found that IRA boat."

"Do we have a description of the yacht, Sir?" enquired Lieutenant Allfrey.

"Not much, I'm afraid. All I know is what's on this bit of paper. She is a sailing boat with burgundy-coloured sails and a ghastly yellow livery. I wonder who wrote this. Obviously isn't keen on yellow!"

"Do we know if she is a Fisher, Sir?" Andy Pringle asked, timidly.

"No, Pringle. She is a yacht, not a fishing boat, lad. Don't you listen?" He really had it in for his young Sub-Lieutenant.

"I think what Andy means, Sir, is whether the vessel in question is a Fisher. It is a type of tubby-looking yacht, Sir."

"Oh. I see. Well, I don't know."

"If she is a Fisher, Sir, I think I know her," said Andy Pringle, with a little more confidence now that he had some moral support.

"What on earth do you mean, you know her, Pringle?"

"Sorry, Sir. I don't exactly know her, but I'm pretty sure we passed her on our way out of the Channel. I'd recognise her anywhere, Sir. She did indeed have a ridiculous, bright yellow colour scheme."

"In that case, I'll want you on watch to make use of your excellent, first-class knowledge of yellow pleasure craft, shan't I, Mr Pringle? See to it that you swap watches if necessary. You'll be on forenoon watch tomorrow, and probably stay on until we bloody well find that yellow tub!"

"Aye, Sir!" replied Andy Pringle very patiently indeed, but not without exchanging knowing glances with Lieutenant Allfrey.

"By the way, Pringle, are you a sailor?"

"No, Sir. I only wish I had taken a proper interest at Britannia," replied the Sub-Lieutenant to his captain's question. He thought he knew the reason for the query and, in the circumstances, was glad he had not learnt to manage a yacht.

"Job for you, then. By your next watch, I want you to have found three volunteers to sail the yellow yacht, in case we actually find it. A needle in a haystack, if you ask me, but we'll give it our best shot. They've got to be highly experienced sailors, if we have any aboard. We can't very well tow the damn thing." Captain Ambrose, on HMS Exeter, already had two eager crew members, both Lieutenants who were willing to sail the clandestine yacht home. But Neville wasn't to know that.

"Aye, aye, Sir."

Moments after that exchange, more friendly this time, new orders came through. The two ships involved would alter course at 19.50 and keep a steady twenty knots until they reached the main shipping lanes, just north of La Coruña. They would then reduce to ten knots. Captain Ambrose had decided that HMS Ambuscade would be the one to penetrate farthest east into the bay, exactly 200 nautical miles. His Exeter would take a slightly different course, heading north at full speed after penetrating 150 miles into the bay. Ambuscade should reach her limit sometime mid-afternoon the next day. Whether she found the yellow boat or not, she too would then steer north-northwest and head for home. HMS Ambuscade should have her Wasp helicopter ready and always prepared to follow up any blip on the radar which might coincide with the course taken by the yacht.

***

It began to drizzle quite heavily just after eight o-clock in the Spanish harbour of Luarca. Jamie, anticipating the rain, had earlier discovered a narrow shelter under the same steps which led down to the harbour and which was close to his original lookout spot. He had tucked himself in as far as he could, feeling even more like a destitute tramp, when the tall blond man appeared on the Hannah's deck again. The Basque looked around for a moment and then went below. He appeared again a few moments later. This time he had his small backpack over one shoulder and appeared to be holding a piece of plastic material over his head to keep the rain off. Jamie watched him step off the Hannah onto the pontoon and make his way up to the road. The little light there was under the dense drizzle was fading quickly, but Jamie saw him walk all the way to the hotel. There, before he vanished into the lobby, Jamie saw the man chuck the material which he had used to keep his head dry onto the street. It was the kind of attitude Jamie loathed. Jamie assumed the man was popping in for a meal, just as he had done at two o-clock. He thought about biting into his second *bocadillo* but kept up the discipline. He might need it more later.

Every now and then, Jamie focussed on the Báltico Hotel entrance. An hour passed and then another, but nothing happened. A couple, holding hands, stepped into the hotel but nobody came out. No Gorka and his men. No Brendan. The lack of action as time went by, the monotonous sound of car tyres splashing along the street, and fatigue began to take its toll on Jamie, and he felt the ominous signs of drowsiness setting in. The drizzle had become very light now, so he decided to take a chance and leave his uncomfortable shelter, if only for ten minutes, and to exercise himself by running up and down the steps a few times. It did the trick. He became alert again and was warm.

By midnight, Jamie concluded that nothing more was going to happen, that the other man was not going to return to the Hannah that night, and that he must surely be planning to sleep at the hotel. How incredibly careless of them! There was no other logical explanation.

Twenty-four hours had passed since he spoke to Bob Bunting. Jamie had forty-eight left. He needed to be positive, and to believe that his farmer friend had managed to persuade someone to take his information seriously. Jamie had to follow this through. He must act now. If the worst came to the worst, he still had Andoni's gun.

He stood up and began to walk down the road. There were still people inside the Mont Blanc café. He could tell by the din, but the tables and chairs on the pavement outside were wet from the drizzle. The gate to the pontoon was still open. As he had noticed the previous day, nobody ever seemed to lock it. That was also terribly careless. However, at the height of the summer season, many of these boatmen would still be ashore enjoying some wine and tapas. Perhaps that was the reason it was left open, but Jamie doubted it.

Jamie walked onto the pontoon confidently, making sure he looked as if he owned the place, and stepped onto the Hannah. He peeped below. Everything seemed in order, just as he had left it the previous evening. He checked the lines and cleats to see what he would need to undo. They too were as he had left them, with just the two bow lines tied to the pontoon. On either side, sets of fenders nudged and squeaked against neighbouring hulls. Jamie loosened the lines which were holding the mainsail on the boom and then checked the jib and mainsail halyards.

At 01.25 Jamie made up his mind. Nobody came. It was no use waiting any longer. Brendan, he was certain, was not going to be seen again, poor man. It was time to go.

Jamie let go first, even before starting her up. He needed her lines released and on deck because he wanted to move the Hannah astern the moment he had the motor turning over. The fenders could wait until he was out of the inner harbour.

Once the Hannah was unattached to the pontoon, Jamie moved swiftly along the deck and into the wheelhouse. He turned the key, waited a couple of minutes, peeping out towards the road to make certain, for one last time, that there was nobody about to interfere, and pressed on the starter button. The motor coughed into life immediately. Jamie promptly moved her astern, very slowly, inching back as straight as he could. The moment the Hannah's bow was clear, he turned the wheel and pushed the throttle forward, just enough to stop her movement astern and to push her gently forward in the water towards the mouth of the marina. As the Hannah moved through the water, Jamie looked to the left, as if he expected there to be anyone at all on the coastguard boat. As on the previous two days, there was no sign of life. There were no alarms, no shouts from the shore, no search lights illuminating the water. This was not a movie. It was real life in a coastal town in Spain and the night, after the last café and bar put the shutters down, was for sleeping.

Immediately the Hannah cleared the old outer pier and was into the beach cove, Jamie turned the wheel a touch to starboard, pointing the bow towards the gap between the two outer breakwaters. Only when he was well clear of these, did he bother switching on the Hannah's navigation lights. As he did, Jamie pushed the throttle forward, urging the motor to move him away from the coast, heading directly north. The further away he got, the less likely it was that he would be followed. There was not much of a breeze, and there was only a gentle swell pushing towards him on the windward side. It had begun to rain again, but that wasn't necessarily a bad thing.

When the chart plotter told him the Hannah was a good two miles offshore, Jamie throttled down and turned the Hannah into the light north easterly. He then hauled the mainsail halyard until the head of the sail was about two thirds of the way up the mast. He was not yet entirely confident he knew how to sail a boat and calculated that, by having less of a sail surface, he would not be in danger of overdoing it if he suddenly met stronger gusts. He then took the jib's in-haul off its cleat, hauled, and set the sail, again to about two thirds. Jamie throttled back and turned the wheel to port, now pointing the Hannah's bow northwest. He put the Hannah on a compass course of 300°, as he told Bunting he would do for six hours. Checking his watch, that would mean until approximately 09.00. If there was nothing much on the radar, he would try to get a couple of hours sleep.

Unfortunately, the Furuno radar put an end to that notion immediately. There was no danger from behind, but the radar showed a whole lot of blips in a section of sea about 15 nautical miles north. Beyond them, inside 40 miles, there were three or four larger targets. Jamie assumed the small ones belonged to a fishing fleet and the stronger blips to cargo ships or tankers. These appeared to be moving both east and west. He could dodge them easily enough and even use the autopilot to steer between them, but the fishing boats concerned him. There was no way he could close his eyes.

You've no option, mate, he thought to himself. In other words, he would have to dose himself with strong mugs of coffee and hope for the best. Even so, he used the autopilot to assist him.

He turned the wheel to point the Hannah directly north and then told the autopilot to steer back onto the original compass bearing of 300°. Within seconds the Raymarine electric steering motor pushed the rudder, and the wheel began to turn to steer the boat north-northwest again. This equipment was functioning perfectly, and it took the Hannah riding gently across the swell. The chart plotter also played its part in comforting Jamie, telling him that he was doing between five and six knots. It was time for that first coffee and to finish off the remaining baguette before he got too close to that fleet of fishing boats.

As he got closer to the blips on the radar, he began to see their lights. He was right. They bore the unmistakable mark of being a group of trawlers, spread over a wide area. The good thing for Jamie was that they were all heading in a north easterly direction. The Hannah, with the course she was on and the speed she was doing, was going to pass well behind them. They were all small-sized vessels, showing an all-round green light above the normal white on the mast, and their green starboard lights were clearly visible. A few more hours of this and the traffic would become less intense as the Hannah ploughed through the swell, further away from the Iberian Peninsula and into deeper waters. Six hours after leaving behind Luarca, Jamie would change course, as anticipated, to begin following a more parallel line to the main shipping lanes towards the Brest Peninsula and the English Channel. It would be full daylight by then, and he would feel more comfortable about closing his eyes for half-hourly or hourly intervals, depending on how far away those blips on the radar were.

***

The two Royal Navy warships reduced speed to ten knots, once they were clear of the commercial traffic, and began their sweep in the Bay of Biscay. One hundred miles east of Ferrol, Captain Ambrose ordered his Sea King to carry out a low-level search, with a series of north to south sweeps within a fifty-mile radius. He sent similar instructions to Commander Neville on the Ambuscade. His Wasp was also to carry out low level sweeps, although its range was much more limited, and the pilot needed to rely a great deal on information from the ship. Consequently, every now and then, he was instructed to head this way or that to identify a possible target.

Those blips on the radars of both HMS Exeter and the Ambuscade became less frequent as the day went on and as they sailed further into the bay, away from the shipping lanes. HMS Ambuscade's radar did fill with a scattering of targets a little north east of them at one point, and they were identified as trawlers. Behind her, and further north, HMS Exeter also detected similar targets. However, neither helicopters nor ships found anything remotely yellow in the water during the middle part of the afternoon.

Nor did Jamie Ryder find any joy in the vessels he spotted as he searched the horizon every half hour with the binoculars. It was now mid-afternoon on Thursday, 1st September. Now and then, his hopes faded a little, possibly due to fatigue and in response to the adrenaline of the last couple of days. It was only thoughts of Ruth that kept pushing his determination to get this done. She would be starting work in exactly one week and he had promised he would be back with her before then.

Had he been an experienced sailor, Jamie would be revelling in these conditions. The weather had cleared up again, after the north Atlantic front passed over them and into France, and there was now a nice, steady westerly breeze. It kept the Hannah cutting an easy path through the waves. Once or twice, a pod of bottle-nose dolphins came to play, and Jamie was certain he might have spotted a couple of orca whales. Those trawlers were possibly after the lucrative, bluefin tuna on their migratory journeys, and those tuna were one of the killer whales' favourite morsels. So much for the dreaded Bay of Biscay.

The autopilot was a wonderful thing. Since Jamie had changed course again at 09.00, telling it to steer on a compass bearing of 20°, the device had given him time to close his eyes, on and off, for the rest of the morning and into the early afternoon. It was then, when he opened his eyes after his last doze, and when he was viewing a small cargo ship heading south a couple of miles to starboard, that his mind became alert enough to do something he had been telling himself not to do in any circumstances, which was to look inside one or two of the boxes and fishmongers' crates that were weighing the Hannah down in the water.

The temptation was too great. He also wanted to have some kind of explanation ready if he was picked up by anything other than a British ship. Jamie was not going to open either of the containers which had been placed on the deck under the tarpaulins. He wanted to avoid risking any damage to the contents by a sudden, belligerent wave. No, all he needed was a peep into one of the boxes below deck, where the galley table would have been.

It was not as easy as he thought. The container was heavy, he needed to move it slightly because Brendan had used layers of thick tape around the top to seal it after inspecting the contents. It had also been secured with two straps. Jamie cut through the layers of tape and managed to release the straps. He removed the top and put it on the chart table behind him. What he saw inside the plastic container confirmed what he already suspected. On top of neatly packed, metallic ammunition boxes containing 9mm bullets there were a dozen or more magazines. Jamie removed a number of these and three or four of the metallic ammo boxes. Underneath, he discovered what these were for, a large number of Brazilian Taurus semi automatics. Jamie didn't bother counting them. He replaced the boxes of ammunition and the magazines neatly, just as he had found them.

Jamie put the top back on the container and returned to the wheelhouse. He checked the compass, the radar, and the chart plotter. The automatic pilot was doing sterling work and there was not much happening. Nevertheless, he went out onto the deck and made a slow, deliberate sweep across the sea and then did a similar, shallow inspection of the sky. The weather had cleared up well and truly and the Bay of Biscay was being extraordinarily kind, with a constant breeze and just a gentle swell. It was going to be a warm and glorious afternoon.

Jamie was concentrating the binoculars mostly in a wide band from southwest to northwest, the direction from which he hoped a friendly ship would approach. He had no idea that two British warships had been hunting for a yellow tub in the water for some time, or that the bigger of the two, HMS Exeter, was soon to set a new course, parallel to his own, on a similar north-northeast heading, but which would take her further away from his position. The Ambuscade would do the same five hours later, at approximately 18.00. Her Wessex Wasp was halfway into a sortie and Ambrose, on the Exeter, had just watched his Sea King lift off from the deck for its second search. The first had been in an optimistically narrow arc, south and south east. This time, it would widen the arena towards the east and north.

Jamie put the binoculars down and stepped halfway down into the saloon. He sat on the ladder and looked towards the bow, thinking. What was going through his mind was whether to open one of the two crates that had been stacked in the fore cabin.

Once again, curiosity got the better of him, although he suspected what they might hold. Therefore, when he eventually prised open one of the unmarked wooden crates and brushed aside a covering of straw, he was not surprised by what he found. There was a slim, sky-blue missile. It was a Russian Strela 2. He estimated there might well have been two or three of them in each crate unless launchers were packed underneath.

Jamie guessed the IRA didn't require any more launchers, but only missiles. He thought back to his training days at Sandhurst when different types of weapons were discussed during seminars. Amongst the weapons the Republican Army was believed to have purchased from Libya, were a couple of MANPADS, man-portable air-defence systems to use against British helicopters. The missiles aboard the Hannah were the lethal ingredient of the same weapon and could be easily purchased for the right price.

Jamie covered the missile over again with the straw and replaced the top of the crate. There was nothing more for him to do, but having seen the cargo, he became even more determined to complete the mission he had set himself. Foolhardy or not, in doing what he had done, instead of simply disappearing by coach or train as far as he could from Gorka and his men in Luarca, Jamie felt good. He was making up for the mess he had made leaving the Regiment. He was doing his duty once more. Aching with fatigue, the thought gave him a great deal of satisfaction and another fillip to get the yellow vessel back to England.

***

At precisely 17.45, Commander Jeremy Neville asked to be put through to Captain Ambrose.

His orders had been to change course to the north northeast at 18.00. He did not have a properly reasoned explanation for his request. In fact, as he explained over the radio to his superior, he just had an inkling that they should give their possible target another two hours. If London's suspicions were correct, and there was indeed a boatful of IRA weapons floating about in the Bay of Biscay, he considered they must give themselves a little longer.

Sub-Lieutenant Andy Pringle had not thought much of his captain until then, especially after being treated like an imbecile midshipman. Now, upon hearing the conversation, he gave the man credit. He liked what he heard, especially when Ambrose agreed to his Captain's request. In fact, Captain Ambrose had already been thinking along the same lines. He would also give it another go, and he ordered the Sea King to make one more sortie before sunset.

At 19.45, approximately half an hour before the sun disappeared under the horizon, Jamie was sitting on one of the tarpaulin-covered boxes behind the wheelhouse, enjoying the evening's orange glow. He had just gorged a tin of baked beans and was sipping at another strong coffee, sweetened with condensed milk. The chart plotter informed him that he was now approximately 90 miles north of the Spanish mainland. Surely, he was safely away now, but how he wished he had some sort of company. Once again, he persuaded himself it would not be too many days before he could share a similar, orange glow of a sunset, from the point just down the path from Trench Lane, with Ruth.

The thought of her again warmed and lifted Jamie. He smiled and let his imagination drift over the surface when he spotted a shearwater skimming the waves in the opposite direction to the Hannah, back to its Spanish cliffs. He wondered if it too had a love waiting for it on dry land. Then, quite suddenly, he heard it. He thought he had, anyway, and leapt into the wheelhouse for the binoculars and the flare pack. When he stepped out on the deck again, he was certain. It was a sound he knew very well, the intermittent hum, followed by a familiar toco-toco-toco. It was a helicopter, and it wasn't too far away.

There was no need for a flare. When he spotted the dark blue shape, about two hundred feet off the water, he knew it was Royal Navy, and it was coming straight for him.

Everyone on the bridge, including Commander Neville and Andy Pringle, let out a loud cheer as the radio on HMS

218

Ambuscade crackled into life when Flight Lieutenant Sam Wells broke the news.

"Right on, Sir! Radar was spot on. Think we've got her. Suspected target dead ahead. Bright yellow. Can't miss her!"

"Well done, Sam! Stand off and report personnel aboard. Don't forget, we suspect she is friendly, but that is still unconfirmed." The radio remained open and two minutes later they heard the pilot and co-pilot laughing.

"No other boat this colour in all the oceans of the world, Sir! One man visible on deck, and he's waving his arms around like he's on a desert island."

"Right. Make contact and ask if there is anybody else on board. Tell the man to keep on the same course and that there's a hot shower waiting for him within the hour. I'll get on to Exeter."

"Yes, Sir."

"One more thing. You've found the prey. Now get back to base. Your big sister will do the rest." Commander Neville was referring to the fact that HMS Exeter would almost certainly send her Sea King to take over.

That was exactly what occurred. Upon receiving news that the yellow boat had been intercepted, Captain Ambrose on the Exeter ordered his Sea King to ferry the three volunteers, two lieutenants and an able seaman, armed and with backpacks bursting with sleeping bags and provisions for five days, to the Hannah. It would then return with Jamie Ryder and any other person on the yellow tub.

As soon as the chopper became airborne, Ambrose gave two orders. One was immediate. HMS Exeter was to set a new course directly towards the Hannah's position. The other was for Commander Neville on the Ambuscade. The frigate was to position herself close to the yellow Fisher, to provide cover and assistance if necessary, while the Sea King did its job. Young Andy Pringle was disappointed. Firstly, he would have to tell the three men who had eagerly volunteered to sail the Hannah that they would not be required. Secondly, he had been looking forward to meeting this guy, Ryder, the one they had all begun to talk about as a bloody hero.

His disappointment soon turned into pride, however. When HMS Ambuscade reduced speed to a virtual standstill and turned to position herself on a parallel course just two hundred yards to port of the Hannah, Commander Neville referred to the yellow tub as Andy's boat. His disappointment then turned into a beaming smile when Neville sent a communication to HMS Exeter. It contained an invitation for Ryder to dine in the officers' mess the moment she was back in port. Lieutenant Andy Pringle felt a calm satisfaction when Neville congratulated him, not only on his excellent work, but on having been so observant, spotting the same Fisher 30 sailing near the English Channel two weeks earlier. He almost chuckled as he came off his watch and stepped down the ladder from the bridge. Once again, Andy remembered the last time he had gone fishing with his old man. The Hannah's yellow hull really did bob along like one of his father's eccentric floats. It was a peaceful sight indeed to finish an unusual day.

***

Sir Geoffrey Howe was at Chevening House, in Kent. He was in a relatively easy mood, looking forward to what could be a well-deserved weekend away from London after too many days of rather tense cabinet meetings and increasingly conflictive discussions with the Prime Minister, Margaret Thatcher.

However, although Margaret Thatcher had nominated Sir Geoffrey to occupy the beautiful Kent mansion for private use in 1983, he also used it for important political and diplomatic reunions. On that particular weekend, he was to host yet another delegation from Spain. It was designed to be a casual, informal dinner this time. The sole objective was to try to lessen tensions over Gibraltar, away from the gaze of the Spanish press. Despite the Spanish Government being profoundly Socialist, there had been signs that Felipe Gonzalez, Spain's tenacious President, had mellowed towards a more pragmatic and common-sense approach to government, and especially to foreign affairs.

With Sir Geoffrey, enjoying a warming sherry before the

pleasantries began, was Nicholas Gordon-Lennox, Her Majesty's Ambassador to Spain. The two men were running through the main points on the agenda for the evening when Sarah Billings, Sir Geoffrey's private secretary, interrupted. There was a call for him. It was George Younger, the Secretary of State for defence.

"A wee bit of news, Geoffrey," began the Defence Secretary jovially, in his gentle Scottish accent. "It might be something for you to talk to your guests about tonight, if the going gets tough."

"Oh?" replied Sir Geoffrey, winking at the Ambassador across the room.

"They've got it. The Navy has got the IRA boat."

"Ah, now that *is* good news. Splendid! Well done indeed! And our man, Jamie whatnot?"

"Safely aboard HMS Exeter and heading for Portsmouth. He's not actually our man, Geoffrey. According to Curwen, he might well be a bloody journalist."

MI5 had not only delved deep into Jamie Ryder's background and ancestry. It had also traced his recent movements all the way to St Mary's, in the Isles of Scilly. Consequently, Mrs Martin, of Annette's Cottage, had been of great help providing the vital information, which was that her guest in mid-August happened to be a journalist investigating for an article. The idea initially puzzled the intelligence service because Ryder had apparently also been job-hunting in two or three very different arenas since leaving his regiment. But then, what could a decent fellow like him have been doing on a boat hijacked by the IRA? He must have been onto something. The question was, for whom? For which daily newspaper?

"Oh, Lord, George! A journalist? Can we keep it out of the papers?"

"That he may be a journalist is only a suspicion, Geoffrey, and yes, it can be kept out of the press for the time being. That is, until he is back on dry land. The Navy has instructions not to permit him to have any contact outside the ship until he has been thoroughly questioned."

"Good. But poor man! He should be given a medal, not have to face an interrogation. And the weapons? Was the boat really carrying weapons?"

"I believe there are weapons, Geoffrey. Not only small stuff and explosives, but anti-aircraft missiles."

"Good grief! That is serious stuff. I insist, and I'm pretty sure the PM will agree with me. The lad must be treated like a hero and not like a damned journalist!"

"Absolutely. Between you and I, Geoffrey, I think the SIS people are barking up the wrong tree or not telling us everything. You know what they are like. They would mistrust even their own pet Labrador. Anyway, the Army is adamant. He may not be an officer anymore, but he is one of them and, as Minister for Defence, I am going to support this Ryder chap all the way."

"I'll have a word with Christopher Curwen tonight after the Spaniards have been put safely to bed. Oh, and George, congratulations all round, especially to those Royal Navy chaps."

"Of course. From what I gather they are cock-a-hoop. Oh, by the way, if you remember, it is believed the boat in question had once belonged to an ex-British Army man, Peter Rennie."

"Yes. Any more on that?"

"No. I'm afraid we have to go with the worst-case scenario."

"Which is?"

"We can assume Rennie's boat was hijacked by the IRA and that he and his wife are most probably dead. Now, as instructed on an SOS note found aboard the boat, the next of kin will be informed in the next couple of days. General Walter Burns, Regimental Colonel of Rennie's regiment, the Coldstream Guards, is arranging a visit to the couple's son, Anthony Rennie. I believe he will be telephoned tomorrow."

"Right. Of course. Now, don't forget. Not a word to the press for the time being."

With that, Sir Geoffrey put the telephone down and resumed putting the final touches to their meeting with Mr Francisco Fernández Ordóñez, the Spanish Minister of Foreign Affairs, and his colleagues from Madrid. Perhaps he could slip in a carrot towards the end of the conference, about collaborating with the fight against terrorism in the Basque Country, and with information about an ETA arms shipment to the IRA from the Asturias port of Luarca. But that would depend upon how cooperative the Spaniards were with maintaining the status quo as regards Gibraltar.

***

The press did get onto the story, of course. They have a way of digging out information of an event before it even happens, and this was a big one, big enough to engage people's attention away from the cracks appearing in Mrs Thatcher's government.

First up was the Daily Mail, on Friday, 2nd September. The headline, splashed across the front page, was "IRA ARMS BOAT CAPTURED IN BAY OF BISCAY". The London Evening Standard was next in both Friday editions. Almost every Saturday newspaper carried a similar story, including the respectable Telegraph and Times. Even so, the Mail kept the pressure on the others by adding juice to the information. It was almost equalled by the Daily Mirror, whose Saturday headline read, "THE SCILLY ISLES CONNECTION" and below, "IRA ARMS BOAT LINKED TO GRUESOME MURDER".

Cath Martin, and her Annette's Cottage, were getting much more publicity than she could possibly have hoped for. A photograph of her, standing in front of her bed and breakfast cottage, appeared in the Mail, the Mirror, and the Express. She was absolutely thrilled and was almost carried away by it all, much to the amusement of the small community in Hugh Town. She was even interviewed by ITV and appeared in a small snippet on the news. Such a nice man was Mr Ryder. Such charming manners, but she could tell he wasn't just a journalist, of course. No, he had not left any possessions in his room.

Luckily for Ruth and her mother, they were not at St Mary's when Alvaro's corpse was discovered by the divers, or when initial investigations indicated the body was of a man who had been crewing a yellow boat called Hannah. Nor were they in

Scilly when the press invaded Hugh Town in a desperate hunt for anything remotely connected with crime and gun running for the IRA. In fact, the first they heard of what had been going on in the peaceful haven called St Mary's, was on their last Saturday in London, before travelling back to the island on Monday 5th, three days before term started for Ruth.

It had been quite hectic, with last minute chores and arrangements, but Mrs Eaton went out for her early morning walk to pick up the two Saturday papers she liked, the Telegraph and the Mail. As she walked through the front door she smelled fresh coffee. Ruth was awake.

"Breakfast, Mummy?"

"Morning, darling. Yes, please. I'll be with you in a minute. But I'll just have some fruit. Don't forget we're lunching with your sister. It will be our last chance to see her before she goes chasing off to Australia."

It was a pure coincidence, but the telephone rang that very instant. It was Ruth's elder sister, Becky. Ruth picked up the receiver and almost pulled it away from her ear at once when the screech at the other end pierced into her just-awake head. Becky was in a high state of excitement.

"Ruthy, have you seen the papers? Gosh, it is just amazing. It's all happening in St Mary's, isn't it?"

"What's so amazing it can't wait until lunchtime? Really, Becky, I've just woken up!" Ruth always found her sister a bit too energetic, and she had a tendency for blowing things out of proportion.

Although they would all be having lunch together in just three hours' time, the conversation between sisters lasted for nearly half an hour. And, yes, much to Ruth's amazement, the information was fascinating, and her sister was not exaggerating this time. The conversation did hover over several subjects, as always between the two sisters, but this time it was mainly about a bloody murder in Scilly. It was unheard of. Their dialogue lasted until Becky asked her sister the most relevant question.

"Isn't your new boyfriend called Jamie Ryder?"

"Well, I wouldn't say he is my boyfriend yet, but yes, that is

224

his name. Why?"

"You really haven't seen the papers, have you, Ruth? He's being talked about as a hero. The papers are full of him and the IRA!"

"What are you talking about?"

"Just read the papers, Ruth!"

The conversation ended abruptly. Ruth slammed the receiver down and skipped into the kitchen, where her toast had now turned hard and her coffee cold. Her mother had not touched hers either, and she was staring at the front page of the Daily Mail, open-mouthed. When Ruth read down as far as the fourth paragraph, leaning over her mother's shoulder, she had to sit down. Suddenly she felt overwhelmed and confused and burst into tears.

"Oh, Mummy. What a fool I've been. I could have got him killed. I did all I could to persuade him to go on that boat!"

Her momentary state of shock was soon followed by a feeling of pride, and it swelled inside Ruth after she read a more orderly and sober account in The Telegraph. Becky's farewell lunch was going to be memorable.

Something similar, but not quite so hysterical, occurred not so far away at the Travellers Club in Pall Mall. It was just before lunch and Samuel, the greying head waiter, had just served Henry Clark his usual sherry in the Coffee Room.

Yes, he would be lunching today and, yes, Samuel's recommendation, a couple of slices of Boeuf Wellington with peppered, crispy French fries would be excellent. Samuel was a little disappointed though. Mr Clark seemed reluctant to exchange a few words, as he usually did in his very kind way. He appeared distracted by something he was reading in the Times, which provided a list of the weapons and explosives believed to have been found aboard an Irish yacht. They included Taurus handguns, AK-47 Kalashnikovs, Semtex plastic explosives and SAMs. Nevertheless, Samuel was prepared to wait for the gentleman to decide which fine wine he would like to accompany his beef.

Jamie's godfather was more than distracted. He was baffled. He had only spoken to Maria, in Tenerife, on Friday evening.

She had again mentioned, in her casual manner, how concerned she was for her son, and about his drifting from one thing and another since he left the Army. As far as she knew, Jamie had gone to Cornwall for a few days to think things over, and that would simply not do. The last Maria had heard was that he was in the Isles of Scilly, of all places. Like any good mother, she worried. Of course, without actually asking for it, his best friend's widow also sought Henry's comfort and support and, if not directly, his advice and help in finding some kind of opening for Jamie.

Now, if what he had just read in the Times was true, and Henry Clark had no reason to doubt it, it seemed Jamie had been keeping himself very active indeed.

Mr Clark suddenly held Samuel's arm and asked him to help him out of the leather armchair, which was behind the pillar and under the bookshelves which contained some of the finest, ancient travel books in the kingdom.

"Samuel. I do apologise. I must go downstairs. I'll take lunch at half past one today, if you don't mind. There is an urgent telephone call I need to make."

"Right you are, Sir. Half past one, Sir. Your sherry, Sir?"

"No thank you, Samuel. I'll go straight into the dining room. Perhaps a Château Clarke?" he said, with a twinkle in his eye.

He liked Samuel to think it was his own wine, and Samuel liked to pretend he believed the fine Bordeaux was from Mr Clark's own vineyards in France. But, of course, it was not the case. The only possession Henry Clark had which was remotely connected with France was a silver fork believed to have been used by Napoleon on the eve of the Battle of Waterloo.

The moment Mr Clark turned his back and walked towards the door, Samuel picked up the untouched sherry glass, looked around to see if any other gentlemen were aware of him, and swallowed the sherry. It was one of the perks of the job.

Maria had just returned from mass and was about to lunch with her daughter and son-in-law. It was not something she was looking forward to, so it was a pleasant surprise to hear Henry's voice again at the other end of the line. However, he usually called on Friday evenings. This was most strange.

"Is there anything the matter, Henry?"

"No, dear. On the contrary. I've news about Jamie."

"Jamie has got in touch with you? Heavens, that is a surprise, darling Henry."

"No, no. He hasn't. But I shall be contacting him the moment I hear he is back in England; I can promise you that. I want to hear all about it from his own mouth?"

"But he *is* in England, Henry. I told you, he is somewhere in Cornwall or in the Scilly Isles. I'm sure I told you on Friday."

"Can you get hold of an English newspaper, my dear?"

"Well, yes. But why?"

"I've a copy of today's Times in my hand. It mentions Jamie on the front page. He hasn't been drifting at all. In fact, I hope you are going to be bursting with pride, my dear. I certainly am."

"What? Why? But we get the newspapers a day late here. Tell me, what has my son been doing."

"Nothing much to talk about, Maria. On the other hand, if you are not sitting down, you'd better."

"Will I need a whisky?"

"Several!"

"Alright, Henry. Stop teasing. I'm sitting."

"According to a reliable source, to the Times in other words, Jamie is currently on a Royal Navy destroyer on his way back from Spain."

"Nonsense! What are you talking about?"

"It is absolutely true. What's more, he has been behaving like me, behind enemy lines and all that," insisted Henry Clark, hinting at his times in intelligence, often working discretely and innocently for British interests in different parts of the world.

"Will you please stop teasing me and tell me what is going on."

"If this report is correct, your Jamie hijacked a boat carrying weapons for the IRA on Friday. I have absolutely no idea what he was doing, or how he got himself into this, but the Times hints at the fact that Jamie has been working as a journalist, and that he had been following up a lead to uncover an IRA gun-running operation from Spain to Ireland."

"No!"

"Indeed! Now, Maria, tell me. Truthfully now, did you know he was working as a reporter?"

"Henry. Of course, I didn't. Now look, this is totally absurd. Are you sure it is our Jamie? I mean, it might just be a coincidence. It could be another Jamie Ryder."

"I doubt it very much. The Times refers to Jamie having been in the Army and names his Regiment. There is no doubt at all. There's even a picture of him in uniform. This is your Jamie alright, and he is being talked about in high praise."

"I *am* going to have a whisky, Henry. This is just too much for my old heart."

"You just enjoy this moment, my dear. You deserve it. This could just be the making of Jamie after his recent disappointments. I'll be in touch the moment I hear more. In the meantime, listen to the BBC World Service tonight. Even if they don't mention Jamie, they are bound to mention the fact that the Royal Navy has captured a yacht packed with IRA weapons."

"My beloved, trusted friend. Thank you. I'll certainly listen to the BBC tonight. Goodbye, my dear. Talk soon."

Lunch at the Travellers was a distinguished and gentlemanly affair. The beautiful, long dining room, with its early nineteenth century frills and mahogany furniture, is an example of what still remains of English taste and class. The long, central banqueting table was laid for at least a dozen guests. They had not yet arrived by the time Henry Clark sat at his usual table by the window, to the extreme east of the hall. Most of the other tables were taken up by solitary gentlemen, like himself. There were no ladies, although modern rules now permitted ladies into certain rooms, as guests.

Once again, Samuel noticed that Mr Clark's mind was elsewhere. It was certainly not on his boeuf Wellington, although he did enjoy his wine. Mr Clark informed the head waiter that, after his usual vanilla ice cream, he would take coffee, this time in the Library. Once again, he would be making a telephone call first.

Henry Clark's second call was to David Brooks, and it was as concise as their telephone communications always had been, not because the man had just sat down to watch some afternoon horse racing on the BBC, but because that is the way things worked in the Service. They agreed that a walk on Sunday morning around St James's Park would be very pleasant indeed. There was no need to decide on a rendezvous point. As on previous occasions in the 1970s, before Henry Clark was retired off, they would meet at Guard's Memorial, facing the Wellington Barracks. Ten o-clock would be fine.

David Brooks was himself close to retiring, but he still owed Henry Clark a favour. It was Jamie Ryder's godfather, in 1950, who had assisted in Brook's recruitment by the SIS, for which he became an extremely valuable member in a series of covert, political operations, including the Iranian coup d'état in 1953, which had been designed to protect British Petroleum's control over Iranian oil reserves. He was also deeply involved, with Clark as provider of contact and tactical information, in the consolidation of Oleg Gordievsky, who filtered documents and photographs related to the Soviet military over a period of ten years, until he had to be hurriedly extracted from the USSR across the Finnish border in 1985.

***

Everything happened rather quickly over the next few days. Much to Sub-Lieutenant Andy Pringle's disappointment HMS Ambuscade was ordered to Davenport. He, Commander Neville, and their fellow officers were going to have to wait for another occasion to meet this Ryder fellow. They also missed the reception given to HMS Exeter when she docked at Portsmouth. There were more family members than usual lined up on the quay to welcome loved ones home from what had begun as a routine exercise, but it was the press, with their tripods and cameras at the ready, which took most of the officers and crew by surprise. They were not there for the destroyer, of course. They were there for the one they were openly referring to as the freelance journalist who had uncovered an IRA operation.

The reporters were also to be frustrated. Jamie Ryder had been transferred, in the same Sea King helicopter which had plucked him off the deck of the Hannah in the Bay of Biscay, to Culdrose Airfield on the evening of Monday, 5th September.

Jamie had been delighted with that plan. He didn't make his thoughts public, but he knew very well that the huge helicopter base in Cornwall was close enough for him to grab a lift to Penzance. He would soon be hopping on the ferry to St Mary's. He gave little thought to the fact that he had been all over the papers, or that they had got themselves into a hysterical muddle interpreting the information available to them about his background and current occupation. Nor was he thinking much about his foolish actions in Spain and on the Hannah, or upon the IRA weapons. His mind was entirely on Ruth and on his promise to return to Trench Lane, in Hugh Town, before she started the winter term teaching in the Isles of Scilly.

What he didn't know at the time was that the arrangement to fly him to Culdrose had been ordered by the Ministry of Defence. In fact, seven gentlemen were waiting to question him early on the Tuesday morning after his arrival at the helicopter base. Two were indeed from the Ministry of Defence. Another, a squarely built fellow in uniform, was from the regiment to which he no longer belonged. A fourth identified himself as a member of British Intelligence specialised in Northern Ireland. There were also two police officers. One of these was Sergeant Marcus Blyth from St Mary's. He wanted to ask questions related to the murder enquiry in Hugh Town. There was a seventh gentleman, dressed casually, wearing a tweed jacket and a cravat. He neither offered his name, nor asked questions. He just appeared to listen and observe from the back of the room. Nevertheless, as Jamie received pats on the back when coffee and biscuits were served after he had replied to questions satisfactorily, the enigmatic gentleman approached and shook Jamie's hand.

"I hope we have the chance for a proper chat one of these days, Mr Ryder," he said, before taking a cream envelope out of his jacket pocket and handing it to Jamie. Without another word, the man wearing the tweed jacket and the cravat departed.

The questioning had been rigorous, especially by the British Intelligence man who delved deep in an attempt to discover what Jamie knew about the IRA. There was little else Jamie could do except be totally open. He had not initially been aware of the terrorist organisation's involvement. However, he was keen to provide his interrogators some additional information, in other words that the IRA's contact in Spain was also connected in some capacity to an Englishman on the island of Tenerife, to a Mr John Palmer. Much to Jamie's surprise, none of the seven men in the room appeared interested in that piece of information, at least not openly.

In the end, when questioning was over and there was a more relaxed atmosphere over coffee, the impression they all gave, as ordinary onlookers, was that they were thoroughly intrigued and keen to shake Mr Ryder's hand. The toughest part of the interrogation had been trying to explain to Sergeant Blyth why he had volunteered to sail to Spain with a complete stranger when he had such a lovely lass as Ruth Eaton crying out for him in Hugh Town. Jamie found it impossible to give a reasoned explanation. However, it was also Blyth who invited Jamie to join him on the afternoon Skybus flight from Land's End Airfield to St Mary's.

"You could be there in time for tea with Miss Eaton," he said, with a twinkle in his eye.

***

The British way of doing things has its failings, but its virtues far outnumber those, and one of the intrinsic attributes of the British people and of its men and women in blue uniform, is their inherent desire to be fair, kind, and helpful. Another is the British organisational skills so often learned school, the ability to make perfect arrangemen Consequently, when the 18-seater Britten-Norman Islan aircraft, transporting Sergeant Blyth and Jamie Ryder, can a standstill at St Mary's Airfield, Ruth Eaton was waitir him. It was past teatime, but the police officer offered J conspiratorial look to which the man they still referred to as *the journalist* replied with a nod of appreciation.

Ruth was standing in front of the airport building, her petite figure dwarfed by an over-sized, blue duffle coat. Her blond, wavy head was covered by a Barbour hat and she had both hands in her coat pockets. It may only have been early September, but there was a cold easterly coming off the Channel. Only when she brought out her right hand to timidly wave at Jamie, as he stepped out of the Islander with his scruffy backpack, did her face light up with the smile he had been longing to see.

They didn't kiss, or hug embarrassingly, but Ruth did hold firmly onto Jamie's hand as he spoke to Sergeant Blyth. Once again, Jamie thanked the policeman warmly and said that if there was anything he could do to help, he would be delighted. It was only as they walked down the road towards Trench Lane that Jamie put an arm lovingly around Ruth. To anyone watching, it was almost as if they had never parted and that they were just a couple returning from an afternoon stroll.

However, they were dying for each other and when they reached the wooden gate, which separated two fields to the east of The Ferns cottage, Ruth could no longer bear it. She turned to look up into Jamie's eyes.

"You came back!"

"A promise is a promise!" he replied.

"Hold me. Oh, please hold me, Jamie."

"Only if you kiss me, my love," Jamie replied, lifting her so
't her green Wellington boots stood on the stile step. He
ed his arms around Ruth and her fingers tugged at his
' bring his lips onto hers.

'st kiss only lasted an instant because Jamie felt Ruth
emotion and then realised that tears were running
'ks. He used his thumbs to gently brush them
'ng the tops of her cheeks.

'hing for you," said Jamie, putting a hand in
' out the cheap, blue necklace with the
'ved on it, the one he had bought with
'oy Gorka, the Basque terrorist.

232

Their next embrace was long, and their lips gave evidence to their feelings, not with great passion and hunger, but with the tenderness of two young people who belonged to each other. It lasted until the clouds began to spit a light drizzle.

"It's raining," said Ruth.

"So?"

"Come on. Mummy's gone to play bridge. She'll be ages."

"Have you just invited me to the boiler room?" Jamie teased, with a predatory look in his eye.

"Oh, I've got a much better idea. You smell of the sea and I'm going to bath you," Ruth promised, jumping out of his arms, and starting to run across the field towards The Ferns, giggling with pleasure.

***

Ruth kept her promise. Hers was a pretty room, feminine, and decorated with taste. A door and two steps led into her bathroom in which a great big, old-fashioned tub of a bath awaited Jamie.

This time, her bursting desire to unbuckle Jamie's belt was slow and deliberate, and she unbuttoned every button on his cotton shirt one by one, not tearing desperately at it as she had done two weeks earlier. Before she made Jamie step into the steaming bath, lit in the fading evening light by candles and scented with aromatic oils, Ruth had already let her own dress drop to the ground, revealing small, round breasts and a preference for silk, French underwear. This had the inevitable effect of rousing Jamie even further, and he sank below the surface of bubbles to hide himself before Ruth knelt on the floor and began to sponge him from behind.

Jamie and Ruth had met only briefly at a cocktail party a little over a month earlier. They had shared no more than three or four days together and yet what was happening to then seemed to be the most natural thing in the world.

When Ruth became more playful with her sponge, Jar closed his eyes and let it happen. Five days ago, he struggling to outwit a merciless enemy. Now he surrendering to the enticing caresses of a beautiful w and she was urging him to respond. He did, the mom stood up to turn the bath taps off before the bubbles overflowed onto the floor. It was her silk underwear that prompted his play. It began when he let his left arm stretch out of the bath, and a wet hand found its way between Ruth's legs, into the inviting space which French undies provide. His touch unleashed her passion and she let him pull her into the bath. Seconds later, Ruth entwined her legs around his middle and they made love for the first time.

**

It was only on the following morning that Jamie remembered the envelope the gentleman in the Tweed jacket had handed him at Culdrose.

Inside, under the Traveller's Club, Pall Mall letterhead, was a short note from Henry Clark. It simply asked Jamie to telephone him on the number he provided as soon as he had the chance, and invited him to lunch at the Club. Once again, Ruth encouraged him. She urged Jamie to go and see his old godfather without fail. How could he possibly have let so many years go by without being in touch? That was something else he loved about Ruth, her sense of duty.

Four days after the school term began, Jamie and Ruth parted company. There were no tears. They both knew they belonged to each other and that their love would grow every time he managed to return to Scilly for weekends.

"Have your Dad's pink corduroys ready for me, my love," teased Jamie when they said goodbye at the crossroads near 'he main school.

'I promise," she said, before adding, "a promise is a 'se!" She blew Jamie a kiss as he made his way towards
'1 Lane. He had one last appointment to do with
'ons into the murder of Alvaro Cousillas, but Jamie
'1 to present the kind Sergeant with a nice bottle of
'ng the ferry to Penzance.

**

'n a glorious early autumn day in London,
'ut into the sunshine from Charing Cross
'ong to 106, Pall Mall. After a curious,
'1e janitor, when he stepped into the

234

lobby at the Traveller's Club, Jamie introduced himself and informed the man that he was a guest of Mr Henry Clark.

"Ah yes, Sir. Mr Clark is expecting you. If you would like to wait in the hall, Sir, I shall inform Mr Clark that you have arrived." A moment later Jamie was shown up the staircase and into the Coffee Room.

Over lunch, godfather and son talked mostly about Tenerife, Jamie's mother, and trivial matters like travel, whiskies, and wines. The adventures which the press had been so keen to report on were not mentioned at all but, prompted by Henry Clark, they did discuss Jamie's frustration at having left the Army. When they touched the subject of what Jamie might do to fill that gap in his career, Henry Clark made Jamie understand that he quite understood his feelings and that he might be able to help, if Jamie would allow him to, of course. It was evident to the old man, from Jamie's body language and the inquisitive look in his eye, that his godson was keen to know more.

Nevertheless, it was not until they took coffee that Henry Clark casually informed Jamie, as if it had been entirely normal, that he had spent a good part of his life, not so much publishing historical articles and a book or two but working for British Intelligence. In fact, he suggested, once again very matter-of-factly, that if Jamie would at any time be interested in serving his Queen and country in another capacity, he knew a gentleman who was keen to meet him.

It was in the Library that they took their coffee and a most excellent French brandy after lunch. It would be quieter in there at that hour of the afternoon, Mr Clark had whispered. Indeed, it was. It was also in that beautiful room, after Samuel had kindly poured them their brandies, that Henry Clark took out a brown envelope from his jacket pocket and handed it to Jamie.

"This is the second envelope given to me in hand since I returned to England, Uncle Henry," said Jamie with a mischievous smile.

"Yes. This one is from a friend of mine, David Brooks. I believe you met him at Culdrose a couple of weeks ago. It was he who handed you the first envelope, my envelope!"

"Ah, the suave and debonair fellow with the cravat."

"Indeed. How observant of you. Yes, he does rather dress up a bit," Henry Clark added with a chuckle, as Jamie opened the envelope.

"Um, Uncle Henry, there's nothing in the envelope!"

"Yes, Jamie. I thought that might be the case. It's typical of David. He has used our old code, very modern technology as you can see," joked Henry Clark, before continuing.

"David knew you were coming to see me today. The empty envelope means that, if I don't call him at three o-clock, you will have agreed to meet him and he will be waiting for you at four o-clock just down the road, where he and I used to get together in my fun days. If you are not interested, all I need to do is telephone him."

"I am interested, Uncle Henry."

At precisely four o-clock, after a five-minute walk from the Travellers Club, Henry Clark stopped fifty yards short of Guards Memorial. David Brooks was standing in front of the memorial, opposite Horse Guards Parade. It was time for Henry Clark to leave David and his godson to have their stroll around St James's Park.

"I hope you won't leave it so long next time before you come and see me again, Jamie.'

"No, I shan't. Thank you so much for a splendid lunch, well for everything, Uncle Henry. I shall call Mama tonight. She will be incredibly happy to know that I have been to see you at last."

"Goodbye, Jamie, and good luck, boy."

Mr Henry Clark turned and began to walk away. He stopped once to look back towards the memorial. The old man was in time to see Jamie Ryder and David Brooks shake hands before disappearing into the evening shadows for their stroll through the park. He smiled to himself, satisfied that he had done his duty.

More books by this author

The Skipping Verger and Other Tales

A collection of short stories set on the island of Tenerife, from the hilarious and romantic adventures of British travellers to intrigue at the start of the Spanish Civil War. An English scientist meets a man with a strange walk. A Scottish artist falls in love with a passionate Spanish woman. Boys get up to mischief in the banana plantations. A British secret agent mysteriously disappears.

A Shark in the Bath and Other Stories

There is a shark in a hotel guest's bath, but sharks aren't the only surprise in these fascinating stories set in Spain's Canary Islands. There's a desperate race against time to arrest one of the Great Train Robbers when he flees to Tenerife. A British revolutionary gets caught up in the illegal transport of human cargo during the dark days of General Franco. A young American is shocked when he finds out why island villagers are convinced he's a ghost. When a pirate's chest was discovered in a cave near a waterfall, nobody could have expected what lay within.

You can find *A Shark in the Bath and Other Stories* and *The Skipping Verger and Other Tales* in Amazon and other stores.

ABOUT THE AUTHOR

John Reid Young was born in London's Welbeck Street in 1957. Although he has spent most of his life in the Canary Islands, home to his paternal ancestors since the middle of the 19th century, he was educated at private schools in England and Scotland. After studying Law and Politics he completed his studies with a Master's degree in Diplomatic Studies. A number of years after working in the UK he returned to the Canary Islands. He is now a family man and owns Tenerife Private Tours with which he finds great pleasure meeting people from all over the world. He has provided his voice to numerous recordings and has translated documents and publications for a variety of clients including the regional parliament. He has published several articles and keeps an historical blog, Travel Stories in Tenerife and the Canary Islands. His first collection of short stories, The Skipping Verger and Other Tales, confirmed his passion for telling a good story.

If you'd like to get in touch, please send a message to reidten@gmail.com with any comments, opinions, requests or general waffle.

Writing under an avocado tree I only get to talk to lizards and hoopoes, so any contact with the real world is much appreciated.

Printed in Great Britain
by Amazon